IN THE
FALCON'S
CLAW

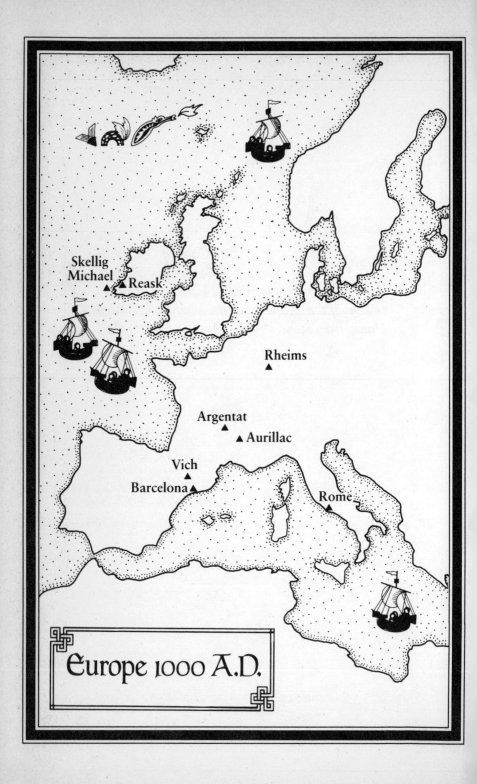

Skellig
Michael ▲   ▲ Reask

Rheims ▲

Argentat
▲
▲ Aurillac

Vich
▲
Barcelona ▲

Rome ▲

Europe 1000 A.D.

IN THE FALCON'S CLAW

A Novel of the YEAR 1000

CHET RAYMO

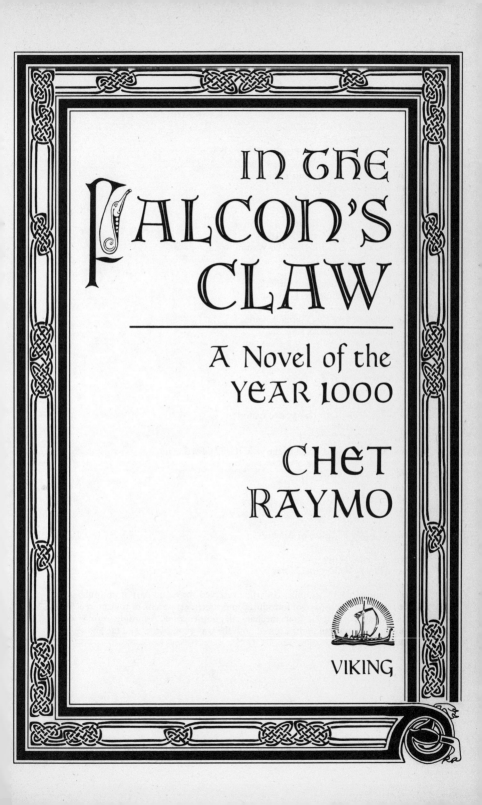

VIKING

VIKING
Published by the Penguin Group
Viking Penguin, a division of Penguin Books USA Inc.,
40 West 23rd Street, New York, New York 10010, U.S.A.
Penguin Books Ltd, 27 Wrights Lane,
London W8 5TZ, England
Penguin Books Australia Ltd, Ringwood,
Victoria, Australia
Penguin Books Canada Ltd, 2801 John Street,
Markham, Ontario, Canada L3R 1B4
Penguin Books (N.Z.) Ltd, 182–190 Wairau Road,
Auckland 10, New Zealand

Penguin Books Ltd, Registered Offices:
Harmondsworth, Middlesex, England

First published in 1990 by Viking Penguin,
a division of Penguin Books USA Inc.

10 9 8 7 6 5 4 3 2 1

LIBRARY OF CONGRESS CATALOGING IN PUBLICATION DATA

Raymo, Chet.
  In the falcon's claw: a novel of the year 1000 / Chet Raymo.
    p.   cm.
  ISBN 0–670–82890–4
  I. Title
PS3568.A928I5   1990
813′ .54—dc20   89–40424

Printed in the United States of America
Set in Sabon
Designed by Sarah Vure
Frontispiece map by Virginia Norey

For my sons, Dan and Tom

And I saw an angel come down from heaven with the key of the Abyss and a great chain in his hand. He laid hold of the dragon, the old serpent, who is Satan, and bound him up for a thousand years and cast him into the Abyss. He shut him up and sealed the entrance that he should deceive the nations no more until a thousand years had passed.

—Revelation 20:1–3

IN THE
FALCON'S
CLAW

God's heart is not easily swayed. Our prayers rise toward heaven like smoke from a vehement fire, and like smoke they are dispersed in the firmament. So desperately do we want to believe God hears our prayers that we often mistake coincidence for answer. But in this world we are answered only with silence; our petitions go unheeded. Evil is sometimes rewarded and goodness often draws misfortune. Only the grave promises justice.

Has that promise been fulfilled for Aileran? By decree of Rome he has been judged a heretic. The Church has consigned his soul to the eternal flames of hell. If Aileran burns, then the promise of justice is a lie. If Aileran burns, then God's heart is stone. It was I who placed his body in the grave—that pitiable body scarred by fire. Into the folds of his winding sheet I sprinkled endive, the herb of invisibility. It was a hopeful gesture—a wish—that in the afterlife he might escape the "justice" of Rome's decree.

It also fell to me to gather up the elements of Aileran's story, the fragments of narrative he so assiduously prepared under trying circumstances. I have the memoir of his early life, which he wrote while alone on the Skellig rock—a ragtag collection of parchments, tattered skins, even scraps of wood, covered over with his cramped and awkward script. These I have collated and copied as best I can. I have letters from his friend Gerbert, and Aileran's replies. I have the narratives that Aileran prepared while a prisoner of Oenu, the bishop of Ardfert, in Ireland, and again while confined by the Holy Office in Rome, and transcripts of his interrogations by the sacred tribunal. Finally, I have the chapters of his story that he wrote during his final residence at Aurillac. All of these I have arranged here into a work that must stand as the sum of his life.

It was not a heroic life. The grand gestures and high ambitions belonged to Gerbert. Aileran's road was more direct—and more dangerous. Of what lay at the end of the road he was not certain, nor was he confident in the journey. Love for God was his burden.

It is said that every herb or plant tells us its use by the form of its blossoms, roots, or leaves. Thus, the hollow stalk of the garlic is effective against afflictions of the windpipe, and the sickle-shaped flower of prunella announces its efficacy as a balm for cuts. A person, too, reveals his character through outward forms. Aileran's eyes were grave and deep, and his soul was a well of sadness. His skin was dark; his character was tragic. He was slight of frame, and like a reed he was bent by his trials but did not break.

I knew Aileran perhaps better than anyone except Gerbert. Our time together was short—it can be measured in months, not years—but few people have shared a more intimate alliance. It seems now that he was near to me all my life, and indeed there were few moments since the time I was fifteen years of age when he was far from my consciousness. At times my thoughts of Aileran were those of a young woman transfixed by love, at other times I thought of him with anger and despair. The residue of our relationship is grief—"the grief of lovers unequally bound."

I watched him die. Thin and wan he lay upon the woodsman's cart when he was brought to me at Argentat. His speech was stilled and his eyes bedarkened like the moon in eclipse. He waited at the porch of death until he saw me, then expired. I blessed his forehead—streaked with blood—his lips, his breast, and washed his body for the grave. How frail he looked, wasted by trials and fasting. I remembered a happier time, when he had thrown off, if only briefly, the afflicting cloak of guilt and given me the sweetest fruits of his flesh.

Why did I—why do I now—love Aileran? He was a sparrow caught in the falcon's claw, a vole goaded by the fox. He was torn between heaven and earth, between the desire for love and the fear of it, between manly strength and abject weakness. He was cursed with equivocation, and his overburdened heart dragged us both down to misery. Yet he alone understood the language of my soul, he alone listened to my voice.

The reader will decide whether Aileran was worthy of my love. As for myself, I do not doubt that certain lives are destined to be entwined. Nor do I doubt that during our time together I had more from Aileran than I gave. Not always in the pages that follow does my own memory of our shared experience match Aileran's. But I have resisted the temptation to let my recollections—or interpretations—intrude upon the integrity of his memoir. Certain details of his relationship with Gerbert and of our time together at Verzenay might have been omitted as indelicate or private, but they are necessary parts of his story. Aileran's words stand uncensored and unrepaired. Here then is his testament.

Melisande

Argentat, Gaul
November 17, 1003

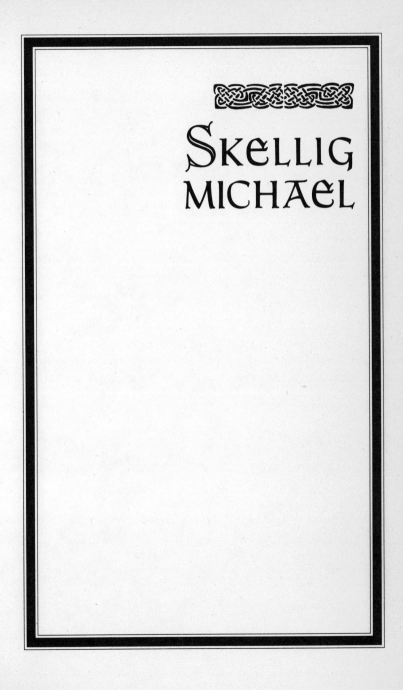

Skellig Michael

Being a memoir of Aileran of Skellig, begun on the 28th day of May in the year of our Lord 998, on the island of Skellig Michael, Hibernia

It is said that I was born beside a peat rick, and that the black juice of the bog accounts for the color of my skin. I think it more likely that I have my dark complexion from my father, a converted Saracen from Spain, who—as Brother No-Ear told me—was washed ashore on Coumeenoole Strand during the great summer storm of the year 940. On that night the wild sea gnawed at the cliffs like a Viking on a bone, and the gale came fierce and unstinting from the west. At daybreak, the wind turned south and the sea subsided. The brothers of Reask, scavenging for wrack, found my father entangled in a shroud of kelp, half buried in sand. His dark eyes were fixed heavenward (said No-Ear) and overbrimming with salt and fear. Of the crew of his ship he was the only survivor.

My father was not the only wrack that came to shore that night. Often in my youth I tasted olive oil from flagons brought to the sand by the same stormy tide. Dozens of the red clay vessels from my father's ship, filled with Iberian oil, were stored in the cellars of Reask, and other hoards of the sweet liquid were cached at Fintra and Fahan. In those days a ship upon the rocks was welcomed as a gift from God, and especially a ship from Spain. Spanish traders frequently plied our shores, with oil, wine, salt, or—most blessedly—ingots of good Spanish iron. For these goods our people traded hides and wool, invariably at a poor rate of exchange. Shipwreck made a dear bargain cheap. I have sometimes wondered if my father's conversion to Christ's faith occurred when the life returned to his eyes on Coumeenoole Strand and he found himself surrounded by Irish scavengers for whom Spanish oil was infinitely more precious than an infidel's life.

I have no memory of my father. He died before I was born, executed by Fergus Mor, the abbot of Reask, for an act of sexual congress with my mother, a young girl fostered to the abbot's care. The circumstances of my parents' unauthorized coupling were never mentioned to me, not even by No-Ear. But the seed of the legitimate husband and the seed of the illicit paramour are equally likely to bear fruit. I came into the world in the autumn of the year 942, with Venus and Mars conjoined low in the morning sky above the very place in the sea where my father's ship had foundered. That conjunction of stars was taken by the abbot of Reask, my mother's uncle, as a sign of God's approbation for his deed of bloody justice, and by everyone else in our community (for Fergus Mor was not a popular man) as the signature of God's unforgiving wrath.

By everyone, that is, except the man who told me of the sign of yoked love and violence that attended my birth. Later, a comet appeared in that same part of the morning sky, causing fear and consternation among the brothers of Reask. No-Ear took me in darkness to the hill of Croaghmarhin and showed me the bearded star in Taurus. The tail of the comet brushed red Aldebaran (the image of the star and comet is my earliest visual memory). The comet is not a portent, said No-Ear; it is a simple gift, a grace of light, whose mysterious coming reminds us of our abysmal ignorance of the workings of the great world.

No-Ear also told me of my mother. She was no more than fifteen years of age at the time of my birth, the daughter of a powerful family of west Munster who had been sent to the relative safety of her uncle's foundation at Reask during a time of troubles. In those days before the salutary unifications of Brian Boru, all of Ireland was embroiled in the squabbles of warring families; no high king sat at Tara, or anywhere else, to impose order on the land. The monastery at Reask was isolated from the worst of the strife, and to the apparent security of our little community the girl was sent. What my mother's family left out of account were the attentions of a certain dark-skinned Spaniard—and, of course, the Vikings. In the year of my birth came a renewed series of devastating raids along the western coast of Ireland by savage Northmen in sleek, clinker-built longboats. The monastery at Reask, with the surrounding countryside, was sacked. Many monks were slaughtered, including Fergus Mor, whose head was placed upon the mast of a Viking ship. My mentor lost only his ear—a story he recounted on numerous occasions, with always grander and more gruesome embellishments. My mother was abducted by the raiders. With the exception of a few holy vessels and flagons of oil, she was the only acceptable spoil of our poor community.

Orphaned by double acts of violence, I was placed by the new abbot, Fergus Beg (the son of the man who slew my father), into the care of an asymmetrical monk, who could hear only half of what I had to say, and who lived long enough to tend me to the age of independence. Of his life I have only affectionate memories, and of his death, even now at the age of fifty-five, black and bloody dreams.

Brother Finnechta—called No-Ear—had two responsibilities within our community: He was brewmaster of the ale and master of the shepherds. In both tasks I was constantly at his side. During the abbacy of Fergus Mor, ale was not permitted to the monks; Fergus Beg relaxed the discipline and allowed ale with meals on all feast days (wine was permitted at Christmas and Easter only, and then only moderately). A part of each year's harvest of grain was set aside for No-Ear's use in the making of the ale; generally this was barley, but sometimes it was oats or rye. We steeped the grain in water, in a wooden trough, then spread the sodden mass on the floor of the alehouse to dry. It was my responsibility, from the time I could lift a rake, to turn the grain and draw it into ridges, so that all parts would dry equally. It was pleasant, satisfying work, and not physically demanding. With the rake I inscribed into the spread grain elaborate patterns of interlaced bands, such as the monks of Innisfallen use to decorate the Scriptures; No-Ear, observing this, would laugh and say, "God's scribe with a rake." At the side of the alehouse was a stone kiln in which the grain was baked to a hard malt. The malt was then ground in a quern, made into a mash with water, fermented, boiled, and strained. For this last task No-Ear used a fine bronze strainer, the bowl of which was perforated in an elaborate pattern of swirls; this strainer was his prized—indeed only— possession, and it was a source of great satisfaction to him that in the Viking raid that cost him his ear he managed to save this valued implement by hiding it beneath his garment. No-Ear's ale was valued throughout the region of west Munster. It was said to be superior because of its smoothness and fine amber color, but the truth is that no ale was quite so intoxicating as his, and for this much-sought-after refinement many goods came to our community by trade.

When No-Ear took me into his charge he was already old, but as strong as a man in the prime of life. He could crumble with his hands a malt cake so hard that any other man must break it with a mallet. Behind the alehouse at Reask was a souterrain, or underground chamber, in which we hid the valuable goods of the community. The entrance was concealed with a large stone that no single man could lift except No-Ear; he raised up the stone from the passageway as easily as a child might tip water from a basin. Yet for all his great strength, he was a gentle man. When he touched the tip of his thick finger to the mash to taste it, he did so with the delicacy of a dragonfly touching the surface of a pool. And his fingers moved upon the strings of the kesh with the gracefulness of a woman. He taught me to play that instrument, and as I played he sang songs of wonderful sweetness:

> *I and Pangur Bán, my cat,*
> *'Tis a like task we are at;*
> *Hunting mice is his delight,*
> *Making ale I work all night.*

> *'Tis a merry thing to see*
> *At our tasks how glad are we;*
> *Pangur bears me no ill will,*
> *He too plies his simple skill.*

> *Practice every day has made*
> *Pangur perfect at his trade;*
> *I too get pleasure day and night*
> *Turning corn into delight.*

In spring and summer we went to the hills above Reask to tend to the sheep and supervise the shepherds, boys no older than myself. It gave me great pride to go with No-Ear to the clochans where the shepherds stayed and stand nearby while he lectured them on their duties. If a sheep had been lost to a wolf, then No-Ear scowled, and I, standing beside, pursed my lips and nodded scornfully, as if to add my paltry authority to his own. On these journeys into the hills No-Ear carried cakes and honey in his pouch, and in the evening, when our work was done, he opened the pouch and spread his treats upon a cloth. "We will have cakes and honey in Paradise," he said. "There will be stars and a warm wind. And leeks and hens and salmon that leap from pool to pool until they swim in a teeming silver mass at the foot of God's throne, and anyone who wishes can reach and take one." He put his arm about my shoulders and drew me close to him. "All of this," he said, "awaits us in Paradise." But it seemed to me then that the blessings he described I already possessed, as I huddled against his great warm frame, permanently sweet with the odors of the mash, and licked the honey from my fingertips. With kesh and song he pulled the cloak of night about us:

> O King of Stars! Eternal king,
> These are the gifts that summer brings:
> Green bursts out on every herb,
> The nimble deer the hound has heard,
>
> The blackbird sings a sweet refrain,
> The kale and leeks are wet with rain,
> The dark and troubled ocean sleeps,
> And in the brook the salmon leaps.

In good weather we slept under the stars, and in the moments before sleep No-Ear taught me the figures of the constellations— the Swan, the Eagle, the Harp, the Plough (which he called King David's Chariot), and all the rest. He knew nothing of the spheres of the astronomers, nor of the zodiac, circles, meridians, and degrees. But there was hardly a star in the heavens whose name he did not know. He showed me the Minnow swimming in the river of the Milky Way, and the small cluster of stars near the wing of the Eagle he called the Dart; these inconspicuous constellations are still as familiar to me as the words of the Pater Noster. In late summer, meteors streaked the sky, stars falling from their spheres; we counted them, competing to observe the greater number. One night I woke before dawn to find the sky raining stars, stars falling from the very zenith as if cast by God's hand. I woke No-Ear and together we marveled at this extraordinary event. So many stars fell that night it was a wonder any were left above to define the constellations.

At no time of my life was I as happy as then, when the wind was from the south and the sky clear to the far horizon. At our backs, the mountain of Saint Brendan scratched its dark hump against the sky; if you went there, said No-Ear, you could touch the stars. Below, near the river known as Donn (that is, "brown") and plainly visible in the light of the stars, was the circular stone wall that enclosed our monastery, divided across, as by a diameter, with another wall, which separated the sacred precinct from the place where we lived and worked. The land was cleared around about and divided into fields, and there were houses of wattle and thatch. Beyond the fields was a marsh, from which our community took its name, and beyond that the sea, silver in starlight, glistening like a polished paten. To the south, piercing the horizon, the island of Skellig Michael rose from the surface of the sea like a knot of deal wood from the bog. There was a monastery on that crag, said No-Ear, and monks lived there like cormorants, with gardens the size of a monk's cowl and an oratory so small that when the brothers assembled for prayer there was not room enough to kneel. No man could live there, he said, who was not a madman or a saint.

Rome
April 26, 998
Sylvester II to Aileran, abbot of Skellig Michael
Sylvester, pope, bishop of Rome, servant of the servants of God, to his very dear friend and son in the Lord, Aileran, abbot of the monastery of Saint Michael on the rock of Skellig, in the province of Munster, Ireland

Letters and delegates have come to us in Rome expressing

honest reservations about certain words and actions that have been ascribed to you, my brother. If these accusations are true—and I sincerely hope that they are not—they would constitute a breach of the apostolic unity of God's Holy Church. It has always been the purpose of our pontifical authority, deriving from Our Lord Jesus Christ and from his servant Peter, prince of the Apostles, to strengthen and uplift the universal faith and hold it firm, even in places as remote from the seat of our authority as your distant hermitage.

We are urged by Oenu, bishop of Ardfert, to confirm your dismissal as abbot of the monastery of Saint Michael—if indeed so small and humble a foundation deserves an abbot at all. However, we hesitate to take rash action lest the reports that have come to our ears have been improperly communicated or wrongly interpreted by ourselves, and therefore urge you, my brother, to respond in your own hand to this injunction.

It is well known that in places remote from our influence it is widely believed that in two years time, when one thousand years shall have passed since the birth of Our Lord and Savior Jesus Christ, the dead will be raised, the world destroyed, and Christ come again in Glory. Even here in Rome many superstitious people entertain the opinion that the end of the world is close at hand, and point to omens in the heavens and on earth. However, it is the judgment of all sensible people, and in particular of theologians and philosophers, that Christians have every reason to expect that the world will endure for a long time to come.

According to our informants, in your own district many of the faithful have adopted needless and foolhardy preparations for the coming of Christ, taking upon themselves unseemly devotional practices that are disruptive of the secular order and normal ecclesiastical observances of the Church. In opposing these excesses, my brother, you act rightly; for it is good that all of Christendom be of one mind on this matter, and rightly in consonance with the authority of Peter.

14

It is not your skepticism regarding an impending Millennium that concerns us, or that concerns your fellow abbots and bishops, but the grounds upon which your skepticism is based. If these have been communicated to us rightly, they provide serious cause for anxiety.

It is said that of the recent wondrous manifestations in the heavens and on earth you have urged a natural explanation. I refer, of course, to the three great comets that have lately sprung from the watery constellations, the earthquakes and eruptions of fire and brimstone that have affected districts of Calabria and Sicily, and the rains of blood, locusts, and reptiles that have fallen upon certain parts of Iberia, Germany, and Gaul. It would indeed be foolish to imagine that this conjunction of extraordinary events were of other than a Divine origin. That these events portend cannot be doubted; what they portend is a matter for scholarly debate. In our own judgment, they prefigure the ascent to the throne of our new Caesar, the beloved Otto, and the auspicious alliance of spiritual and temporal power in Rome. With the establishment of a new and Godly empire these miracles soon shall cease.

You rightly reject foolish preparations for the coming of Christ. But take care, my son, lest you reject also the *possibility* of such an event. God has the power to supersede nature at any time. Certainly, if He so willed—and we firmly hold that He has not—God could bring the world *even now* to its just conclusion.

It is not for you to choose in these matters. Let us remind you that the Fathers of the Church have applied the Greek word for "choice," *haeresis,* to all opinions contrary to Holy Scriptures and the teachings of the Church of Peter. It is well known that the views of the heresiarch Pelagius, who denied the power of God's grace in the world and who was rightly condemned by the Council of Carthage, are still broadcast in the countries of the Celts. We caution you not to give voice to these pernicious opinions and to moderate whatever tendencies you have shown toward a denial of God's power in the world. Your opinions are all the more dangerous in that your reputation for holiness—which extends even to this city—lends them a certain authority which they do not deserve. We do not forget that, as Tertullian has taught us, many ravening wolves will come in sheep's clothing, and those with the outward appearance of Christians will sometimes spread treacherous thoughts to infest the flock of Christ.

Beware of the chain of anathema of the Lord and of Peter. But do not doubt that the damage of your untoward preaching can be redressed through the gift of Roman compassion. We wait for your expression of abdication to our will, and if—God forbid—that abdication is not forthcoming, we fear lest you might find yourself, by the prescribed anathema, a companion of Judas in the Tartarean depths for eternity.

Written by the hand of Nicholas, notary and secretary of the Holy Roman Church, in the month of April, in the first year of the pontificate of Lord Pope Sylvester II.

☧ *Gerbert,* who is also Sylvester, bishop of Rome

The heretic Pelagius was right: The doctrine of grace corrupts. If we are saved only by God's grace, then we must become beggars at his table. We must grovel and whine and play to be his favorite. And those who hold the power of the dispensation of grace—Gerbert, with his miter and triple crown—by them we are also oppressed. If Pelagius is damned, then so am I. Better to be damned with an honest heretic than to share Paradise with swaggerers and fools.

Gerbert, the friend and the companion of my youth, my teacher in the arts of geometry, arithmetic, and astronomy, who once saved my life at risk to himself, now calls me "Judas." Gerbert, now pope of Rome (who calls himself "Sylvester"),

16

dispenser of God's grace and arbiter of salvation, demands my "abdication." This man who was my tutor in the brothels of Spain now threatens me with anathema and consigns my soul to "Tartarean depths" for denying miracles.

"We make our own miracles!" That is what Gerbert said to me one morning in a certain house at Vich, in Catalonia. We were young, and on our own in the world, although ostensibly constrained by the rule of the monastery of Santa Maria de Ripoll. It was the last hour before dawn and I had gone looking for my friend. I found him in a room of quavering curtains, in bed with four women. "Look," he cried. "It is like the miracle of loaves and fishes. I began the night with one mistress, and through the dark hours she has been miraculously multiplied. First two, then three, now four. Enough for all!" With a wave of the hand he invited me into the bed. "We make our own miracles," he said. "Come join us. My pretty friends have the skill to make Lazarus rise from the dead."

Gerbert was not so certain then of God's plan for the world. Nor was he so solicitous for the salvation of my soul. His nakedness, and that of his companions, was mesmerizing. As I watched, one of the women moved her mouth to the organ of his sex. I could not cease to look, to admire the audacity—even the beauty—of his sin. But in his gaze my soul felt sullied. I was scandalized by his sacrilege, by his blasphemous references to the miracles of Christ. And now he accuses me of blasphemy!

It was not from Pelagius that I received my doubt about the efficacy of God's will in the world—my *haeresis*, as Gerbert calls it—but from No-Ear, my mentor at Reask. "There are no miracles but one," he often said, "and that one miracle is Creation." If a monk of our community fell sick, the abbot called us all to the oratory for prayer. But No-Ear went instead into the fields, to the brook, to the forest, and returned with balms and salves. "The miracles are all about us," he said, "in the water that refreshes, in the herbs that restore the balance of humors, in the leeches that draw out the fevered blood. When we pray, we should pray to thank God for the gifts he has already given us, not for those we foolishly believe we need."

No circumstance of my life was more fortunate than that as an orphaned child I was placed into No-Ear's care. Fergus Beg, the abbot of Reask and the son of the man who slew my father, gave me a second father out of his own company, and no child ever had a more solicitous parent. No-Ear would often say: "There are three kinds of service that can burden a man—serving a bad woman, serving a bad lord, or serving a bad land." This was by way of telling me that his own service was not burdensome, and that I, too, might enter into the same peace. To women he was indifferent; he served, he said, only Mary, Mother of Christ. His lord, the abbot, asked of him only ale. And our land at Reask, although not rich, was fair enough—the forest thick with wood, the soil black, heaps of carrageen upon the shore, and always a fat badger for the pot. These same gifts he shared generously with me, and invited me to share his service to the abbot and the Virgin. This I would willingly have done had not the worm of concupiscence begun to pester.

The source of my affliction was several years older than me. So often did she inhabit my youthful dreams that even today I can evoke her presence by closing my eyes. Her name was Maire. Her father was a cousin of Fergus Beg who was allowed dispensation to build a house on monastery land. It was a favor not generously repaid by the father, who was indolent; but the daughter worked hard as a goatherd, and to see her among the animals, her skirts jacked up about her thighs, her white calves splattered with mud, was my heart's delight. From the time she came onto our lands my thoughts went swimming away into her sphere. I dared not approach her, but I was never at a loss for finding opportunities to be nearby, where I could watch her out of the corner of my eye.

Her red-blond hair, the blush of her cheek, eyes that seemed forever about to turn in my direction, the curve of her breasts beneath the soft linen of her shift—these were the elements of my fantasies. Perhaps after all she was not so beautiful as I remember, but against an awareness of my own awkwardness she seemed impossibly unattainable. I was ever conscious of my dark skin, my limbs like brittle sticks, and the wild tousle of my hair—unsuitable attributes against her perceived perfection. At night I lay in the darkness of my bed and hungered for her with a longing that amounted to a physical pain. And worse than the agony of my lust was the burden of my sin, and the fear lest No-Ear should discover my shameful secret.

It is clear to me now that my affection for Maire was no secret within our community. The clumsiness of my speechless courtship, my tongue-tied mutterings when I was challenged in her proximity, my scatter-brained distraction from my work, must have been obvious to all. But no one spoke to me of this matter. During the abbacy of Fergus Beg our house was somewhat lax in matters of sex, and in any case I was not yet constrained by any vow. Perhaps it was thought best to let me expend my passions early, in this harmless way, so that when I came to the profession of the vow of chastity at the age of twenty—for it was generally assumed that I *would* profess—I would be better prepared for a continent life. And so my anguished longing for Maire went on for months with no conclusion or remission. A thousand times in my imagination I went into her bed; a thousand times I was delivered by my conscience from that almost perfect bliss into the fires of hell. And never did I know if she was aware of my obsession.

❧

Is memory Satan's gift to Adam? Without memory our thoughts would be forever fixed upon Heaven, the paradise to come, and our actions measured accordingly. But because the life we have lived continues to exist within our minds, we turn backward, away from God, to a reconsideration of the events of the past, which we worship as the Romans worshiped gods inherent in the hearth and home. These idols of memory are a pagan pantheon that we carry within ourselves.

Here in the darkness of my Skellig cell I can evoke a thousand deities of memory—foremost among them Gerbert and Melisande, but also the minor deities of youth, gods of sky, sea, bog, and glen. *I am sent to the strand by the sun-flecked sea to collect beach pebbles and bits of quartz to ornament the grave of Fergus Mor.* Now, after more than half a century, I recall each stone, see its colors, feel its heft in my hand. *I carry charcoal to Conall, who tends the furnace where iron is made from the red earth of the bog.* I see the metal run like molten gold into the clay, and hear the heave and whoosh of the leather bellows as it drives air through the fire. *I bring to Abbot Fergus the bleached skeleton of a curlew, found high on the hill in the yellow bloom of gorse.* He smiles and blesses my forehead; my eyes are fixed upon the sheaf of scarfskin that blemishes the abbot's neck; the bones of the bird rattle in my hands.

I carry in memory the plan of the cashel at Reask, each twist and turn of the thick walls, the corbeled buildings of stone and rooms of timber, the kiln where we baked the malt, the drains that carried water to the outer ditch, the graves with their magical inscriptions on stones that were themselves like recumbent bodies. I recite, as a kind of exercise, the names of the monks, rehearse the features of their faces, the separate timbres of their voices at the recitation of prayers. I hoard in memory each childhood gift I received from the brothers of Reask—a trap for mice, an elfin effigy in deal, a bright amber button pierced with two round holes. And I recall and relive the exquisite idolatry of Maire—not a reasoned love or adult passion but a thing of spells and enchantments, a young mind helplessly in thrall. Against this store of *lares et penates* Heaven pales.

One bright winter's day I set out for Saint Brendan's mountain, the mountain from whose summit Brother No-Ear had said you can touch the stars. I went without permission on a boy's adventure. The journey took longer than I expected; it was past noon when I reached the base of the mountain, and nearly twilight when I achieved the summit. From the top of the mountain I discovered a world of unimagined immensity, although I know now that what I saw is only a tiny part of Ireland, and Ireland only a smaller part of the great world. But then, in the eyes of a youth who had never traveled more than a few miles from Reask, the sea, the distant peaks, the lush valleys and hilltop forests, the islands (including far-off Skellig), seemed impossibly remote. My vista carried me from Ardfert to Ballinskelligs, from Reask to Innisfallen. I gazed in wide-eyed wonder that so much earth had been provided by God for men.

At the summit of the mountain was Saint Brendan's cell, a small stone oratory, its roof now fallen, where centuries earlier the saint had come alone to pray before setting out on his famed voyage upon the western sea. Here, I thought, a person might live in the presence of God and free from sin. Near the oratory was a spring, now clogged with stones. I knelt in the grass and removed the stones one by one, arranging them in a kind of wall about the spring. The water began to trickle out again into a clear pool rimmed with cress. From somewhere on the mountain a curlew called. Briefly, I tried to pray, as I imagined Brendan might have prayed, but could form no image of the God who might hear my prayers. Instead I plaited a cross of reeds and fixed it on the stones above the pool, holding it in place with pebbles of bright quartz. And then I began to remember Maire.

So long did I linger near the site of Brendan's cell that soon the light was departing and cold thick clouds descended on the mountain. Within the clouds every direction seemed the same.

Blindly I began my descent. The terrain was steeper and more dangerous than what I had encountered on the way up, the ground stonier beneath my bare feet. I stumbled and was bruised. I began to hurry, recklessly, downward, and soon found myself upon a narrow ledge with no foothold below. I dislodged a stone and it fell beyond the precipice; there was no sound of stone striking against stone, only silence. Nor could I go back up. No rock or twig gave purchase to my hand; the soft earth crumbled between my fingers. In darkness and cloud I was trapped on the edge of an abyss, and for the first time in my life I began to be truly afraid. I wept bitterly in the knowledge that my predicament was the consequence of my sin. It was then that I made my prayer. I promised God that if He saved my life I would never again look upon Maire. And almost immediately I saw a goat standing not five feet away. The goat turned and began to move upward along a small track. I saw that the way was passable and followed, to the shoulder of the mountain and then down the other side, until I emerged from the cloud and saw far off in the light of a waxing moon the familiar crescent of the harbor at Reask, and farther off still the star-crowned crag of Skellig.

Now began the struggle to remain faithful to my promise. God had saved my life and I must keep my end of the bargain. But the struggle was unequal. My obsession with Maire was overwhelming, stronger even than my love for God or my gratitude for the "miracle" of the goat. I held to the alehouse, the refectory, or the oratory, any place where I was unlikely to see her, and busied myself with work. I was being made physically sick by a longing over which I had no control. The more desperately I sought to avoid her, the more painful was my longing. At last I began taking long walks to put myself beyond reach of temptation, and on one of those walks I encountered her in the fens near the sea, setting and clearing traps for hares. I followed, hidden, watching. She moved across the grassy marsh in a kind of dance, her red-blond hair floating on sunlight, her feet barely touching the soft earth. In one of the snares she found a heavy buck, as long as my arm, trapped but not dead. Maire took the animal by the nape of its neck and freed it from the snare. Weakened, or paralyzed with fear, the hare made no attempt to escape. She held it against her breast—its head on the bare skin of her neck—and stroked its back, all the while rocking gently on her knees. Her eyes were closed. Her fingers furrowed the hare's thick pelt. She rocked and wordlessly sang, and her hair fell down across her face and covered the head of the hare. She rocked and sang, and my body moved in sympathy with hers, until, against my will, the sin of infidelity to my promise was compounded by another. I knew from that moment that my soul was damned to hell. Wretched, I continued watching. She whispered. She whispered to the hare. The beast kicked out with its powerful hind legs and the spell was broken. Maire pushed the hare against the ground. From the girdle of her shift she took a short bronze knife and plunged it into the animal's neck, unloosing a spurt of blood.

A boy lives two lives: one private, one public. Even as I suffered my private obsession, Abbot Fergus took care to see that my public self was prepared for eventual profession. For a few minutes each day between the hours of Lauds and Prime I was given into the care of Brother Donatus to learn the Roman alphabet. In the yard next to the oratory was set up a stone cross, and along the spine of the stone were incised the Latin letters. I traced these with my finger (remembering how Maire's fingers had furrowed the hare) until the shapes and forms were graven upon my mind. There was a kind of magic in the way these twenty-four characters could be arranged into words sufficiently numerous so that everything in the world had a name—and not just every *thing*, but every action and quality:

A fierce wind from the south
Plows up the white hair of the sea.
I have no fear that Viking ships
Will cross over the water to me.

Brother Donatus wrote out the verse one word at a time with the charcoal clenched in his fist like a bronze knife, and the wind and the spray seemed to leap out of the thick black letters and blow about me, promising, by Viking sword, my necessary penance. Our monastery possessed two fine books, kept in a bronze cask. When I had learned the Roman letters and the vocabulary of simple words that Donatus drew with charcoal upon stone, I was given access to the books. One of them was the Divine Office, the prayers a monk must recite each day; the other was a chronicle of the lives of Irish saints. I was greedy and quick. I soon mastered both texts. I read them over and over again until I could say the words and turn the pages with my eyes closed. At last Donatus forbade any further reading lest the books should fall apart in my hands, and gave me instead the few Greek words that he possessed.

My favorite story in the Book of Irish Saints was that of Modomnoc and the bees: *Modomnoc was a monk of Saint David's in Wales, and a beekeeper. When he decided to remove himself to Ireland his bees followed him across the sea, humming in a small cloud about his boat. When he reached his destination and established his new hermitage, he had all the honey he could eat.* Later, when I became abbot of Skellig, I tried to bring bees to the island without success, and I remembered the story of Modomnoc and wished for swarms with the fidelity of his. When I could have used a miracle, my bees were dispersed by the wind. But it is the nature of bees to resist the new hive, and it is the nature of the wind to blow. The honey, I have discovered, is miracle enough.

24

Skellig
June 2, 998
Aileran, abbot of the monastery of Skellig Michael, to Gerbert,
pope, bishop of Rome

Gerbert, bishop, greetings from your friend and son in Christ.
The people who live in this part of the world have a saying:
Twenty years growing, twenty years in prime, twenty years
declining, twenty years dying. I approach the fourth of my
allotted scores of years and feel each day more emphatically the
encroaching darkness that will ultimately engulf my life. You are
but slightly younger than myself—although my guide and
teacher in philosophy and the ways of the world—and thus you
will not be unsympathetic to my infirmities and diminishment of
faculties, for these inevitably afflict every person of our years.
Perhaps you will allow, then, as to an elder brother, a certain
informality that would be inappropriate in a younger man
writing to his lord, the pope. Indeed, I fear that by the time my
letter reaches you, and almost certainly by the time I have had
your reply, I will have passed from this world to whatever state
of grace or oblivion lies beyond the grave. (And there, you see,
dear friend, my condition gives me dispensation to confess to you
my deepest fears and doubts—and the anguish of heart that
comes with the extinction of love. Yes, the extinction of love; for
now, after a lifetime of loving, my heart is shriveled up like a
mushroom in the pan.)

I am alone. My monks have deserted me. I am left on this
island with no companion but a goat. My congregation consists
of gulls, cormorants, and kittiwakes. I preach to the wind.
Outside my cell sits the young, ashen-faced monk who brought
me your letter. He trembles as he waits for my reply. Below, at
the cove, his companions huddle beneath their upturned boat on
a ledge of rock, anxious to depart. What are they afraid of? You
will laugh, my lord—you who were once contemptuous of *my*
innocence, *my* naïveté. They are afraid of *me*. They have heard
that I possess magic. They have heard that I have traffic with

Satan and that through Satan my hands and feet and side have been marked with the false stigmata. They have heard that I deny Christ, that I celebrate the Eucharist with a host made of flour mixed with semen, that succubi visit me in my sleep, and all other manner of foolishness. Dear Gerbert, my companion in reason, all of this is because I have dared to say that certain "signs" do not signify, that certain laws of nature will not be superseded, and that in two years time Christ *will not* come. And for *this,* my friend, I am chastised by you, my lord bishop, the pope. I am told to acquiesce to superstition by the very person who instructed me in the art of reason. I laugh at the splendid symmetry: As I have been brought low, you have been raised to the pinnacle of Christendom. Here on this island I huddle next to a goat for warmth; you confess emperors. I scribble in a cramped hand on whatever scraps I can find; you issue anathemas in bold script on parchments dripping with wax.

Let me describe to you my situation here, for nothing could be more different from the pomp and ostentation of Rome. My island stands off from the coast of Ireland by a distance of ten miles, in the Western Ocean, and the sea is seldom calm. Indeed, your letter waited at Ballinskelligs, on the far-off shore, for seven days before a crossing could be made, and—God protect them!—it may be another seven days before the messengers can return to the mainland. There is no proper landing place on the Skellig, only a crevasse in the cliff that provides a boat scant shelter from the sea and a slippery wave-washed shelf of rock. From the landing one must climb hand over hand, by the agency of steps cut into the face of the cliff, a distance of one hundred times the height of a man, to the monastic enclosure, which is situated on walled terraces near the eastern peak of the island. The climb from the sea is arduous and terrifying. My present frailty precludes that I could leave this island even if I wished to do so; I could no more descend from this place to the sea than I could ascend bodily into Heaven.

Our foundation—now mine alone!—consists of half a dozen

cells, made in the shape of beehives from unmortared stone. They are empty now, save for one small cell standing off from the others, in which I live. I venture out of my cell only to tend my garden, a pitiful plot of soil built up from rotten rock and seaweed, on which I grow cabbages and leeks. For water, I have two springs that are never dry, and from my goat a bit of milk. It would seem, Gerbert, that what I have is far less than what is required for a man to live, but I live well enough. From my doorway I look out upon sea and sky—an always varied prospect of which I never tire. My sea is the same sea that receives the waters of the Tiber. The stars above my cell are the same stars that shine upon the palaces of Rome—although here, as you well know, the Great Bear walks higher in the sky. (Do you remember that night on the road in Languedoc when you taught me to measure celestial degrees with the fingers of the hand?) I have ceased to say the Mass. I have no bread or wine. The bronze chalice encrusted with the pearls of mussels I have buried, lest the occasional visitor to this island should take it from me. The body of Christ and the blood of Christ have abandoned me.

Nevertheless, it is said by people in the regions about that I possess the consecrated host, which I keep hidden in a cask of dung, and that with it I work my magic. If it rains unceasingly on the mainland and the hay rots on the ground, they say it is my doing—the magus of the Skellig. If there is drought and the grain withers on the stem, then that is my doing also. I am the Antichrist who stirs up mischief in preparation for the second coming of Jesus Christ. Gerbert, if you believed all that is said about me you might expect to see the beast that John tells us will rise from the sea with seven heads and ten horns. But instead I am an old man with cataracts upon his eyes and boils upon his skin. My belly is in constant pain and my stool is like caked malt. If I possessed magic, I would cast the spell that would loosen my bowels.

A fear has taken hold of the people. They are convinced that the end of the world is near, and certain clerics of this diocese

27

whip the fear into a frenzy. Monasteries grow rich with the hawking of relics. There is an excess of self-flagellation and the practice of penances of the most severe kind. The monks of my own house, whose life was already hard, begged me for a sterner discipline, and, when I refused, began to plot against me. The irony! The more I deny the miraculous, the more I am accused of miracles. The more I invoke reason, the more I am accused of sorcery. And the greatest irony is this: Gerbert, the friend of my youth, who once laughed at my gullibility and provincial piety, now commands me to give full rein to pious superstitions.

You insist that the remarkable concurrence of comets and other improbable phenomena are miracles, divinely inspired and sent by God as signs. But is it not best to modestly say that we do not know the cause of these phenomena? It is said that Saint Kevin, in order to cure a sick youth, caused a willow tree to bear apples. If a willow tree bears apples, then that is indeed a miracle, for it is the nature of willows to bear catkins only—as you, old friend, once so patiently instructed me. But can we be sure that the tree was a willow? And that the fruits were apples? Such miracles, it seems, are always out of reach of our direct examination. Let me give you an example of how "miracles" arise. There is a spring on this island that, it is said, I have caused by my magic to issue blood. Now, I had a cup of the so-called blood brought to me and I tasted it; it is water colored with iron. For my trouble in tasting the water, the story is spread about me that I live on this island by drinking blood from a spring that I have caused to flow out of the rock. What am I to do? If I say black, I am accused of white. If I say sweet, my detractors hear bitter. If I stand by a river where the salmon leaps, it is said that I make fish fly like birds.

The salmon flies because it is the nature of that fish to fly. And if stars fall from the sky it is because it is the nature of stars to fall. When it thunders, philosophers are no braver than the rest, but if we look for the *cause* of thunder let us consider not the rumbling anger of the gods but currents of the air. I detract nothing from God; for whatever is, is from Him, and by Him. The events of each day—the birth of animals and men, the growth of plants, thunder, rainfall—are all (according to Augustine) "daily miracles," signs of the mysterious power of God at work in nature. Because of the fullness of Creation, all natural things are filled with the "miraculous." The universe is capacious with astonishing events, events that often defy human understanding. But because something is not understood does not mean that it is miraculous. We must listen to the very limits of human knowledge, and only when reason breaks down utterly should we refer things to God.

If I am skeptical, it is because I have been—with you—a student of philosophy. I honor God, and I honor his creation. If I do not go about in search of "miracles," it is because I find wonderment enough on this acre of rock. Those who charge me with *haeresis* are far from here and are the dupes of hearsay. You are farther yet, in a city puffed up with the pride of Babylon. The fingers of your hands are heavy with gold; your shoulders stoop under the weight of silks and ermines; your table overflows with sweetmeats and game; courtiers and courtesans vie for your attention. Gerbert, who calls himself Sylvester, do not accuse *me* of "choosing." I choose nothing. I have nothing. I live by a simple Rule, given to us by Father Columbanus: I rise from sleep, I work, I pray, I sleep again.

Aileran, abbot

It is said of Saint Kevin—who made apples grow on willows— that when he lifted the host at the celebration of the Eucharist he saw in his hands the body of a beautiful child. There are no willows on this island, and no apples. Nor is there bread for a host. But in my dreams I have seen the child. The child is thin and perfectly formed. His hair is a tangle of golden curls and his skin radiant. His genitals are delicate and not yet coarsened by puberty. He smiles, and his eyes shine like two white pearls. He holds out his hand to me, and when I reach to take it, the hand becomes a viper smeared with blood. I awake in the darkness of my cell. My body shivers with cold. The straw is damp beneath me. *Domine, Domine,* I whisper. I listen for the child's voice and I hear the hiss of the wind.

Gerbert's messenger is on his way, back to Babylon-on-Tiber. So anxious was he to be rid of my island that he did not wait for a calm sea but commanded the oarsmen to row out onto a rising swell. Surprisingly they did so willingly, and looking back would not have been surprised to see this island wreathed in diabolical light. They have heard, perhaps, of the "Satanic lights" that appeared in the sky the first time I preached against the fear of an impending Millennium. My text was the Second Epistle of Peter, chapter 3, verse 8: *But, beloved, be not ignorant of this one thing, that one day is with the Lord as a thousand years, and a thousand years as one day.* I cautioned my little flock against precipitous superstition. I asked them not to be swayed by the general hysteria that had taken hold in the region hereabouts. But the brothers murmured among themselves; they had heard that the bishop of Ardfert had urged his congregation to prepare for Christ's coming. The monks of Innisfallen had begun a regimen of bread and water, and the abbot of that house had added Monday to the Wednesday and Friday fasts. At Ballinskelligs the hours of sleep had been reduced by the abbot to those between the tenth hour and midnight, and in the remaining hours of darkness the monks recited psalms. One of the brothers at Ballinskelligs was said to have pierced his palms with a nail in imitation of the wounds of Christ. When my own brethren heard these things, they felt ashamed. They begged me for sterner mortifications. It did not seem right to them that the monks of the mainland should be more rigorous in their discipline than the monks of the island. I warned them against the sins of ignorance and pride. *The Lord is not willing that any should perish,* I preached, *but that all should come to repentance.* And that night, as if to prove me wrong, the sky to the north of the island danced with flames. Luminous curtains of rose and green light undulated on the horizon, as from distant funeral pyres. Higher in the sky, against the Plough, were corpse candles of yellow and crimson. The monks took refuge in the oratory, and the walls reverberated with the fervor of their prayers. The lights, they believed, were the work of Satan.

Once I watched such lights in the company of Gerbert. We were on the road from Aurillac to Santa Maria de Ripoll in Catalonia, where we intended to study at the renowned library of that monastery. It was a spring night; the road was warm with the heat of the day and the air redolent with the odors of flowering trees—heavy, smothering odors such as I had never experienced in Ireland. My head swam with a kind of intoxication. I was inordinately happy, with the kind of happiness that comes only with a first full awakening to the world. I was twenty-four years of age and my companion two years younger. I felt young and helpless in his company— foolishly, pleasantly helpless. If he had asked me to dance in the road I would have done so. He was less tall than I, more fair, and there was something of the air of a woman in the way he carried himself. His hair was thick and blond and neatly trimmed; he was clean-shaven. The color of his eyes was the same *glaisín* blue as the wool of his cloak, and his thick, full lips never ceased trembling with excitement. A silver bracelet dangled down across his hand, and now and then with a wild stab of his arm he would send it flying back into his sleeve; his fingernails were as smooth and bright as the silver. I thought I had never known anyone so beautiful, and in his presence I managed not to remember the coarseness of my own features, the angularity of my shoulders, the shambling awkwardness of my gait. I was in love—with Gerbert, with Gaul, with the perfumed night, with myself.

Among his few possessions Gerbert carried a small volume of Pliny's *Historia naturalis,* copied in his own hand, and when we saw the lights in the sky he showed me where they are described by Pliny—the aurora borealis, Pliny calls them, the northern dawn. The lights are occasionally seen as far south as Rome, but—says Pliny—they are an almost nightly occurrence in the lands of the Hyperboreans. As we hurried toward our destination and our hospice for the night—was it at Castres? or Carcassonne?—Gerbert read aloud from Pliny, passages full of wonders, of things I had never heard and countries I had never seen. I had come far, from Ireland, the remote perimeter of Christendom. I was learning new things. At Reask I had marveled at the breadth of knowledge of Donatus; now I realized that there was more to know than Donatus had ever dreamed. An endless road of knowledge opened up before me; wonders beckoned. With my new companion I would rediscover the wisdom of the ancients. In Spain we would unstop the fountains of philosophy. I skipped and stretched my legs to match Gerbert's rangy, impatient stride.

That night on the road with Gerbert was not the first time I watched the aurora borealis. I had seen the aurora once before—although I did not yet know it by that name—from the hill above Reask on the night of the Poet. The year was 958; I was sixteen years old. The Poet came to Reask from the east with stories of tripartite warfare between the Dál Cais of north Munster, the Eóganacht of the south, and the Norse at Limerick. Mathgamin mac Cennátig, king of the Dál Cais, and Móel Muad mac Brian, king of the Eóganacht, had laid claim to the high kingship of Munster. As the two Irish chieftains and their forces exhausted themselves in mutual slaughter, the Norse sought by opportunistic alliances to extend their influence. Many towns and monasteries had been sacked, hostages had been taken. As if to emphasize the authenticity of his descriptions of these violent events, the Poet waved his mutilated hand, which lacked all of the digits except the little finger. I stared with fascination. The hand was like a cudgel. Where the fingers had been cut away the skin was black and purple and streaked like bacon with thick white scars. The one remaining finger protruded at the side of the hand at an odd angle, like an iron nail.

The Poet was young, one of that fraternity of versifiers and balladeers who went about the country giving voice to the hopes and fears of the people. He was like a badger—wild, bristly, and darting. He laughed; he laughed almost continuously; even as he recounted the most gruesome details of a battle he hissed out little barbs of laughter. His burning eyes leapt from listener to listener as if he were the Paraclete and we were the Apostles gathered in the Upper Room. The Poet recounted how huge men with gleeful grins hacked at each other with broadswords and axes. He told us how at Sulchóid tenscore houses had been burned to the ground, and how in the lands about Cashel a thousand cattle had been rounded up and driven north. He told us how at Emly the abbot and thirty monks were placed in a cow byre and the building set afire. The Poet danced about, acting out each adventure, his blackberry eyes bulging with a fever heat, his cheeks flushed, his hair flying like flame. Brother Donatus sulked with envy of the Poet's narrative gifts. Fergus Beg rolled his eyes and slapped his fist into his palm with delight at each of the Poet's revelations. The brothers nudged one another, laughed, or shrieked with terror. And I . . . I could not take my eyes from the hand.

When the stories were done, Fergus Beg announced a relaxation of the Rule which prescribed that monks eat in moderation. Brother Niall, our cook, was instructed to prepare a feast—our guest would be honored at the evening meal. The Poet gleamed. His fat, flecked face was like a pudding. He lay back in the grass and threw his arms akimbo and roared at the sky, a great thunderstorm of a laugh, and the monks who stood about gaping were the recipients of mocking winks and a barrage of guffaws and chortles.

But Fergus Beg had in mind a joke of his own. When the

brothers and their guest were gathered in the refectory, the abbot made a speech about how ordinarily the monks partook only of bread, a little milk, and a bit of broth, but that this evening, in honor of our celebrated visitor, we would dine on meat. In came Brother Niall with an oaken platter held high over his head. With great ceremony, he placed the platter in front of the Poet. On it was a mouse, roasted on a tiny willow spit, garnished with butter and wild garlic. The monks sucked in their breaths to hold back their laughter. Solemnly, Fergus Beg gave the Prayer:

> *God's blessing on Munster.*
> *A blessing on her peaks,*
> *On her bare stones,*
> *On her shadowy glens.*
> *A blessing on every treasure*
> *That is produced on her plains,*
> *The food that comes to our table.*
> *May no one be in want of help.*
> *God's blessing on Munster.*

And the Poet, who had as yet made no sign, pushed back his bench and stood. He let his nut-black eyes rest briefly on each person at the table. He scratched his teeth with the nail of his solitary finger, bowed with exaggerated graciousness toward Fergus Beg, and declaimed:

> *The abbot of this holy house*
> *Extends his welcome with a mouse.*
>
> *Not with fish, nor eggs, nor wine,*
> *But with* rodentia *divine.*
>
> *His hospitality, I'll confide,*
> *Is known in Ireland far and wide;*

Owls and kestrels, if they're able,
Flock in numbers to his table.

Come dine on mouse, you'll not get fat,
Join Abbot Fergus—and his cat!

With that, the Poet sneezed out a great spray of laughter across the table, and everyone, including those of us who listened at the windows, roared with him. Brother Niall marched in with bowls of wheat cakes, barley bread and butter, stirabout made from new milk and honey, boiled white and black puddings, and a salad of watercress and brooklime. Brother No-Ear contributed a brimming crock of his freshest ale. Fergus Beg invited all to partake of the feast. The Poet heaved forward and ate as if he had a wolf in his belly, and the banter and stories continued until time for Vespers.

It was a dark hour of the night when I rose from my pallet in the alehouse to go into the yard to relieve myself. The night was clear, as black as *dubh-poill*—the inky-dark sediment at the bottom of the bog pool—and streaked with stars. The grass was wet with dew, and soft and cold under my feet. I leaned against the wall of the milking house and sent my rush of water sizzling into the dung. In the intensified silence that followed the last trickle of my stream, I heard a whisper, which at first I took to be the lowing of the cows. It was a man's whisper and it came from just beyond the outer wall. Silently I moved to where the wall of the milking house abuts the cashel, and with the angle of the wall for my support and putting my feet into the chinks between the stones, I lifted myself to where I could look down out of the monastic enclosure. Two people stood below me, so close together I could make out only a single mass of hair. One figure leaned forward so that the other was corralled between his arms and the wall. His mouth was pressed against her ear. His body rocked gently against hers. It was the Poet and Maire!

I dropped to the ground and ran. Across the compound. Past the alehouse, the refectory, the cook shed, and the cells of the sleeping monks. I let myself out at the gate, and cursed the squeak of the bolt as I drew it back; in my ear it was as loud as the shriek of a slaughtered lamb. I ran through the gardens, the field of oats, and the upper pasture, until I was in the rough furze and the prickles stabbed at my feet and scratched my naked calves. Only when I reached the top of the hill did I stop, falling exhausted onto the ground, terrified at the sound of my heaving breath. *His mouth was against her ear. He touched her bare breast with that horrid hand. His kithless finger, like a thin stiff penis, had brushed her lips.*

On the night of the Poet, through eyes wet with tears, I saw the lights of the aurora shimmering on the northeastern horizon. I thought it must be Limerick burning. I cursed the Poet. I cursed Maire. I cursed the Dál Cais and the Eóganacht and the foreigners of Limerick. All of it, the lights, the battles, the scene by the cashel wall, seemed part of the same treachery, the same wickedness. In the cold, crimson flicker of the aurora the fields about Reask glistened like the scorched skin of a roasted pig; even my own body seemed a thing of scar and gristle, as ugly as the stump of the Poet's hand. *Bualtrach! Bualtrach! Bualtrach!* I pounded foul, hopeless curses into the ground. My anguish seemed unendurable. I did not yet know that the troubles of the Munster kings—and the ugliness of the world—were about to overwhelm us.

Two weeks after the Poet went away from Reask, Brother No-Ear woke me in the first hour of the dawn. He was agitated.

His eyes were as wide and white as two boiled eggs. He shook the sleep from me violently and dragged me into the yard. My head spun as in a mixed-up dream. The monastic enclosure was in turmoil. Monks skittered about like frightened hens, their sandal straps flapping the flagstones. Cattle bucked and bellowed. Through the gate in the outer wall people streamed into the cashel, driving goats and pigs before them. No-Ear pointed. And then I saw them, on the hill where a fortnight earlier I had cursed the earth—a line of men like pales, like a copse of leafless trees, their weapons glinting in the slanted light.

Taking hold of my hair, No-Ear dragged me to the kiln where we dried the malt. Saying nothing, he jammed me inside, and with an unanswerable thrust of his finger made it clear that I was to stay. He went away, and in a moment returned and heaped grain and straw on the sill of the oven. The illumination from outside was almost extinguished, except for thin red slats of light from the rising sun that slotted in through chinks in the unmortared stones. I pushed into the backmost corner of the kiln, my knees against my chin and my arms lashed about them. Against my back the stones of the kiln were still warm from the baking. Even in this first hour of the morning the air in the oven was stifling and scented with grain; in my state of excitement I sucked in gulpfuls of fetid breath and my lungs burned.

I closed my eyes and listened, trying to quieten the clutch and wheeze of my own breath. Voices were indistinguishable—a panicked chattering of jackdaws and tits. And then, like the roar of the sea, a great *barrán-glaed,* or war-whoop, rolled down the slope toward our little rath. The wall, I knew, would be of no use to delay the onslaught; it served only as protection against wolves and weather. The roar of the wave washed over the cashel wall into the compound, and for a moment I expected to hear the clank of metal upon metal until I remembered that we had no weapons. Now the roar was in my head; I could hear nothing else; the world outside seemed strangely silent. The huge turmoil behind my eyes would not subside; I opened my eyes to shake out the terrible bellowing. I saw the blood-red slats of light. And I heard her cry.

Putting my eye to a chink in the wall of the kiln, I looked out into the yard. At first I saw nothing but the head of a bearded soldier in a helmet strapped with hoops of iron. As the soldier moved from the kiln I saw that in his left hand he held Maire and in his right a battle-ax. He dragged Maire to the milking house, and threw her to the wall, holding her face against the stones with his spread hand. He lifted the ax and placed the shining blade against her neck. I thought he meant to cut her, but instead he hooked the tip of the blade beneath the collar of her shift and with a jerk of his arm ripped it from her side. I saw the white of her breast, and the hollow of her waist, and was paralyzed with fear and shame. I did not want to watch, but I could not stop watching. I could see that she was screaming, but heard nothing except the roar in my head. And then the soldier hesitated and looked to the right, and I saw Brother No-Ear approaching with his arm raised, and in his hand, held like a weapon, was the bronze strainer. I knew instantly that it was not to save Maire that he meant to do battle with the soldier, but to protect *me*, to keep *me* from coming out from my hiding place, to keep *me* from protecting *her*. The soldier swung his ax and the strainer went flying, and then I saw that No-Ear's severed hand still clutched the handle. The monk dropped to his knees, grasping the gaping stump of his arm, and with the same spiraling swing of the ax the soldier brought his blade down upon No-Ear's back, and there was a gush of blood such as follows a new calf into the world, and No-Ear fell flat onto the ground. I vomited. My stomach collapsed like a bellows, and the roar in my head became so loud that I thought my skull would shatter. But still I could not move. Still I watched while the soldier had his way with Maire, thrusting again and again against her nakedness, and when he was finished, he twisted her hair in his fist and smashed her head against the stones.

I did not crawl out of my hiding hole until nightfall. All day I stayed in the oppressive oven until I thought I must pass out from the stench of my own vomit, urine, and excrement. I heard nothing. I saw nothing. *Did God do this? Did God do this?* Over and over the question formed deep in my bowels and, rising toward consciousness, burned like acrid smoke in my throat and nostrils. Brother Donatus had said that nothing happens except by the will of God. Had God done this? Had God severed No-Ear's hand? Had God rammed Himself again and again into Maire's split flesh? Had God vomited his abominable blessing upon our small corner of the earth?

When I came out from the kiln, the night air struck me like the cool rush of the Donn stream. I crossed the churned-up yard to the milking shed. Maire's body lay where the soldier had dropped it, bespattered with mud. Her hair was matted with blood. A dried red rivulet curled at the corner of her mouth. Her eyes looked into mine—no, *beyond mine;* they were fixed on the soot-gray clouds that hung over Reask like a shroud. I covered her nakedness with straw.

There was no one alive at Reask. Even the animals lay slaughtered in slurries of blood. No-Ear's body was rent by a chasm of gore. I found his beautiful bronze strainer trampled in mud and dung, still clutched in his severed hand, and carefully pried it loose from the cold and blooded fingers. The door of the alehouse banged in the wind; I hooked it shut with the leather thong. Behind the alehouse, the great stone slab that covered the entrance to the souterrain had been lifted aside, and I knew that the books and the bronze cask were gone. The thatched roof of the refectory was consumed by fire, and smoke curled from inside the four simmering walls as from a hearth; looking in, I found the charred body of Fergus Beg, bound to the smoldering black boards of the great table. Horribly mutilated corpses littered the precincts, one of them that of my teacher Donatus; no one had been spared. Near the gate was a pile of severed heads, stacked neatly as turf.

❈

I had lived all my life within sight and sound of the sea. Often I had walked the strand gathering wrack, or at low tide dillesk and carrageen from the rocks. Never had I entered the water, nor could I swim. Now, leaving the putrescent wreck of Reask behind, I stumbled blindly along the marsh path to the shore, to the place called the Wine Strand. The wind-hurried sea thumped its flint-hard fist on the sand, slapped the plum-colored strand with the flat of its steel sword. I threw off my clothes—rags fouled with sickness and death—and stood naked at the edge of the tide. *Fuck God!* I cried. *Fuck! Fuck! Fuck Him!* And the wind roared, and I was both pleased and terrified that the wind might carry my obscenities to His ear. I was alive. That was my punishment. I was alive because I had cowered in a shit-hole while everyone I loved was butchered. No-Ear had thought to save me, to keep me from emerging from my hiding place, but there had been no danger that I might move. I was a coward. I had *watched* the bearded soldier rape Maire. I had *watched*! I did not even have the courage to close my eyes.

Were they Eóganacht? Or Dál Cais? Or Norse? What alliance had we violated to deserve their savage reprisal? What part did we play in their lunatic wars? It made no sense. Reask had been destroyed with as little consequence as when a man crushes a louse between his fingers. *Nothing happens except by the will of God.* So it was God who had crushed Reask. God had crushed our little community between his fingers, and only I had been spared because I cowered in a shit-hole. Reask had been pinched between the fingers of God until it was a smear of blood, with nothing left but dung and flies—and me. *Fuck Him! Fuck Him!* And I cried. I cried until my face was caked with tears and salt and spray.

I walked into the sea. I wanted it to wash away the foul crust from my skin—the crust of blood and excrement. I walked out into the tide until the sea was at my shoulders and the waves broke into my mouth, and I gagged and coughed on the taste of salt. A swell lifted my feet from the bottom, lifted me as No-Ear might have hauled me up by the nape of my neck, and when I came down the bottom was not there. I was underwater, in Tartarean darkness. There was no up or down. Salt burned in my nose, and it seemed as if all the waters of the seven seas had rushed into my lungs. I would not fight. I would sleep. I would sleep in the cleansing sea, and my body would become as clear and transparent as a jellyfish. Ethereal, matterless. Drifting clear. And then, at the moment when I knew I must die, a great panic took hold of me and I began to thrash about. The surface! Where was the surface? I pushed and flailed for anything solid, landward, enduring. And the black sea offered no resistance.

Rome
September 2, 998
Sylvester II (Gerbert) to Aileran, abbot of Skellig Michael

Gerbert, bishop of Rome, servant of the servants of God, to his friend Aileran, abbot of the monastery of our Lord and Savior on the rock of Skellig, in the province of Munster, Hibernia

Your letter assumes much and answers nothing. You have been accused by your bishop of dangerous heresies. The charges are buttressed by a full dossier of evidence, compiled in large part from the words of your own sermons. The dossier has been examined by theologians appointed to that task from among the doctors of our own household. We must tell you that they find in your words much that is contrary to the teachings of Christ's Church as defined by the Holy Fathers and the Councils. But we did not act precipitously upon their advice. No. Out of consideration for our past alliance, we wrote to you, my brother, and asked for clarification. Far from dispelling the accusations, you have hurled them back into our face. You spite us. You insult us. You presume a position of moral superiority. You flaunt the unnatural simplicity of your present eremitical circumstances and wear your white martyrdom impertinently.

As your compatriot Father Columbanus taught us: "A religion is idle that is decorated with prostrations of the body; equally idle is the mere mortification of the flesh." A false asceticism can be a prop for pride, and the incautious anchorite can soon be puffed up with self-satisfaction and think himself superior to all men. Mortifications are no substitute for humility. To live with Christ, we must become dead to our own will. Therefore, Aileran, do not mistake your cell for the Church, or your island rock for Christendom. A proper asceticism must be founded on the Rock of Christ, and that Rock is Peter.

Since by the grace of God we have assumed this pontifical authority we have had but one purpose: to see God's Holy Church made one in peace and charity. This is a work of the utmost urgency. The world has become corrupt. Christians make war against one another. Secular princes are set against bishops, abbots against emperor. Monastic houses have become citadels—the *militia Christi* has become of sad necessity a *militia mundi*. Ecclesiastical properties are sequestered by princes. The countryside is racked with violence, hunger, and distress. There is terror everywhere. Secular strife is compounded and abetted by discord in the Church. The Churches of Alexandria and Antioch have been forfeited. Constantinople has removed itself from Rome. Asia and Africa are lost to our authority. Parts of Spain and the countries of the north know nothing of Roman judgment. Recent popes have led lives of licentious debauchery. One of our predecessors in this Holy Office lived incestuously with his sister, consecrated deacons in his stables, and made a bishop of a ten-year-old boy; another of our predecessors cut off the hands of the cardinals who voted against him. Bishops sell privileges to fill their personal treasuries. Priests live openly with concubines. It is not difficult to understand why so many of the faithful anticipate the imminent conclusion of the world. O lamentable world! O lamentable Rome!

It is our duty to restore the world to Christ, and to prepare the Church as Bride for the Bridegroom, adorned in white garments and pure as snow. In past centuries this Eternal City gave to the world great popes, Leos and Gregorys, the shining stars of our ancestors. And what shall I say of Gelasius and Innocent, who in their scholarship and eloquence towered above the worldly learning of the schools. If the Roman Church is to preserve her stewardship over all other Churches, as appointed by our Savior, then she must be worthy of respect, she must excel all others in virtuous living and wisdom. In this great work we have the support of our new Caesar, Otto III, who seeks to unite in one great Christian empire all the nations of the earth, a German prince who has appointed a Frank to the See of Rome, the first since Christ founded His Church upon Peter's Rock. In assuming this heavy responsibility we have taken the name Sylvester II, in memory of our predecessor who at the time of Constantine administered a great Christian empire bounded by Contantinople and Rome.

If the world is to be restored, then Christ's Holy Church must speak with one voice. It is our will that all peoples ruled by the administration of our clemency shall practice the religion which Peter the Apostle transmitted to the Romans and which endures to this day. As Christ Our Lord tells us, there shall be but one flock and one shepherd. Against all heretics we will endeavor to enforce the *consensus ecclesiae,* and we will endure no personal visions of the faith that threaten ecclesiastical unity by ignoring scripture, tradition, or creed. The alternative is continued anarchy, terror, and despair.

I shall ignore the element of doubt you expressed in your letter concerning the immortality of the soul; those doubts are not given expression in the dossier that has been given us. It is only with your public influence upon the faithful that we are piously

43

concerned. In particular, it is your teaching on miracles that perniciously infects the unity of the Faith—your denial of God's power to suspend the laws of nature if and when He chooses to do so. If God ordains through the agency of Saint Kevin to cause a willow tree to bear apples, then most certainly He has that power. Undermine the confidence of the faithful in such miracles and you must inevitably plant seeds of doubt concerning the greater miracles of the Incarnation and Resurrection, upon which our Holy Faith is founded. Dismantle the universal affirmation of the Faith—the common order of the *consensus ecclesiae*—and you release upon the world the terrible malignancies of violence and blood that you have yourself witnessed. Do not believe, Aileran, that any secular administration can alone preserve the order of the common good. Only a *conceptus* has the power to give unity and peace—and that *conceptus* is the Holy Faith consigned by Christ to Peter and defined by the councils of Nicaea and Constantinople.

I will temporarily withhold action. I urge you to moderation. Again I ask for your abdication to our will. Do not, Aileran, let reason unenlightened by faith lead you on the road to perdition. You say: "If I am skeptical, it is because I am a student of philosophy." Give mind to the words of Paul to the Colossians: "Beware lest anyone deceive you through philosophy and vain deceits in the ways of men." We do not need philosophy when we have Jesus, nor do we need unbounded inquiry now that we have the Gospel. Reason must be ruled by faith. The most dangerous heretics come tricked out in philosophy.

Many years have passed since we were last together. On that occasion, as you must often recall, we intervened on your behalf. Our intervention averted a terrible physical tragedy to your person. Consider now, Aileran, that our present intervention has as its only goal the aversion of a spiritual tragedy. If once your body stood in danger of impairment, now your soul risks the eternal injury of hellfire. We fondly remember our former comradeship. Do not doubt that our concern is grounded in anything other than the kindest fraternal affection.

☧ Farewell. *Sylvester II*, Gerbert, Pope, bishop of Rome

What I first noticed about Aurillac were the colors. At Reask, in Ireland, the world was rendered in shades of green, brown, and gray. But in the lands of the monastery of Saint Gerald in south-central Gaul, I saw blues and violets, yellows, ochers and orange, pinks and vermilion. The valley simmered and steeped in liquidy hues, blushed and pied with the rainbow smoke of summer. Azure fleabanes and scarlet poppies carpeted the meadows. Between the meadows and the forest were orchards: apples, pears, plums, and peaches—yes, peaches!—each contributing generous dollops of pigment to the mural landscape. I saw blue-green stands of almond, walnut, and mulberry trees, although I did not yet know the names of these exotic plants, nor had I yet tasted their fruit. And medlar, laurel, fig, and quince. All of this was laid out before me as I approached Saint Gerald's along the road from Limoges. I had traveled for several days through the densely forested valleys of Limousin. Now, at Aurillac, the stygian forest opened out before me as into a paradisial garden. At the center of cleared and richly cultivated lands I saw the buildings of the monastery and the town, disposed as by the hand of a master artist. From the bough of a tree by the side of the road I plucked a peach; I turned it in my hand, enjoying the delicious convexity and color of the fruit—yellow flushed with rose—and brushed its downy skin against my cheek. I bit into this marvelous thing, sank my teeth deep to the pit, and let the juices run down my chin and neck. Never had I tasted any food so succulent.

This, I thought, is Eden. This is the garden of our first parents and foolish were they to have lost it by sin. The pity of it! Donatus had told me the story of Eve and Adam in their chaste nakedness. And the snake, coiled and purple, the color of a bruised thumb. The fruit, succulent and sweet. The Fall. The irrational, impetuous sin. The loss, the penance. Eve standing up to her neck in the waters of the Tigris, her hair floating on the stream. Adam fasting in the Jordan. The loss! I closed my eyes and for a moment, as always in those days when I closed my eyes, came the terrible dream. The stinking hell of the kiln. The obscenities and murders. The blood-brown flower of Maire's violated flesh, the rivulet of dried blood at her mouth. The severed hand grasping the bronze strainer—like a blood-soaked glove. Sinking, flailing, grasping in a sea of blood, sucked down into the dung-thick slime at the bottom of the sea. And then—God's pity—cast up on the sand, scrubbed clean. I was drowned in the waters of Adam's sin, and by a lucky wave tossed up again onto the Wine Strand as clean and naked as the day I was born. The pall of gray-black clouds had cleared and a fair moon moistened the plum sand. Reask was destroyed. In all of the great world I knew only one place that I might go. At Aurillac in Gaul was the monastery of Saint Gerald, whose abbot, Colman, was the brother of Donatus. Donatus had often described that monastery to me, told me of its reputation for learning and its library of marvelous books. Gathering my rags and the bronze strainer, I put my back to Reask and set out for Aurillac. The strainer bought my passage from Ireland to Gaul; for the rest, I relied upon my wits and pity.

The buildings of Saint Gerald's shamed the huts of Reask. It would be weeks before I had fully explored the many compartments of the monastery, learning my way through the maze of doors and connecting passages, creating in my mind a kind of map: church, cloister, dormitories, refectory, kitchen, cellars, warming room, infirmary, visitors' hospice, and abbatial house. And more! Arrayed about the central core: the bakery, brewery, drying house, kiln, winnowing shed, mill, granary, bath, laundry, and latrine. Gravel paths and fig trees. Kitchen garden, herb garden, and medicinal garden. Monks' cemetery. Pigsty, goat stalls, sheepfold, gooseyard, and cow byres—in the soft evening hours filled with a consoling murmur of bleats and mewings. Here at Saint Gerald's were arrangements for the satisfaction of every want of soul and body, set out with order and tidiness: woven thatch, polished wood, blanched stone. This, surely, was the Heavenly City spoken of by Father Augustine, "freed from all evil and filled with all good." Or so it seemed to my incredulous eyes, to a young heart hungering for something safe and certain. (I did not yet know that every good contains within itself the seed of evil, like the pit of the peach, and that the greatest goods contain within their rose-blushed skin the nut-hard core of eternal pain.) Full of unbounded optimism, I approached the porter's house and heard the monks singing in the church a familiar Latin psalm, but in a kind of chant such as I had not heard in Ireland: *He delivereth me from mine enemies: yea, thou liftest me up above those that rise up against me: thou hast delivered me from the violent man.*

On the day of my arrival at Saint Gerald's I was received by Abbot Colman. He was eager for news of Donatus. Tearfully I told him of the fate of our community at Reask and of my last glimpse of my teacher, his brother—the butchered body, the severed head like a clod of turf, carrion for crows and jackdaws. Colman listened, saying nothing, rocking slowly in his chair. He was a small man, smaller and older than Donatus, and heavier, with pouchlike cheeks knitted with blue veins; not a hair on his head, but with brows as bushy as a calf's tail; and fat pink lips, like Donatus's, pursed as if forming a Latin vowel. When I had finished my account of the raid on Reask and the subsequent butchery, he put his hand upon my knee and said consolingly in Irish: "Straw is consumed by fire, but clay is hardened. You are clay. You will be made strong."

And as I had hoped, he invited me to stay. He placed me in the care of the winemaster, Brother Madalberta. I was given a bed in the novices' convent—a bare gray room above the infirmary, with three small windows that looked out across the monastery wall to the vineyards—and two clean shirts, sandals, and an outer garment of sturdy coarse cloth. Madalberta tossed into the fire the rags I had worn on my journey: *"brocamas, aoileach,"* he said, in the dialect of Reask—"filth, shit." He put back his head and laughed a sawing sort of laugh, his fat tongue clenched between his teeth like a ripe plum.

I understood nothing then of the language of Aurillac. Several of the monks were Irish, and with them I could converse, although their dialects were strange to my ear. For the rest I relied upon fragments of Latin. For Madalberta, I recited what prayers I knew. *In nomine patria et filia,* I began—and he roared with laughter. "In the name of the *nation* and the *daughter,*" I had said. In the weeks that followed, in the tutelage of Madalberta, I spent long hours with my Latin grammar and memorized the Credo, the Pater, and the prayers of the Mass. I recited the stories of the saints that I had learned with Donatus, and Madalberta corrected my errors of grammar and pronunciation. There was at first little time for instruction. Soon after my arrival came the harvest and the pressing of the grapes; we buzzed about our work like bees in the hive—with Madalberta as our queen, issuing orders, correcting, instructing, goading. But afterward, through the months of winter, spring, and early summer, my duties as Madalberta's assistant were few: We maintained the cellars, Madalberta tasting the vintage and turning the casks as required like a harpist carefully tuning his harp; he supervised the carpenters who built the casks of oak and the smiths who forged the iron hoops, and sometimes it was necessary that I caulk the casks with pitch; we walked the vineyards, and Madalberta taught me how to prune the vines and support them on their poles, and how to recognize the insects and musts that might harm the grapes. And as we went about these pleasant tasks he gave me the Frankish tongue and smoothed the ragged edges from my Latin, and showed me how to conform my life to the bell and the Rule of Saint Gerald's.

⬡

The Rule! Life at Saint Gerald's was organized more regularly than at Reask, according to the canons of Benedict. As I was not professed, I was excused from the observance of the Rule, and in particular from the rigor of the Night Office, but nevertheless I was soon swept along by the regular tide of prayer, study, and work that characterized the monastic discipline. It was a kind of life that suited me perfectly, as an antidote to the chaos and disorder I had recently experienced at Reask and on my journey from Ireland. Here was a rhythm, a kind of music, which I soon came to understand was attuned to the rhythms of nature, to the seasons and the cycle of night and day, so that together prayer and work, winter's cold and summer's heat, light and darkness, constituted a kind of polyphonic harmony, a "joyful noise," stirred up out of the earth and the elements, and formed in our lungs and in the chambers of these buildings, as in the pipes and wind box of an organ, a music rising to God's throne. My body was a passive instrument, one of the many in that house, upon which the music was played: a throbbing, a pulsing, as regular as a heartbeat, as melodious as the song of a thrush, which encompassed in some mysteriously capacious way all of Creation and yet was as private and intimate as a dream. The making of this music was—as the abbot reminded us—the *opus Dei,* the work of God, and the reason for the existence of our community: the buildings, the orchards, the cultivated fields carved out of the trackless, wolf-infested forest. If the music ceased, said Colman, if it was blown away and dispersed by the wind, then the power of Satan would prevail, the forest encroach upon our Paradise, and the sin of Adam overwhelm the world.

We rose in darkness in the eighth hour of the night for the Night Office, which the monks gathered in the church to sing—psalms, glorias, and alleluias, a long and demanding discipline which I struggled to follow in the novitiate, nodding and dozing. In winter, the time of darkness between the Night Office and dawn was used by the monks for study or for reading; in the short nights of summer there was barely time to go to the latrine before the celebration of Lauds, which was sung at daybreak. During the day, the monks stopped whatever they were doing for the communal prayers of Prime, Tierce, Sext, and None. Vespers was sung at about five or six o'clock in the evening, usually by candlelight; we called that office the hour of the candle, *lucernaris hora.* Compline, before bed, was completed with the abbot's blessing and dismissal. Meals, too, were like a part of the Divine Office, taken in silence but accompanied by a reading, perhaps something from the lives of the desert fathers or from Cassian's *Institutes* and *Conferences.*

"A wise man is known by few words," said Madalberta, quoting Proverbs, and he encouraged me to silence in anticipation of the time when I would embrace the Rule. He himself spoke only when required as part of his responsibilities, or for my instruction. And so I kept my lips sealed and listened. And I heard the music; and I learned to hear. The chanting of the monks. The bell. The vines bending in the wind like Aeolian harps. The birds: the cuckoo and the corncrake, the warbler and the lark, and at night, like a *nocturnae solemnitates,* the swish and croak of the roding woodcock's amorous flight. And there was another sound: the insistent, petulant urging of the flesh, the murmur and coo issuing from my genitals and resonating in my head, the small incessant voice of sex like a flow or purl that spoke every time I closed my eyes—at night, in the darkness of the church, as I bowed my head at meal prayers, in the musty cloister of the cellar—Satan's contemptible plan, nagging at my soul the way a dog yaps at the legs of a laggard cow, driving me away from the arms of Christ into mortal sin and the fires of hell. And if I allowed myself to listen for even a moment, the image would come, the scurrilous and unwelcome image of the soldier and

Maire, the dark power of his sex, the whiteness of her skin, the violence and beauty of ultimate evil, terrifying and enticing. In this unceasing battle against my soul's pollution I was assisted by the Rule, which fragmented my life into a succession of full moments, each anticipating the next, and kept me tired.

Madalberta told me this story of our founder, Gerald of Aurillac: *On a certain occasion Gerald became enchanted by the charms of a pretty peasant girl who lived upon his estate. He arranged to meet with her for an evening rendezvous. When they came together, God made her appear so ugly that his passion was abated and he let her go. Saved from sin by a miracle, and fearing a recurrence of temptation, he arranged her marriage, freed her from his service, and bestowed upon her a plot of land.* Such stories were meant to strengthen the young novices in their struggle against impure thoughts and actions, but in fact they stirred the embers of lust. The Rule provided a more effective assistance in our battle against Satan: A candle burned all night in our dormitory, and our beds were interspersed with those of older monks. And so the two simultaneous necessities of sin—vigor and solitude—were denied us. Busyness, silence, humility, prayer: These were the elements of our microcosm, and when at the end of my first year at Aurillac Madalberta read me the Rule and asked if I was prepared to live by it, I could answer with a willing and unhesitant "yes."

I would not be allowed to profess until the age of twenty. But once each year Madalberta read me the Rule of Saint Gerald's and repeated this formula: "Behold the law under which you wish to fight. If you can observe it, enter upon the life; if not, you are free to leave." I did not leave. I was happy at Aurillac. I thrived on the Rule. I fought the battle, and by and large I won. Madalberta did not—could not—replace No-Ear in my affections, but he was a man of admirable rectitude and steadiness. He

51

lived the Rule with unflinching fidelity, and although at the time of the harvest and the crushing of the grapes we were excused from many of the offices, he found time to make them up even if it meant going without meals or sleep. With him I learned the meaning of the rule of silence. The Rule quotes Psalms: *I held my peace and was silent, even from speaking good things.* At first this puzzled me: We do not speak evil lest we sin, but why do we not speak good things? In the spare economy of Madalberta's speech I saw that most of what comes from our mouths is idle chatter that serves no other purpose than to fill time and spin frivolous, cobwebby threads of connection with our brothers. Madalberta spoke only when his words had substance; for the rest there was purposefulness and action, and it became clear to me that out of his silence came strong bonds of trust and respect between himself and the other monks. Madalberta possessed happiness without frivolity, joy without silliness.

In the summer of my nineteenth year the weather was perfect for the grape. A month of drenching rains was followed by long unbroken weeks of generous sunshine. As the days passed and the grapes swelled like plums, Madalberta's eyes began to glow with the gleam of a fine vintage wine. By August the weight of the harvest threatened to bring the vines down from their poles, and I spent many hours in the vineyard propping and tying the grapes. It was work such as might occupy the saints in Paradise. I went into the vineyard in the heat of the day with a midday meal of figs and honey; the earth was soft and hot under my bare feet, and the sun put a delicious fever in my cheeks. The woolen garment we were provided for our summer labor was lighter than our winter tunic, but still I sweated as I tended the vines, a rich full sweat that made my body glisten like the watered earth. Below, in the valley, the bell called the monks to Sext and None; my own thoughts answered only the bell of the vine—until the moment that I saw *him*.

He lay asleep in the grass at the end of the row of vines. He appeared to be about my own age or a little younger. The sun fell full upon his face, which was fair and fine, and framed as with new brass by the tangles of his blond hair. He wore a shirt of polished white linen and leggings dyed crimson (the color that in Ireland we obtained from the plant called *roid*). His shoes of supple goatskin were tossed to the side, shoes too fine to be those of a traveler, and any thief could have made off with them while he slept. After I had stood gaping for a moment I became embarrassed and turned back to the vines, which I trimmed and propped. When next I turned to look at him he was awake, up on his elbows, grinning broadly and watching me.

"What is this place?" he asked.

Aurillac, I replied.

"AU-ril-lac. Au-RIL-lac. Au-ril-LAC." He rolled each round syllable upon his tongue as if he were tasting grapes. "Then *that* would be Saint Gerald's," he said, pointing into the valley.

I nodded assent.

"And who is this Gerald?" he asked.

I told him of our founder, Gerald of Aurillac, a lay count of Aquitaine and a man of enormous wealth (it was said that he could travel from Puy-Griou to Salat, a journey of a week, sleeping only in his own castles), who was nevertheless noted for his piety, charity, modest dress, and simplicity of life.

"It is easier for a camel to pass through the eye of a needle than for a rich man to enter heaven," said Gerbert—for, yes, it was *he* whom I had found sleeping.

I became defensive: *There are miracles* . . . I began, and halted, tongue-tied.

"Ha!" cried Gerbert. "Yes, of course there are miracles. There would be, wouldn't there? There are always miracles. Let me guess. A deer comes to lie unafraid at his feet? A cloak given to a beggar becomes a garment of silk? A woman is made ugly by a miracle and thereby the saint's virtue is saved?"

He grinned. He was handsome—his face unblemished, almost

plump. His lips quivered. He was playing with me, for indeed each of the miraculous episodes he mentioned was associated with the life of Saint Gerald. I parried, uncertain how to respond: *Gerald used his wealth to build this place,* I said. I felt the fool.

"Yes," Gerbert responded. "Yes, of course. That's one way of stretching open the needle's eye, of making it large enough to allow passage for the wealth-laden soul. With a place like this to one's credit"—he gestured to the monastic buildings baking yellow in the sun—"one could march comfortably through the needle's eye with one's whole kit and retinue."

I blushed; I was frightened and angry. *We have relics,* I stammered.

"Hmm, yes." Gerbert studied the valley, the monastery, the gardens, the vineyards, and the orchards. One would have thought they were his own. And then he added: "And what would they be? The relics, I mean. A tooth, the paring of a nail, a hair from his head? Yes, of course. All those little bits and snippets of dear old Gerald. It's amazing there was anything left of him to stick in the ground."

That's blasphemy, I said. A *sin.* I walked away from him down along the row of vines.

"Wait!" he called after me. "Wait. I was only having a bit of fun."

He caught up with me and stopped me with his hand on my shoulder. I jerked from under it.

"Listen." He was suddenly apologetic. "I confess that I do know this place. I was born not far from here and lived for ten years in this very monastery. I know Saint Gerald's as well as the lines on the palm of my hand."

And he showed me his palm, unfolded it under my nose as if it were a small map, and then offered me his hand.

"I've been away," he said. "Traveled a bit. Now I'm back. Back for good. I'll take the vows. Have you professed? Are you a monk here?"

I studied his eyes, as blue as the sky. His eyes were open,

honest. I took his hand, and shook my head in a negative answer. *I am a novice,* I said, *but soon I will take the vows.*

"Ah! Ah, grand!" He took my elbow and steered me toward the monastery. "That's wonderful. I like you, I really do. Perhaps we can profess together."

I found myself hoping that it would happen as he said. His closeness made me feel somehow cleverer, less alone. I was heartened by the touch of his shoulder brushing against my own as we tramped down the dusty path toward the vineyard gate. I had never had a comrade of my own age. Perhaps this beautiful, effusive young man would become my friend.

"Wait! Wait!" he suddenly cried. He turned and strode gracefully back up the path. "I forgot my shoes!"

Gerbert was a natural scholar. Already he had mastered the Latin grammar. His proficiency was such that he was assigned to assist certain of the older monks who struggled to learn the rudiments of reading and writing. Languages came easily to him. He spoke fluent ecclesiastical Latin, of course, and the *lingua romana* of the region around Aurillac. He understood without difficulty the dialects of Aquitaine, Languedoc, and Burgundy, and had a good smattering of the Germanic tongues and the languages of the Basques and Bretons. I could speak to him in Irish and he understood, almost intuitively, the meaning of the words and the rules of the grammar. *An capall,* I would say, indicating a horse. *"Na capaill"*—he grinned, making the plural. And then in a rush: *"An capall bán"*—a white horse—*"na capaill bhána"*—white horses. His lips trembled with excitement when he caught a glimpse of the internal structure of a language. When visitors arrived at Saint Gerald's from far-off places, Abbot Colman often asked Gerbert to act as interpreter, and even if the language or dialect was one he had never before encountered, he could usually provide a fair translation of the speech. His gift for languages meant that book-learning came easily to him. He could quote the Rule verbatim, and all of Psalms, and—most eloquently—the Song of Solomon. "In my bed at night I sought him who my soul loves," he might declaim at some odd moment, giving me a conspiratorial wink, and then rattle off a dozen verses of the dialogue of the Bridegroom and the Bride. He loved knowing the stories of how things came to be, and he was passionately interested in the past. He often regaled me with tales of Charles Martel or the court of Charlemagne. And almost alone among the monks of Saint Gerald's, he was proficient at the manipulation of the Roman numerals.

For a year we shared the novitiate with half a dozen younger boys and a few older monks. But except for the hours of sleep, we were seldom together; our responsibilities kept us apart—I with the vines, Gerbert with the business of interpretation and translation—and at prayers and meals we were assigned to separate places. But on those occasions when we were alone together there was an easy camaraderie between us. Gerbert paid no mind to the rule of silence. He chattered incessantly. He spun tales. He reeled off lines of verse. And he teased. I blushed and ripened in his sunny disposition. Occasionally on a Sunday or a Feast Day we walked together in the vineyard where we first met, or higher on the hill to the edge of the forest. Below us the vines fell away in ranks to the sparkling silver thread of the river on the valley floor. "Catch the foxes for us, the little foxes, that make havoc of the vineyards, for our vineyards are in flower," he recited from his favorite book of the Scriptures. Or he would tell me of places he had been in his travels—Lyon, Saint Maurice, Saint Gall—and of the places he wished yet to go, there, down the valley of the Cére River, beyond the hills.

To Ireland? I asked.

"No, not that God-forsaken place. South," he exclaimed, pointing toward the sun, "south to the pear grove of Augustine."

The most astonishing thing about Gerbert was his physical

ease. In a place where touch was forbidden he dispensed touches like gifts. He would fling his arm about my shoulders and whisper some hilarious thing in my ear, or he would take my hand to drag me off to spy on the girls of the village. He would poke and tease the younger novices or tousle their hair, although never in the presence of our monitors. There was an exuberance to his flesh, an excess of physical feeling. Sometimes while changing his clothes or preparing for bed he would stand naked, and we—the younger boys and I—did not know whether to gape or avert our eyes. He was handsome: skin full but firm, limbs well proportioned, penis neither flaccid nor fully erect. He appeared in those moments of casual posturing like a statue of the pagan Romans, shiny pink marble, at once decadent and chaste. Whether he did this to shock us or out of an unpremeditated immodesty I do not know.

Oh, Gerbert! What sweet torment you caused me. You were the fox in the vineyard. Your guile was like honey. Even when you were out of my sight I carried your image with me: Gerbert of the yellow curls, bent over a parchment, puzzling out the meaning of a Latin text or learning a few new words of Greek, the tip of the quill pen touching your trembling lips.

In the autumn of my twentieth year I was allowed to profess. In the presence of the abbot and the assembled monks I vowed before God and his saints to be stable and obedient and to live like a monk. This I promised in the names of Saint Gerald and Abbot Colman. And when I had made the oral promise, I wrote it out on a slip of parchment and placed it upon the altar stone that covered the relics of Gerald. Three times I said this verse: *Accept me, O Lord, according to your promise, and I shall live according to your rule, and let me not be confounded in my expectation,* and three times the assembly repeated it after me. Then I prostrated myself before each of my brothers in turn and begged his prayers. And when I came at last to Colman, he lifted me and said: "Donatus would be proud. He is with the saints and martyrs in Heaven, sanctified by his own blood and the Blood of Christ. Red martyrdom was the most precious gift Our Lord could have granted to Donatus. Live now in such a way as to honor him." And even then, at the moment of profession, when my thoughts should have been entirely with Christ and my will completely obedient to his Holy Church, even then I thought of Gerbert and wished he might share my pride. The Rule forbade the exercise of one's own will; yet even as I professed obedience to the Rule, my will rebelled. I was puffed up with an awareness of my *self*, as water fattens a sponge, and tried to imagine myself as I might appear in *his* eyes. The Rule quotes Proverbs: *There are ways that seem right to men, but they lead to the depths of hell.* And I knew then, even in my first moments as a monk, that I would not live in the fullness of the Rule. Even then the fox was moving among the vines.

"You are a monk," said Gerbert, when we were next alone. "Now the Rule requires that you must always be thinking of your sins. What a delicious rule—to be obliged always to be thinking of sin. Ha!" And he gave me a mock jab in the ribs. It was the last time he would touch me for a long while. We were almost never alone. Upon profession I was moved out of the novitiate into the monks' dormitory, away from Gerbert, and my duties as Madalberta's assistant kept me busy. It was October, the month of the vintage. The grapes were to be cut, carried to the winery, and crushed in the press. For this Madalberta organized gangs of workers from the village, and it was my task to supervise them in the field—men and women, young and old. It was exhilarating work, an intoxicating harmony of color and motion, redolent with the sweet smells of grapes and sweat. When the grapes were in the press the women crushed them with their feet, skirts tucked up at the waist. The juice we let out into casks we had prepared during the previous winter and spring. Some of the casks were stored in the cellar of the monastery. Others went to the village of Aurillac. The excess were sold to merchants who moved them on convoys of carts or boats to the cities of the Rhone, or to Bordeaux—from where it is possible that some of our Aurillac wine made its way to Ireland.

At about this time the count of Aurillac returned from a journey to Italy with the gift of a book for the library of Saint Gerald's—*De fabrica mundi,* "The Frame of the World," by Victorinus of Pettau. This was a rare work from the third century, inscribed on vellum and bound in leather, and unknown to any of the scholars at our house. Colman assigned Paulinus, one of our more learned monks, to prepare a commentary, with Gerbert as his scribe. Of what happened next I know only the rudest outline. Gerbert, it seems, in transcribing the commentary of Paulinus, found that he did not agree with the interpretation of his older brother. The book of Victorinus is based upon the theory of numbers, of which Paulinus knew little and Gerbert much. For example, Victorinus begins his story of the Creation on the fourth day and draws threads of connection with the history of salvation through the various figures of the number four: the four elements, the four seasons, the four animals before God's throne, the four gospels, the four rivers of Paradise, and so forth. There was a subtlety in the way Victorinus compared the days of Creation with the days of the week and in his use of days to represent generations and millennia. Much of this—according to Gerbert—Paulinus failed to understand or misconstrued. Gerbert prepared his own commentary and showed it to Paulinus, who became enraged and went directly to the abbot to complain. Colman called Gerbert before him. "No one doubts your talents," the abbot chided Gerbert, "but you must not presume to teach your superiors. The Rule requires that the young monk make his will subservient to his masters." Gerbert protested, asserting the correctness of his own interpretation of Victorinus, and trembled with indignation. Colman was unswayed; he relieved Gerbert of service to Paulinus and required him instead to transcribe books of financial accounts—dull, stultifying dog-work. And then Gerbert did something rash; he slipped away from the monastery and went to the castle of the count of Aurillac, with his commentary on *De fabrica mundi* and part of that of Paulinus. He hoped to convince the count of the correctness of his views and entreat intercession with the abbot.

There was a sickness in that house, which the count had brought with him from the south. Already a dozen members of the count's retinue had become infected, and half of those had died. The master of the house himself lay mortally ill. Gerbert was asked to leave, but he stayed on, lingering with the servants, hoping for a chance to bring his case before the count. For two days he remained at the castle of the count of Aurillac, until forcibly retrieved upon Colman's orders. During those two days, his body fell prey to the invisible scourge.

When I heard that Gerbert lay dying, I asked for permission to visit him. I was refused, for my friend was held in the strictest quarantine. I volunteered then to be his nurse, as assistant to the infirmarian. It was in this way that I came to his bedside. What I found was shocking. Gerbert was flushed with fever, his fair pink skin turned scarlet and black. He shook uncontrollably in the bed. His arms and thighs were pocked with foul pustules that oozed venom. In his terror-stricken eyes I saw that I was recognized.

"I'll burn in hell," he stammered, forcing the words past his swollen tongue. "I'll burn in hell."

I could not answer; I shook my head helplessly.

He grinned, a savage frightened grin; his eyes swam with fear. I fixed upon the whiteness of his teeth as the only omen of hope in the disorder of his ravaged face.

"I'll burn in hell," he said again, and then again, in Irish, "*Dóim . . . ifreann.*"

The glowing ash of his cheeks, the tongue like a fiery coal he could neither swallow nor eject, the white diabolical grin: *God forgives,* I whispered.

"If He does, He is a fool," blasphemed Gerbert.

And I knew then that nothing I could say would alleviate his fear. With a sponge and cold water I bathed his body, cooling the festering toadskin flesh. I thought of the psalm: *You brush men away like dreams, they are like grass that flourishes in the morning, and in the evening it is mown and withered.*

Skellig
November 2, 998
Aileran to Gerbert, bishop of Rome

Gerbert, greetings.

For a fortnight a gale has raged about the Skellig, throwing sheets of stinging black spray over the highest pinnacles of the island; the wind is from the west, out of the sea, and lashes the island with a whip of thongs. I cannot leave my cell. I have little to eat: a few bird eggs, taken uncooked, leeks, a bit of rancid butter, a bite of cheese. And for drink, only an occasional swallow of goat's milk and the salty mix of rain and spray that collects in the niches of my stone cell. I have become very weak. I meditate and I pray. I cast my prayers onto the wind as a stranded sailor casts into the sea messages scratched on bits of wood or bone. I am intent upon recollecting the past, and in the darkness and silence of my cell (I no longer hear the roar of the wind) my memories are bright and vivid. Do you remember the day we met, in the vineyard above Saint Gerald's? You wore a shirt of white linen and crimson leggings. Your goatskin shoes were cast aside in the grass, and when we went below to the monastery you almost forgot them. I close my eyes: I feel the heat of that day on the back of my neck and taste the dust in the air. The dust is sweet, flavored with the scent of the vines. Thirty-six years! So much has happened.

I recollect Brother No-Ear and Maire, and the terrible events that ended their lives. I remember Madalberta, his good and gentle silence. And Melisande! Day and night I dream of Melisande; sometimes when I wake in darkness I put out my hand expecting to find her asleep at my side, as once we slept together in the cottage by the river at Verzenay. And of course, Gerbert, I dream of you: not as pope of Rome, or archbishop of Rheims, or abbot of Bobbio, but as a novice at Saint Gerald's, full of lively confidence and animal spirits. I remember your profession of vows, and how when you prostrated yourself before me and asked my forgiveness you looked up and winked. And I remember your commentary on Victorinus, and the pestilence your pride brought upon our house. Your beautiful pink skin was pocked with sores and your eyes were instruments of fear. *I'll burn in hell*, you said. Do you remember, Gerbert? A dozen of our brothers died of the infection you brought into our house, including Paulinus, and you were saved. In shame, you threw the offending commentary onto the fire. And then, weeks later, when the scars of the pox had faded from your skin, you wrote it out again from memory and placed it in the library of Saint Gerald's.

And *will* we burn in hell, Gerbert? You and I? Tertullian tells us that all souls, saved and damned, will reside in the *inferi*, or underworld, until the time of resurrection. Even those souls that are destined to be saved, he tells us, must pay "to the last farthing," until the coming of the millennial kingdom, when the damned will be cast into Gehenna and the saved will enter into eternal blessedness. Are we saved? Or damned? What is the balance? Does the scale of our lives tip toward the bosom of Abraham or toward the abyss? Ah, Gerbert, that is the great conundrum: We have no way of knowing whether we are saved or damned. The theologians of Rome, working day and night upon the wondrous abacuses that you brought back from Spain, could not solve the calculus of our sins. But—if my accusers and their frenzied flock are right—we shall not have long to wait before the answer is given. We shall not linger in the *inferi;* we are—say my very own monks—the generation that is born to the Millennium, and upon our deaths will come the end of time.

I am ordered under threat of excommunication to appear at Ardfert to answer the charges against me. The representative of the bishop arrived here together with your own courier. I refused to return with them, nor would they wait for my replies. The season is late; it will now be spring before they can return to the island to take me by force. And you, Gerbert, must wait for this letter. You will see that it is written on the back of the order from Ardfert, wherein are listed my alleged crimes against the faith. You will find what is manifestly a tissue of contradictions: According to these assertions, I make God subservient to nature, and I identify nature with God; I deny miracles, and I am the instrument of Satanic magic; I reject the authority of Scriptures, and I falsely quote Scriptures to support my heretical views; I am derisive of the authority of my superiors, and I have failed to assert my own authority as abbot. How could I *not* be guilty of one or the other of these errors? By now the order of excommunication has perhaps gone into effect. The calculus of sin has been superseded. I am damned by edict. My soul is consigned to the abyss by episcopal decree. The lawyers have drawn up a document, signed by the bishop and bearing the seal of his weighty ring, and doubt is rescinded: By powers deriving from the Keys of Peter, signed in Ardfert and confirmed in Rome, I am condemned to burn.

And the irony is this: My true *haeresis* is more profound than any charge listed in this document. My apostasy is indifference. I do not fear the fires of hell, nor do I long for the *perfectio* that will come with the resurrection of the body. I am weak. Death skulks in the corner of my cell; at night I hear his impatient breath. The bishop has forbidden that food or drink be brought to the island, and what I have is conserved in pitiful piles. It is unlikely that I will survive the winter. Death's bright eyes shine; he weaves a shroud of the wind in anticipation of my demise. And then? Tertullian uses the term *refrigerium* to refer to the state of the blessed in heaven, and *carcer* for the place of the damned. The first suggests a cool drink, rest, refreshment, bathing, meals, and the relaxation of games; the second, a prison. You, Gerbert, enjoy the first, even now in Rome. No theologian of the afterlife ever imagined a *locus refrigerii* more delightful than the palace of the pope. And I have chosen the prison. Willingly I languish in this wretched cell. Having fled the comforts of the world and embraced a hermit's solitude, why should I desire heaven or fear hell? This rock is my heaven *and* my hell. Of what will follow my death I know nothing. I am indifferent. It is indifference that is my true crime. It is for this that I should be dragged in chains to Ardfert.

You say to me: *Do not mistake your cell for the Church, or your island rock for Christendom.* I do not. But I have seen enough of the world. I have tasted the sour justice of the Church and the bitter peace of Christendom. I have been stung by the *consensus ecclesiae.* You desire a world restored to peace, in which all men act according to the inspiration of Christ. To achieve this you would have us all become children of God, wrapped in the swaddling clothes of the creeds of Nicaea and Constantinople, and utterly dependent upon his earthly vicar, the pope of Rome. Within your pontifical *conceptus* we must move and act, and we are saved or damned in accordance with the vicar's will. I ask: Must we become children to be saved? Is it not better that we are *sons* of God, rather than infants? The son is liberated from the father. The son is responsible for himself and is saved or damned by his own actions. You ask for my abdication to the will of the Church. You ask me to become again a child. Then what have the years been for? What of the happiness and the pain? When I watched Maire's murder from the kiln at Reask, when I bathed your fevered body with a

sponge, when I fled with Melisande from the burning cottage—
what was it all for if not to become an adult? And when I came
at last to this rock, this barren island in the sea, what was it for
if not to live by an unalloyed act of the mature will? If I am
damned by the sin of Adam and saved by the vicar of Christ, then
. . . what was any of it for?

Gerbert, I do not know if I am right or wrong. I do not know
if I will burn in hell, or if my life shall simply go out like the flame
of an extinguished lamp. I only know that I shall die on this rock
where I have known the consoling magisterium of the wind and
the sea. I have little to show for a long life. I have a chalice that
is buried. I have a pile of scraps—parchments and vellums—
scribbled over. These are intended for you.

Aileran, monk

✦

At Narbonne we came to the sea. A sea unlike any I had
seen—not the wild western ocean that lashed the strand at Reask,
nor the gray wind-flecked sea I had crossed between Ireland and
Gaul. At Narbonne we saw the blue of sapphires, the green of
emeralds, glass turned molten and poured flat by the sun, colored
by cobalt and copper. This was the sea at the heart of the world.
The Mediterranean! Bounded by the great cities of Christendom—Rome, Constantinople, Antioch, Athens, Alexandria. The
sea that bore the travels of the apostles Peter and Paul. "Rome!"
said Gerbert, pointing to the featureless eastern horizon. And as
if he would swim to Rome right then, he stripped off his garments
and ran into the sea. He dove and frolicked like a dolphin.

I could not follow. I cannot swim. Nor could I have stripped
off my clothes so casually there in the light of day. I studied his
cast-off garments scattered on the sand. The sandals of soft
leather. The blue cloak, white shirt, and saffron leggings. And
bright against the blue of the cloak, the silver bracelet. Not
monkish things. When two weeks earlier we had left Saint

Gerald's we were two monks together in like garments of brown wool. In our satchels we carried an extra cowl and tunic and a bit of food. And somehow, as we traveled, Gerbert became miraculously transformed. His monk's robe vanished, and in its place appeared a shirt and leggings of fine linen. A silver bracelet. Books. Fresh fruit. Coins. Conjured as if by magic. As we moved along the road he gathered to himself bright and beautiful things. And then he was standing before me on the strand at Narbonne, the water glistening on his skin, his wet blond hair plastered on forehead and cheeks. He picked up the silver bracelet and slipped it onto his wrist.

"These are the same waters that lap the Irish shore," he said, tossing a headful of spray into my face.

They seem gentler, I replied.

"They are the same, the very same," he insisted. "All the waters of the earth are one."

And in the sand he drew a map like a quartered circle. "Asia"—he pointed to the right half of the circle—"Europe"—the upper quarter on the left—"Africa"—the lower left-hand quarter. "And surrounding the dry land is Oceanus, the great sea that covers half of the terrestrial sphere."

He was lecturing, magisterial. With his spread fingers he drew a broad circumference to the circle and showed me how the waters of the Mediterranean are connected to Oceanus by a narrow strait between Spain and Africa—the Gates of Hercules.

"Here is Aurillac," he said, pointing, "and here is Narbonne, and here"—he jabbed his finger into the sand—"is where we are going. Santa Maria de Ripoll."

Our journey had its beginning when Borrell, count of Barcelona, made a pious visit to Saint Gerald's. Borrell was a rich man, stout and darkly handsome, fifty years of age, and passionately interested in learning. He owned much land in Catalan and southern Gaul, and he was known in those regions as a generous patron of the Church. It was natural that Abbot

Colman should extend to him a generous welcome and introduce him to Gerbert, the brightest light of our house.

Borrell was much taken by the young monk's gifts of grammar and rhetoric, and drew him out with subtle disputations. He asked: "Paul writes that flesh and blood cannot inherit the kingdom of heaven. How then is it that the body will rise on the last day?"

Gerbert answered quickly: "This mortal body is perishable, but the body I shall put on at the last day will be imperishable. Paul spoke only of flesh corrupted by the sin of Adam. My body at the resurrection will be like a new garment, of bleached cloth, bright from the loom and uncorrupted by sin."

It was typical of Gerbert that he spoke of *his* body, rather than of the resurrection of bodies in general; Borrell took note of this, smiling. "Then at the resurrection shall *your* body eat and sleep?" asked Borrell. "Will it experience pleasure or pain? Will it have genitals?"

Gerbert responded: "Abbot Colman has gathered here at Saint Gerald's a splendid library of early Christian works. Among them is a book known as Esdras, which speaks at length of the resurrection of the just. *In odorem unguenti*—they shall have perfumed ointment. And they shall dine *in convivio* at the marriage supper of the bridegroom—*epulari nuptias sponsi.* From this, then, I take it that my resurrected body will have the fullest capacity for the pleasures of the flesh. Nowhere in Esdras, nor in any of the Scriptures, do the authors speak of pain. *Inibi non pluvium, non frigus*—neither rain nor cold. Imagine, if you can, flesh of silk, woven with threads of purest light. There will be no shadow of the world—no *umbra saeculi*—to blemish it. Flesh of silk! Anointed with perfume!"

So it went, for several days, as Borrell teased and tested Gerbert. And my young friend relished the opportunity to flatter and amuse this important person. An invitation was forthcoming. At the end of his visit, Borrell extracted from Abbot Colman permission for Gerbert to travel to Catalan to extend his education. The young monk would be entrusted to Atto, the bishop of Vich, and he would study at the nearby monastery of Santa Maria de Ripoll, where a substantial library of classical and Saracen texts had been gathered. It was an unusual request on behalf of a monk so recently professed. The required *licentia* was obtained from Colman only upon the promise of a substantial gift of money from Borrell. And Borrell, at Gerbert's urging, suggested to Colman that the young monk should have on his travels a suitable companion.

Flesh of silk! Bleached with salt, perfumed with oranges and figs. "I shall cross this sea to Rome," said Gerbert on the strand at Narbonne, gesturing to the east. "To the city of light, to the city of marble . . . to the center of the world."

Is not Jerusalem the center of the world? I asked, pointing to the map that he had drawn on the sand.

"Ha!" he laughed. "A fine observation." I smiled, pleased that I had pleased him.

He trembled; he was still naked. "But the map is only a convention, drawn on flat sand. A map can be deceptive. The earth is a sphere"—he took an orange from his satchel—"like this fruit. The sphere itself has a center, but the surface of a sphere has no center"—his hands caressed the orange—"or rather the center is where you make it."

He tossed me the orange and picked up his white shirt.

"The center is where power lies," he said. "In the days of Solomon power resided in Jerusalem, and Jerusalem was rightly said to be the center of the world. Today there are two contending seats of power, here and here"—he showed me on the map—"at Constantinople and Rome. But Rome . . . Rome is the natural center; look, it is centrally placed in the Mediterranean Sea, which is like the bowl at table from which all the guests sup."

He drew radii in the sand: "Rome was once the most powerful city on earth, and it must become so again."

We slept that night on the sand at Narbonne. The stars seemed dangerously close—not the distant points of cold light I knew in Ireland. *What is that star?* I asked, pointing at the red heart of the Scorpion. It was a star I knew, that I had learned from Brother No-Ear, and as soon as Gerbert told me its name I recognized its constellation—the claws, the curled tail, the stinger—but here the Scorpion was high in the sky, and in Ireland it was near to the horizon. It was, of course, as Gerbert said. The earth is a sphere, enclosed within the sphere of the stars. Somewhere on the surface of the earth Scorpius is directly overhead—somewhere south, in Africa or beyond. Every point on the surface of a sphere is like every other, every point has its own zenith star. Above our heads that night we saw the star called by Pliny the Star of the Harp; we felt its light. We felt the wonder of creation in every pore of our bodies. Paradise seemed superfluous; it was enough for flesh and blood to inherit the earth.

There is a saying: Old age comes not alone. It comes with companions from the past, memories like shades and specters that dance about us in the dark. There are certain events in our lives that impress themselves upon our consciousness so deeply that they acquire a kind of corporeal permanence, a materiality as real as the flesh of one's own hand, and these, too, stay with us into old age, as real as any memento of youth that is kept in a chest of oak and cedar, enduring, almost physical talismans of our happinesses and sorrows. Such was the time when the count of Barcelona held the flame to the serving boy's hand. And such was the moment the following morning when I met Gerbert among the olive trees and saw upon his face the look of confusion and shame. These episodes I must now recount.

When we came at last to Catalan we made our way immediately to the palace of Borrell. This splendid residence was situated on the cliffs above the sea, near the place where the brown waters of the Llobregat River muddy the glasslike transparency of the Mediterranean. The castle was more grand than any I had seen, and the gardens that surrounded it were like Eden, with—as the Bible tells us—*every kind of tree, enticing to look at and good to eat*. We were given a room of our own in a tower looking out to sea, a place too grand to be fit quarters for monks bound to Christ by vows of poverty. It contained a bed of oak, as broad as five of the cots at Saint Gerald's, with a mattress and coverlet of down. Opposite the bed hung a tapestry, woven in a Moorish pattern with rich colors, and below the tapestry was a painted chest large enough to hold a man. Gerbert provided an explication of the startling scene that appeared on the front panel of the chest: *Venus, Juno, and Pallas Athena appear nude before Paris, who must decide which of them is the most beautiful.* Never before had I seen such a picture; never before had I seen a representation of the unclothed human figure. A side panel of the chest depicted another woman, also naked—"Venus," said Gerbert. The goddess was throwing a book into the fire; the title of the book was *Remedia amoris,* "The Remedy for Love." Within this provocatively decorated chest Borrell had placed a number of fine garments. Upon our approach to the castle Gerbert had put on again the monk's cowl and tunic; these he now quickly exchanged for Borrell's fine offerings and—I am ashamed to admit—enticed me to do the same. But not before we cleansed from our bodies the dust of the road. Two oaken baths were brought into our room by servants of Borrell and filled with hot water from brass basins. We soaked in these tubs like two joints of lamb stewing in pots on the fire. "The troubles of the journey are washed away," sighed Gerbert, lolling deep in his bath. "This . . . *this* is contentedness." I was ambivalent about sharing his pleasure; the journey from Aurillac to Barcelona had been the happiest time of my life.

Dressed in garments of wool spun fine as silk, we explored the castle. We imagined that what we saw were satisfactory accommodations for a Saracen prince, for surely no finer possessions might be found in the palaces of Alexandria. My eyes gaped wide at furnishings and tapestries grander than any I had ever seen. Gerbert, however, pretended as if such wonders were familiar.

He strode from room to room, pouring forth a steady stream of explanation: "This chair is in the style of Granada; see the decorations carved into the rosewood seat: they are letters from the alphabet of the Moors."

What does it say? I asked.

"God be praised," he answered without hesitation, and I wondered that he should be able to read such characters, although I now believe that in this matter, as in others, he supplemented his incomplete knowledge with the fabrications of a rich imagination.

"Look at this!" he exclaimed. "It is Roman!"

It was the statue of a young man lacking head and arms, every feature of the body so perfectly rendered that the stone seemed alive. Gerbert ran his hand across the smooth marble. "No one has been able to make statues such as this for a thousand years," he said. "Look!" He touched the penis with his hand and laughed.

Borrell entered—an imposing man, tall, erect, and elegant.

"You like my statue?" he asked. "It is Roman, of course. We found it in the gardens. This place was a Roman camp long before my ancestors acquired the property; the grounds are littered with the detritus of Roman empire."

"Who is it?" Gerbert asked. His hand rested delicately on the shoulder of the headless Roman.

Borrell answered: "I am not certain. I suspect it is the torso of Antinoüs, the favorite of the emperor Hadrian. Look. See how the artist has turned the calf slightly out, with the ball of the foot barely touching the pedestal . . . very graceful. I have seen similar statues in Italy, often with the features of Antinoüs."

Borrell paused. He circled the statue, letting his fingers brush lightly against the marble. He continued: "A beautiful boy. Hadrian ordered the youth's likeness carved on half the statues of the empire. Perhaps this one represented a god—Apollo or Orpheus—a god with the features of Antinoüs. It is unfortunate that the head is missing. The eyes, the hair . . . ravishing, on the figures I have seen."

Gerbert asked: "Who was he . . . this Antinoüs?"

Borrell answered kindly: "The *cupido* of the emperor, a Bithynian, I believe. When the boy died, Hadrian declared him a god, to be worshiped throughout the empire."

I did not then know the meaning of the word *cupido,* but Gerbert accepted Borrell's information with apparent nonchalance.

Then Borrell asked Gerbert: "And *you?* Would you like to be a god . . . a companion of Apollo . . . divine Gerbert?"

My friend answered, laughing: "I am happy enough to be a mortal."

A fine dinner was prepared in our honor. Borrell presided, ensconced in an armchair at the table's head, attired in a long Moorish shirt of embroidered silk. Gerbert sat at Borrell's right and I on his left. Next to Gerbert sat Blanca, Borrell's daughter, who was somewhat older than ourselves, and on my left her twin brother, John. Down along the table were seated a dozen other men and women of the count's household, and at the table's foot, with the weary bearing of a queen exhausted by the labors of ruling, Lutgarde, his spouse. The table was laden with every food: pimentoed pig, mutton flavored with cloves, peppered chicken, vegetables and fruits, and puddings and pies. There were as many servants there to serve as guests at table. One of these, a thin, fair-skinned girl in a honey-colored dress, captured my imagination. It was her eyes that charmed me: as deep and timid as a doe's. I endeavored not to mind her, but wherever she moved in the room my eyes involuntarily followed. And music! Three musicians entertained us . . . a strange, elaborate music of notes and chords, as intricately woven as the lines of the Moorish tapestry in our bedchamber or the embroidery of the shirt of Borrell. I longed that I might have a kesh and try for myself some of these Catalan tunes. Wine flowed freely, and as Borrell and Gerbert became inebriated they began to engage in a punning banter of double meanings. This repartee immensely amused the guests; Blanca and John blushed and laughed. The women, especially, were taken by Gerbert, and when he sang . . .

Under the hawthorn in the green fields
There lay a lady with her love
Until the cock crowed—day is near!
God, God, how early comes the day.
Would it be that the night should never end,
And that my friend should never leave my side.
Would it be that the cock should never crow.

God, God, how early comes the day!
My sweetest friend, in the tall green grass.
Kiss me, come, while the birds are singing,
No man's envy will make us afraid.
God, God, how early comes the day.

. . . they smiled and nudged their partners. Blanca flushed crimson in the face of Gerbert's smile—*Kiss me, come,* he sang, and moved his hand near to her bare shoulder, letting only the silver bracelet touch her skin. But it was to Borrell that my friend gave his most solicitous attention.

Throughout this musical interlude the girl in the honey-colored dress stood opposite me, against a tapestry depicting a scene of the hunt.

"Brother Aileran has taken note of Joveta," said Borrell. "I think he is quite smitten."

I did not expect this; I had not taken part in the joviality. I stiffened and demurred. *Joveta! So that was her name.* The girl checked herself and listened, like a deer that has heard the distant bay of a hound. Gerbert grinned broadly; I was ashamed and could not look at him.

The count put his hand upon my shoulder and said immodestly: "You can have her, you know. You need only ask. She is my servant; she will do as I say."

I shook my head in dissent; I wanted to be away . . . on the beach at Narbonne . . . in the vineyard at Aurillac.

Borrell continued: "Did not Saint Paul say, 'Slaves, be obedient to your masters, as if you had only to please men.' So you see, you need not be afraid of violating your monkish vows; I present her to you with the authority of Scriptures." He looked to Gerbert and laughed. My friend encouraged him, saying to me: "Paul also says, 'Masters, make sure that what your slaves are given is just and fair.'" And then he added: "Or, in Joveta's case, just and dark."

Gerbert laughed lewdly. Blanca, John, and the others laughed with him. Joveta had not moved—she was a deer frozen in fright.

She is not a slave, I said, *but a servant.*

Gerbert was quick to respond: "A linguistic quibble! As you well know, dear Aileran, the word 'servant' derives from *servus,* which is Latin for 'slave.'"

"And a quibble in law too," said Borrell. "She will go with you if I command it. There is no law here save my own."

No, not that, I answered quietly, *she need not do that.*

"That—or more!" trumpeted Borrell. He was drunk, triumphant. He took from the table a candle in a silver holder and beckoned for one of the serving boys to come near him. The boy moved forward, hesitantly; he was very young, no more than twelve.

"Put your hand into the flame," said Borrell to the boy, as gently as a father might ask his son for a kiss.

The boy stood rigidly in his place. Borrell beckoned with his hand, inviting the boy to the flame, an imperious gesture, and his face became suddenly white and fierce. The boy came forward and lifted his hand to the taper, his eyes locked with the eyes of Borrell.

Even then it seemed to be a dream, a terrible paralyzing dream, until I caught in my nostrils the stench of burning flesh. At the same moment, Gerbert leapt from his seat and pushed the boy's hand from the flame. He glowered at Borrell and then delicately ministered to the boy, massaging butter into the scorched skin of the palm. The count made no move to interfere, nor did he seem annoyed with Gerbert's interruption of his demonstration; rather his eyes glowed with satisfaction, and something else—was it admiration? In the confusion Joveta escaped. Blanca and John watched wide-eyed as Gerbert tore from the hem of the tablecloth a strip of clean white linen and wrapped the boy's hand. I excused myself and slipped away, shamed by my passivity; always, it seemed, I was destined to be the watcher of evil, made impotent by fear!

That night Gerbert did not come to our room. I woke alone in the huge bed, still in the clothes I had worn at supper, wet with sweat and the sinful residue of dreams. Rising, I stripped off the polluted garments and returned to my monk's cowl and tunic. And then I went to look for Gerbert. I found him in the garden, among the olive trees. He sat with his back to the sea and his arms wrapped tightly about his bare knees. His clothes were not those he had worn at dinner; instead he wore a familiar shirt of embroidered silk.

Where were you? I asked.

He did not answer. His lips trembled, and his eyes were at once astonished and afraid.

I turned from him. *I am going,* I said. *I am going on to Vich. Come with me if you want.*

Did I love Gerbert more than I loved myself? Did I love myself more than I loved God? And if the answer to both questions was yes, then it followed that I loved Gerbert more than I loved God. These troubling thoughts were much on my mind as we traveled to Vich. I was determined that when we reached our destination I would find a way to give myself more fully to Christ.

Our journey took us away from the sea and up into the hills along the wooded valley of the Congost River. Gerbert was unnaturally silent and distracted, and inclined to linger. I hurried us along. At the crest of the ridge, near the village of Centellas, we achieved a distant view of the Pyrenees, a range of magnificent snowcapped peaks that seemed to demarcate the very edge of the world—towering marble pillars supporting the azure dome of the sky. I remembered the map that Gerbert had drawn on the strand at Narbonne; with his two hands he had pushed up a ridge of sand to indicate the mountains that divide Gaul from Spain. How much grander was the *real world* than Gerbert's pitiful representation! How much grander these shining peaks and harboring valleys than those little heaps and hollows of sand.

The town of Vich is situated in an amphitheater of hills in the valley of the river Ter. It is a thriving, vibrant town, alive with the chatter of diverse tongues, a place of the mingled cultures of Moors, Jews, and Christians, tossed up helter-skelter like wrack on sand. At the center of the town a broad plaza had been cleared of houses and a new cathedral was being built. Masons, quarrymen, carpenters, sculptors, bricklayers, and hod carriers moved busily about the precincts. A crypt had been dug and walled with brick and stone, a massive foundation that would support the soaring nave of the new cathedral. Our residence was nearby, in a building adjacent to the bishop's palace, a single spare room arranged for by Borrell: two small beds, a table, and a small window closed by wooden shutters that opened onto a yard where stonecutters produced a never-ending cloud of dust. Ostensibly, we were entrusted to the care of the bishop of Vich, but we never met him, nor did he impose the slightest stricture on our movements; his attention was fully occupied by the construction of the cathedral. In any case, we did not stay long at Vich, although Gerbert would frequently return, and eventually I would join him. Our objective was farther up the valley, at Ripoll, where a monastery practicing the Rule of Benedict had assembled a most remarkable library.

At Santa Maria de Ripoll we were assured accommodation in the guesthouse and access to the library by letters of introduction from the count of Barcelona. Borrell's influence was considerable even here, in the foothills of the Pyrenees, sixty miles from his castle. In the quick acquiescence of the abbot to our most presumptuous requests I sensed a reprise of the power that had caused the boy at Barcelona to put his hand into the flame, and began to see that Christ and Caesar are unnatural bedfellows. In answering God's call to a higher life the soul must loose its bonds to Caesar; there can be no bending of the Rule. At Santa Maria de Ripoll we were tolerated but not condoned. The abbot closed his eyes to our transgressions, but did everything in his power to isolate us from the life of his house. My strenuous efforts to integrate myself into the practice of the local Rule were rejected. Books were placed at our disposal, and bedding, but not prayer, nor the life of the bell, nor the obligation of obedience. I felt dirtied by our privilege, and most particularly by how it had been obtained. However, my reservations were not shared by Gerbert. He relished the license that accrued to us because of our alliance with Borrell. He used it shrewdly to further his own objectives. And in the end perhaps he was right, for soon we both found at Ripoll things that occupied our minds and hearts totally. For Gerbert, it was Ovid and the manuscripts of love—the *Amores,* the *Ars amatoria,* and the *Remedia amoris.* For me, it was a vision of natural law, achieved by the Greeks and given perfection in the schools of Islam. I was also drawn to Ovid, but not, as Gerbert, to the erotic poems. It was the *Metamorphoses* that attracted my passionate and unwavering attention.

Gerbert discovered in Ovid an explicit and fervent tutor in the arts of love. He often quoted to me one or the other of Ovid's salacious lines: "Hands won't be idle, and fingers will explore those hidden parts where love's fire has been ignited by Cupid's darts." With these poems as his guide, he set about to experience new territories of the senses. It was something more cerebral that I found in the *Metamorphoses*: a sense of the possibilities of change in a universe of infinite complexity. From Ovid I learned that nothing is ever quite what it seems; that no person's identity is wholly secure. Ovid's gift was to take a profoundly depressing world, polluted with sin and racked by evil, and transform it into a richly textured poem of delight. In Ovid's vision of reality, all of nature is capable of miraculous transmogrifications, in which matter and spirit, gods and mortals, mix and mingle: *Nothing remains the same. Nature, the great inventor, ceaselessly contrives new forms from old.* Ovid is an optimist who honors the senses, who imputes sufficient subtlety to matter to dispense with the need for an immaterial divine. He is a Midas who embraces base creation with a touch of gold.

We were often engrossed in our respective books, perfecting our Latin and our wits on Ovid's verse. And later, when walking in the hills or eating in the town, we tossed back and forth favorite passages, Gerbert from the books of love, and I from the *Metamorphoses*:

> "Wine makes men apt for passion, ignites desire;
> Venus in her cups is fire on fire."

> *Across heaven's arch runs a road,*
> *easily seen on a starry night;*
> *it is called the Milky Way,*
> *and rightly famed for its glow of white.*

> "Once in woody Ida roamed a bull, milk-white,
> between its horns a single mark of black;
> each heifer in the herds of Gnossus and Cydon
> yearned for that burden on her back."

Now I am swept on the surging sea,
all canvas spread;
in all of creation no thing
endures, all things flow instead.

"Do not withhold your promises,
by promises women are seduced;
call as your witness any god you please—
Jupiter smiles on lovers' perjuries."

Then Phaëthon saw the world ablaze;
he could not bear the heat—
the air was like a furnace's breath,
the chariot white hot beneath his feet.

And so it went, for months of passionate study and play; we were inordinately happy, and so might we have remained, had not "love's fire . . . been ignited by Cupid's darts."

Perhaps the events I now record should be left unwritten, but honesty compels me to include them. Gerbert, my friend and tormentor, if these pages come at last into your hands, excise from them what you will, but first these events must be given life here, as part of this chronicle, for without them there can be no understanding of what follows. For it is to *you*, I now understand, that these pages are addressed; it is to you that I wish to explain myself, to give an accounting of my life, to evoke whatever reward or censure my life deserves. If there is a judgment beyond the grave, then these pages will be superfluous. Into that final dark night I must go unexplained and unshriven, but meanwhile, in *these* dark nights in my cell on this barren rock, throughout these long winter nights of condemning wind and terrifying solitude, two judges sit to listen to my carefully contrived catalogue of justification and sin. Their names are Love and Guilt. Their faces change; sometimes they wear the faces of the grave—death's-heads clothed with decaying flesh and caked blood; at other times the faces are those of Gerbert and Melisande, radiant and uncorrupted. Over and over in their presence, in total darkness, I call up the past. Again and again I tell them my story. And I watch the faces: *Is the story true?* Gerbert, you will decide.

When I was a young priest at Aurillac, having taken orders in my thirtieth year, I was given the use of a Penitential. This book listed for the confessor appropriate penances for a multitude of sins. More than half of the sins listed in the penitentiary manual were sins of the flesh—a most astonishing catalogue. Self-abuse, illegitimate unions of young people, adulteries of the married state, guilty relations between laymen and nuns, monks and laywomen, monks and nuns: All were foreseen and penalized. Here also were listed the appropriate penalties for the brother who lies with his sister, the son who has guilty relations with his mother, the father who deflowers his daughter, sodomites, lesbians, and men guilty of bestiality. Every sort of aberration was anticipated, and even the priest with long experience in shriving sinners found in the Penitential a revealing compendium of deviation. And with the list of sins and penances came this advice: *Many crimes are enumerated in this penitential which it is not proper to make known to men. Therefore, the priest should not interrogate the penitent about all of them, for fear that he will fall yet further into vices of whose existence the sinner had formerly been ignorant.* And, yes, Gerbert, it was in your company that I lost my ignorance and my innocence, and that the crimes of the Penitential became real. It was in your company that I had my first lessons in the *ars amatoria*—that I was introduced to an unexcised catalogue of fleshly sins. Only once before had I witnessed a carnal act—the rape of Maire—in a context of extreme brutality. Then you, Gerbert, with Ovid as our guide, introduced me to an elegant debauchery.

The decay of our happiness at Ripoll began with Gerbert's absences, on journeys of several days or weeks to Barcelona and Vich. He went wordlessly, and returned without report. I was both curious and jealous. About his long absences from Ripoll Gerbert said nothing. When I questioned, he merely smiled. He was engaged, he said, in "study." At last I asked if I might accompany him on one of his excursions. He shrugged. "If you wish," he said. And so it was that we came together to Vich and to the house by the river Ter. It was at the height of summer, and the air was scented with fruits of the orchards and the vines. A cool breeze blew from the river, causing the translucent curtains that hung throughout the house to move and sway. I was dizzy with fear and curiosity. And with drink. We had drunk wine with supper, and Gerbert had purchased more wine in a goatskin flask to carry with us. (*Where did you get the money?* I asked. He shrugged. As on the road from Aurillac, Gerbert seemed magically to acquire whatever he needed.) The women of the house were dressed alluringly and immodestly; their diaphanous gowns hid few of the secrets of their sex. As we entered, they moved quickly to embrace Gerbert, to proffer him their attentions. He laughed, and made jokes, and fondled each of them in turn. He seemed to me then infinitely attractive and desirable as he moved among them, caressing their silken skin. His silver bracelet danced among them like a butterfly seeking a flower on which to alight. I watched, determined to model my actions after his own. I was impassioned by the possibility of what might happen, but paralyzed with timidity and fear. And then Gerbert was gone with two of the women, one of them only a girl, into the maze of quavering curtains. The women who remained turned to me and my bones went cold with cowardice. Gathering courage fortified by wine, I chose one of them, a woman many years my senior, and let her lead me away.

What I began that night in the house on the river Ter became, in our remaining months at Vich and Ripoll, a tempestuous part of my life. At the monastery of Santa Maria, in the gardens, cloister, or library, I wept and lashed my soul, begging God's forgiveness. A thousand times I resolved to turn from sin, to do penance of the most extreme kind, and to make my life a thing of Christ-like purity. But always the itch of the flesh returned, at first with a sting as slight as that of a fly pestering a cow, and then the sting grew in intensity until the longing became irresistible and in my sleeping and waking dreams I laid plans for new and more salacious experiments . . . for all of which I found at Vich ready companions. I might have cried out with Ovid's Medea: *I am led against my will; reason calls me one way, desire beckons another; I know the better course and approve it—but I follow the worse.* And the nadir of this descent, the unabsolvable corruption of innocence, was yet to come. Of that, Gerbert, you will require no accounting of mine.

One evening in the spring of my twenty-fifth year, while we were still resident at Ripoll, Gerbert returned from Vich with a companion.

"See who I found along the road," he said.

It was Joveta, the servant of Borrell, who had been offered to me by her master. The girl stood quietly at the door, with downcast eyes (she had been brought surreptitiously to our chamber by Gerbert).

"She has run away," said Gerbert. Gently he removed the cloak from her shoulders. Joveta's dress was in tatters—it was the same honey-colored dress she had worn on the evening of our banquet in Barcelona. Modestly, she placed her arms across her breasts.

"See," said Gerbert. "See what that bastard Borrell has done."

He turned the girl so that her back was to me. Her shoulders were marked with a fret of bloody stripes. I was stunned and hurt. I felt keenly that what had happened to the girl was somehow the result of my own indecencies.

Did he do this to you? I asked. *Did Borrell do this?*

"She cannot answer you," said Gerbert. "She is dumb."

He went to the basin and filled it with cool water from the water jar. "Come." He beckoned the girl to the window.

The moon was in the waxing phase, the evening air scented with rose and honeysuckle. With great tenderness Gerbert sponged the girl's wounds, wiping away the dried blood from the unbroken skin. He was suddenly exuberant. "Look!" he exclaimed. "A four!"

And indeed in the flesh of the girl's shoulder the lash had accidentally incised the figure of the Saracen numeral. Gerbert had recently discovered this remarkable way of writing numbers from Moorish sources and for several days had been enthusiastically experimenting with the new system. Now he traced the figures onto Joveta's skin—one, two, three . . . the blood-red four . . . five, six—and where the seventh numeral might have been he kissed her, after first wetting his lips with water. All the while I looked into the girl's eyes, prepared to accept her accusation, but saw only bewilderment and fear.

"No man's envy will make us afraid," said Gerbert; it was a familiar phrase, but I had forgotten its source.

Gently he removed the remnants of Joveta's dress, letting them fall at her feet, so that she stood before us naked. Reaching from behind he removed her arms from her breasts and carried them to her sides. "My soul thirsts for you," he whispered to Joveta, "my flesh longs for you. I gaze upon you in the Sanctuary, and see your beauty and glory." Blasphemously he quoted Psalms.

The girl was beautiful. I could not cease to look at her. Never, not even during our most intimate debaucheries at Vich, had I felt such a stirring of the flesh as I felt now—and such an overwhelming sense of shame.

"Take her, she is yours," said Gerbert, echoing Borrell. "She probably came all this way seeking you—her blushing gallant, her savior with the sad eyes."

I could not move. *She* . . . , I began, but faltered.

Gerbert took the girl's face between his hands. He stroked her lips with the flats of his thumbs, and said, "You are not afraid, are you? You are glad to be rid of that bastard Borrell. You are glad to be here with your friend Aileran, aren't you? Aileran will not hurt you. Aileran is your friend. He will help you get away."

Joveta's eyes moved searchingly; she seemed to beseech something from me.

What? I framed the question soundlessly.

Joveta did not—could not—answer. Gerbert moved her to the edge of the bed. With the wet sponge he wiped her breasts, her belly, and her sex, and followed his ablutions with kisses.

"My lips will praise you," he said, again quoting Psalms.

I was sickened. Not with shame, but with desire.

Rome
March 3, 999
Sylvester II (Gerbert) to Aileran, of Skellig Michael

Gerbert, bishop of Rome, servant of the servants of God, to Aileran, on the rock of Skellig, in the province of Munster, Hibernia

Since our last letter we have heard nothing from you. Whether you have chosen to ignore our communication or have been physically unable to respond we do not know. But other messages regarding your case have come to us here in Rome. On Christmas Day arrived a letter from the bishop of Ardfert, informing us of your excommunication from the Holy Church of Jesus Christ. It is requested that this action be registered and confirmed in Rome by our pontifical authority. Further, upon his return, our courier brought word of unacceptable excesses among your compatriots in anticipation of the Millennium. The clergy, we are told, incite among the people a false fear of impending judgment and have used this sincere but unwarranted power to consolidate certain holdings of land and enrich the treasury of the Church.

What are we to do? If it were not for the personal affection we hold for you, these distant affairs would scarcely warrant our attention. Certainly, there are pressing matters nearer to hand. We seek with our lord Caesar, Otto III, to bring certain provinces in the south of Italy within the compass of the Christian Roman empire. Dangerous political and spiritual alliances of Venice with Byzantium must be checked. We endeavor to bring King Stephan of Hungary into the Roman fold and thereby thwart the advance of Byzantium Greeks into that quarter of Europe. We are engaged in important negotiations with King Vladimir of Kiev and King Olaf Trygvvesön of Norway, seeking greater conformity in those lands to Roman usage; and especially, in the latter case, for the substitution of the Roman alphabet for the pagan runic if Norway is to take its proper place as a Christian nation. Our dream is of a united Roman Christian empire reaching from the Tagus to the Tigris, from the lands of the Hyperboreans to the tropic of Africa, one in worship, one in peace. I ask you, is it not in opposition to the divine work of unity that the present diversity of laws reigns, not only in each region and city, but sometimes in the same household and even at the same table? Would it not be more pleasing to Almighty God that all men should be governed by a single law, under the rule of a single pious king, who was himself subservient to the Keys of Peter? Would it not be greatly to the profit of concord within the City of God if there were no Barbarians and Scythians, no Franks and Germans, no Romans and Byzantians, no slaves and free men, but one body of Christ made up of many parts? Christ is all and is in all.

And now, in the face of this noble and taxing work, comes the vexing matter of the excommunication of Aileran, abbot of Skellig—perhaps the smallest monastic establishment in Christendom, presently occupied by a single monk. So you see, brother, how strong are the bonds of our former friendship, that we are turned from the urgent agenda of the extension and consolidation of Roman hegemony—and from conversation with kings—to address ourselves to a squabble of Celts on the remotest fringe of Christ's kingdom. Our dilemma is this: Protocol requires that we support our bishops in the promulgation of edicts of excommunication, and yet in certain of the circumstances that led to this particular excommunication—those unseemly and uncivil agitations in preparation for the coming of Christ—we find ourselves in sympathy with Aileran, abbot of Skellig. And again, love for our brother disposes us to be anxious concerning the fate of his soul, now destined for the eternal fires of hell by excommunication and exclusion from the fold of Christ.

And therefore we have taken this decision: We shall not arbitrarily interfere with the edict of excommunication promulgated at Ardfert. However, we have written to our brother the bishop of Ardfert, urging caution in the matter of Aileran, and in the matter of the millennial agitations. In particular, we have cautioned him concerning the safety of your person, and have urged that you be transported to this place, that we might personally ascertain the nature and extent of your apostasy and prescribe suitable admonitions and punishments. We have assured our brother the bishop that he shall have ample representation in the course of our deliberations and that both the letter and the spirit of his edict of excommunication shall guide our actions.

Aileran, friend, I urge you to act prudently in allowing yourself to be conveyed hither. We are concerned for the physical health of your body and the well-being of your soul. Be assured that we shall be solicitous in our ministrations and do everything in our power to restore you to favor in the eyes of Christ's Holy Church and in the eyes of God.

This letter is conveyed to Aileran with sincere affection. Written by the hand of Anthony, notary and secretary of the Holy Roman Church, on the third day of the month of March, in the second year of the pontificate of Lord Pope Sylvester II.

☧   *Gerbert,* who is also Sylvester, bishop of Rome

A week ago visitors arrived on the Skellig. When they found me in my cell they could not tell if I was alive or dead. Nor was I myself certain if my life had departed. For a long time I had lain immobile in darkness, in a fever, possessed by deliriums that might easily have been mistaken for hell or heaven. At times I was tormented by demons of the vilest sort: satyric creatures with androgynous bodies, gross phalli, and mouths like vulvae—they pinched and snapped at my body as crows peck at carrion. At other times my dreams were of a seductive sweetness: showers of pure light, a warmth that filled my breast, and music of the most delicate purity. From these torments and raptures I was lifted by the hand of Gerbert's servant.

I did not know the day, nor even the month. The sun shone full upon the sea, and the sea was as smooth as beaten bronze. My faithful goat stood at the entrance of my cell, her paps dry, her gaunt body like a bag of bones. Birds wheeled and dived above the island: kittiwakes, gannets, guillemots, puffins, and razor-bills, in ranked, sun-bright choruses, like Seraphim, Cherubim, Thrones, and Dominions. Through the newly opened eyes of one raised from the dead, the Skellig rock seemed a fit place for God's throne. My Roman rescuer had waited through the long winter at Ballinskelligs, and now on the first calm sea of spring had come with two companions to obtain my reply to Gerbert's previous letter ... and to deliver another. More important than the letters, he brought food—in contravention of the proscription of the bishop of Ardfert—cheese, butter, bread, blood puddings, wine—and so it was that Roman power reached to the ends of the earth to restore to health a single human body tethered to life by a slender thread.

Yes, Gerbert, it is even as you wish. The balm of Rome extends from north to south, from east to west, from shore to shore of the circumferential sea, and perhaps even beyond this westernmost island of Europe to the Isles of the Blessed and the antipodes. Is this the vision that guides you: Christ's healing ministry applied to the fevered brow of a starving monk on an ocean rock—the miracle of the loaves and fishes repeated by your representative to produce for my physical salvation a great ripe lump of Munster cheese, sweet butter, wine, and a delicious blood pudding? Shall your proclamation, issued in Rome on a slip of parchment, raise this Lazarus? Restored by your pontifical dispensation, shall Lazarus find happiness in food and drink, in diving birds and healing sun? Your messenger and his companions stayed with me for a week, carefully tending to my needs; they did not leave until my vigor returned. In that time they sensed, if I am not mistaken, something of the austere silence and majesty of this place that has kept me here for so long. There is an old Irish saying: *Three candles illumine every darkness— knowledge, nature, truth.* I have lived here for ten years in the light of those three candles. Nothing more is needed.

And now I am urged by you, Gerbert, to allow myself to be conveyed to Rome. I sent away your courier with a rejection and the promise of a letter. I will not leave this place willingly. I now have food enough to live for some months. I will reside on this rock until the breath leaves me.

Melisande. Now it is time for *her* story. It is time to bring her alive on these pages, while I still have breath and life. It is time to watch her eyes, here in the darkness of my cell, and discover if the story that I tell is true. Perhaps the story of Aileran and Melisande was a dream devised by God to lure me into a deeper rejection of the divine will, or as a test of my resolution and purpose. Or by Satan . . . No! Not Satan. Satan could not have had the goodness to invent Melisande, nor could he have laid for me so sweet a snare. It is true; it is because of *Melisande*—all goodness and beauty—that I turned from God. Oh, the paradox! Gerbert led me into the cesspits of sin, and *there,* in the fleshpots of Vich, and especially in the affair of Joveta, whom I coveted and violated in imitation of my friend, I found God. Though her eyes were full of fear and pleading, I took her, no less culpably than the soldier took Maire; when I had finished I recognized in Gerbert's approving look the magnitude of my sin, and in the fullness of my shame I embraced Him. But Melisande lifted me to the portico of Paradise, and from that lofty prospect my soul fell Godless into eternity. God, it seems, is the necessary correction for evil, but in the goodness of my love for Melisande there was no room for God.

In my twenty-eighth year I was sent by my abbot to the castle of the count of Argentat, to provide instruction in poetics, music, and Latin grammar for his daughter, Melisande. It was not an assignment I welcomed. For three years since my return from Spain I had lived at Saint Gerald's in strict accordance with the Rule. In reaction to the vile depravities of Vich, my life took on an order and a simplicity that allowed me to devote myself entirely to study and prayer. When I prayed I felt a particular intimacy with God, who showed Himself to me as an image of order and simplicity not unlike that of the Rule itself. The tumultuous passions that had governed my soul in Spain quieted. Sleeping, eating, study, prayer—these became the fixed components of my day. The practice of the Rule was like an extension of my own heartbeat. I could no more have ceased to love God, or ceased to pray, than I could have stopped my own heart from beating. The itch of my flesh was quelled by knowledge, and the desire for beauty satisfied by nature. How quickly and effortlessly the days and months and seasons passed, as if all of nature lived in accordance with the bell of Saint Gerald's. The sun rose, the cuckoo sang, the grapes ripened, the stars plied their courses, all in subjugation to our Rule. I was content that I should pass all my days in the sweetness of that simplicity. And then came the call from Argentat. I protested. I begged dispensation. Father Colman reminded me of the appropriate chapter of the Rule: *Whatever a brother is asked to do, even though he deem it impossible, he should undertake meekly and obediently.* The abbot was importuned to supply an appropriate teacher to the house of a necessary patron of our monastery. No other monk in our community possessed the required arts. Meekly, I obeyed.

Argentat lies some thirty miles from Saint Gerald's as the crow flies, but the road takes one down along the valley of the Cére River to its junction with the Dordogne, and then up the Dordogne, perhaps doubling the distance. There is a forest track into the hills and across the ridge that separates the two valleys, but wolves and brigands make it unwise for a person to go that way alone. Guillaume, the count of Argentat, owned vast tracts of land in the valley of the Dordogne, between Auvergne and Bordeaux. The seat of this domain was a massive square tower house at Argentat, set among extensive gardens and vineyards. Upon my arrival I was ushered into his presence in the family quarters on the top floor of the house. Although the building itself lacked refinement or distinction, the rooms were richly furnished with carved furniture and bright brocades. Guillaume was a man of some sixty years, with features as fit and rough as his castle, but affecting in dress and demeanor a certain unsettling propriety. With his son, Riculf, he had won vast estates by force of arms, and now sought other ways of extending his properties and the influence of his family.

The most useful instrument in that program, Guillaume

informed me, would be his daughter, Melisande. Her physical allurements were satisfactory, he said, indeed highly to be prized, and her chastity unblemished. What were required were certain cultural refinements: music, the ability to write poems and letters, and most especially a command of the languages that would enable her to move effectively in the powerful courts of Gaul. I would be given a year to teach her such things; then, the following winter, Guillaume would introduce Melisande to the courts of Lombard and Burgundy. The duke of Burgundy, in particular, had recently lost his wife of thirty years; he would be looking for someone young and attractive to take her place. Guillaume would offer him a woman of such comeliness and talent that the Burgundian lord would readily strike a propitious bargain.

As Guillaume told me these things—with a crude and astonishing frankness—he was clearly measuring my own capacities for his program. He asked several probing questions, disguised as jest, regarding my concern for matters of the flesh, to which I replied with a satisfactory indifference. He had heard, he told me, of my "devotion to the Rule," and of the "spartan holiness" of my life; these things, he assured me, I would continue to enjoy at Argentat. A small hermitage had been prepared for me at the edge of the forest, not far from the castle; food and drink would be provided in whatever quantity I required. Except for four hours each morning, when I would instruct Melisande in the company of her maid, my time would be my own. The books of his modest library were at my disposal. ("They are of no use to me," he laughed. "It's all hen-scratch. I can't read a word.") At the end of two months he would expect suitable progress. Then, calling to another room, he introduced me to his own wife, his third, Mechtild, a plain girl of fifteen years. "The same age as your pupil," Guillaume noted with satisfaction. "There is no question of teaching *this one* to read," he said, boldly caressing her. "She has all the talents necessary to be mistress of *this* house."

From the first moment I saw Melisande, some part of me, not yet conscious but deeply felt, knew that I would love her. My thoughts were of certain biblical verses I had learned from Gerbert: *How beautiful you are, my love, your eyes are doves. Your lips are a scarlet lace and your speech sweet.* Her skin was fair but glowed with an inner fire, like polished amber. She was slight and pretty, her green eyes solemn, even somber, but I saw in them a quickness and curiosity, and a cautious restraint. Her dark hair, tied at the neck with a braided ribbon, fell nearly to her waist. Her outer tunic was of soft red wool, dyed with the root of madder, and the undergarment a becoming yellow, the color of the madder blossom. The tunic was tight-fitting, laced at the side, and pulled close at the waist with a sash of embroidered silk. I could not help but admire the fashion of her dress; it was not ostentatious, nor as rich as her father's wealth might warrant; she wore no ring or necklace, no jeweled ornament in her hair; her demeanor was simple, yet no one would mistake her for other than the daughter of a *potentes*, the child of a powerful house.

Our lessons were strict and formal. We met in a quiet anteroom on the lower floor of the house. Melisande's maid sat against the back wall, working an embroidery on a collar of white linen. It was agreed that our lessons would be in three parts: first, instruction on the harp and the theory of music; second, the elements of Latin grammar and the rudiments of writing; third, poetics, for which I followed my first inclination and chose as our text the Song of Solomon. We began each morning at the seventh hour, when Melisande and the women of the house had finished morning prayers, and we continued until midday, with appropriate breaks for refreshment and walks in the gardens of the castle. From the first, I was impressed with how adroitly Melisande followed my instruction. I was required to say nothing twice, and her fingers on the strings of the harp or with quill on parchment were as nimble as her mind. I set for her each morning an exercise on the harp, involving the tuning of the strings or the practice of short airs. As she played, I carefully supervised her posture and the disposition of her fingers on the strings. I made comment as necessary upon the melody or sweetness of the music, what in Irish we called *binnius,* and harmony, or *cuibdius.* We began first in the style of the dance tunes of Ireland that I had practiced since my early youth, and then advanced to the Frankish music of the district of Aurillac, decorated with certain of the embellishments I had learned in Spain. Of our study of Latin there is little to say; we began with a simple vocabulary and inflections of person, tense, and number. I formed the words with my voice or with the stylus on wax, and Melisande imitated my manner. There was a seriousness in her study; she seldom smiled or laughed. I watched her intently—the cloud-slow movements of her head, eyes, and mouth, the way she held her body gracefully erect, the grave but comely dance of her thin fingers on the strings of the harp. Melisande's purposefulness inspired in me a similar resolve, so that I found myself becoming, almost against my will, a stern and taxing teacher.

In our study of poetics, however, the text soon wove between us a delicate and dangerous thread of communication. As Melisande's Latin improved we read together from Solomon's Song, she taking the part of the Bride, and I the Bridegroom:

"A sachet of myrrh is my Beloved; he shall lie all night between my breasts. My Beloved is a cluster of henna flowers in the vineyards of Engedi."

You are beautiful, my love, and fair! Your eyes are doves.

"How beautiful you are, Beloved, and how pleasant! How green is our bed."

The beams of our house are cedar, and the rafters fir.

"I am the rose of Sharon, and the lily of the valleys."

As a lily among thorns, so is my love among the daughters.

"As the apple tree among the trees of the wood, so is my Beloved among the sons."

With these verses as our guide, I instructed Melisande in consonance, dissonance, metrics, and harmony. Together we reframed the verses, using meter and rhyme. Our fingers worked with the styluses on a wax tablet. And as the tablet passed back and forth between us, I was ever conscious of the distance that separated our fingertips, a gap that slowly narrowed but did not close.

A cell of thatch and wattle had been prepared for me at the forest's edge—a place of contentment and charm. Quite contrary to my original expectations, I found the long hours of solitude in my new hermitage a welcome departure from the constant companionship of the monks of Saint Gerald's. Only in the mornings, during lessons with my eager pupil, did I share the company of others. Occasionally, Melisande's brother, Riculf, rode near to my hut. He never spoke or otherwise overtly acknowledged my presence. He reined his mount before my door, the beast's great hooves pacing, and then, driving his heels violently into the stallion's flanks, thundered away. Once, while gathering reeds by the river for my pallet, I watched a falcon snatch at a thrush on the wing. The thrush fell not far from me, among the reeds. I retrieved it, wounded but not dead, and held it in my hands. Riculf approached on his horse, the falcon hooded on his arm. He spoke no word. I examined his face for some clue to the cause of the anger that transformed his features, but saw none. His unkempt hair was partly contained by a leather cap, not unlike the falcon's hood. Behind his close-cropped beard his face was marked with the scars of pox. He was perhaps the same age as I and powerfully built; his legs against his steed's flanks seemed more like the sinews of the beast than the legs of a man. I offered him the bird. He spit onto the ground at my feet, then drove his horse violently through the reeds at the river's edge, sending up great torrents of spray. What animosity he bore me I did not know.

As the weeks passed I gave to Melisande what I knew of the art of poetics, and I began to employ the long golden afternoons writing verses of my own:

> A hedge of trees
> Surrounds my hermitage;
> A blackbird sings
> (An announcement I shall not hide);
> Above my lined book,
> The trill of chorusing birds.

> In a gray cloak, from bushtop,
> A cuckoo chants.
> (An invitation? A warning?)
> May the Lord bless me
> And protect me from folly
> As I write in the greenwood.

From my hut at forest's edge, I often looked down upon the life of the castle. Riculf and several of Guillaume's men-at-arms sometimes went falconing along the river, and even from my distant prospect the silver bridles and bright caparisons of their mounts moved in colorful consonance against the green backdrop of the river reeds. In the castle yard the women worked at distaff tasks: They sheared the sheep, washed the fleece, carded the wool with thistles, combed and spun it; the flax, harvested in sun-bright fields near the river, was brought to the castle yard and steeped, washed, beaten, and spun. All of these activities passed in a silence imposed by distance, as a kind of pantomime played out on a faraway stage. Among these *divertissemente* I never ceased to look for the figure of Melisande, working with the women at the wool or flax, extracting honey from the hives, or playing childlike games in the castle gardens with her young stepmother, the wife of Guillaume. Her presence anywhere within the mute pageant of Argentat became the consuming focus of my attention.

Gerbert, how trivial you would have considered my pastimes at Argentat. An hour's walk along the river might be given up to a catalogue of smells—perhaps with a forethought to a poem: the honey-sweet scent of the lime trees, the savory fragrance of the elder bushes on the bank, the woody incense of the meadowsweet, the biting weedy smell of the river itself, the pungent odors of compost and dung. Of what consequence were such activities compared to the political and ecclesiastical reforms that occupied your time? How quickly you had risen in the hierarchy of power upon our return from Spain: first, your mission to Rome, in the company of Borrell and the archbishop of Vich, in the matter of reviving the archbishopric of Tarragona; then, the patronage of Pope John, who, impressed by your gifts of wit and rhetoric, sent you to the court of Otto I, as tutor to the son of that great lord; next, scholar to the house of Aldebero, archbishop of Rheims; revision and extension of the curriculum of the schools, with the introduction of the Arabic numerals you had so admired in Spain, and the construction of a wondrous clock for Magdeburg cathedral, the fame of which had spread even to the remote fastness of Argentat; and then, before your thirtieth year, at the designation of the emperor himself, you became abbot of Bobbio. The imperial palaces of Pavia, the *castelli* of Rome— these were the venues of your ascendancy. Against the quicksilver luster of your career, the earthen grayness of my life at Argentat would have seemed dull indeed. But to me, my life seemed neither gray nor dull. There was never a moment when my mind was not intent upon my surroundings. The tapestries of air and earth that adorned my hermitage were ever changing. Colors, textures, sounds: these intricately woven patterns required—from the new teacher of prosody and song—a constant exegesis. And even a simple catalogue of scents might lead at last, through the winding path of a poem, to the *eau* of rose and lavender with which Melisande combed her hair.

My thoughts of her became indistinguishable from my prayers. *You are beautiful, my love, and fair! Your eyes are doves.* How often had the monks of Saint Gerald's sung those very words as an antiphon for the Feast of the Assumption, the sweet music filling the cool darkness of the church. *I charge you, daughters of Jerusalem, by the roes and hinds of the field, not to stir my love, nor rouse her, till she pleases to awake.* My love for Melisande inspired in me that same paradoxical sense of fullness and vague longing that I had often felt as I woke in deepest hour of the night to join my brothers at Matins. Oh, Gerbert, you are the theologian, you are confessor to Christendom: Was my longing a sin? This fleshless passion that gathered to itself words and glances as a bee gathers honey for the hive? These touches that were not touches, passing from her hand to mine, and mine to hers, as warmth on the page of a book or vibration on the string of the harp? And once, when she had gone, I turned over her tablet, to find on the reverse, smoothed but still readable in the soft wax, a fragment not Solomon's:

> *My heart answers*
> *The cicada's quickened call . . .*

Yes, my love for Melisande was an antiphon. *Stay me up with flowers, restore me with apples, for I languish with love.* I felt no shame, no sense of sin. God is love, says the apostle John in his first epistle, and anyone who fails to love cannot know God.

A summer storm rolled across the valley, flinging sheets of rain against the castle walls. The curtain puffed and billowed at the window of the small room where we held our lessons. With each rumble of distant thunder Melisande's maid stirred anxiously and pulled her gray wool cloak tighter about her shoulders. Melisande was gay, in a dress of rose linen bound at each shoulder with a bright brass pin; a milk-white apron was gathered in her lap. She worked at a translation of Psalms from the Latin of Jerome into her own tongue. Guillaume, her father, entered, with Mechtild, his young wife, and Riculf, his son. He took the book from Melisande and studied it. The words on the page were meaningless to him.

"Read this," he said, and thrust the text into Melisande's hand. He pointed to the Sixth Psalm.

She looked to me. I nodded encouragement.

She began: "God, do not punish my . . . do not punish me in your anger, or . . ." She showed me the troublesome word. I translated: *Reproach, scold.*

"Or scold me in your anger . . . fury."

She looked to Guillaume, who indicated that she should continue.

"Pity me, O God, I have no strength, heal me . . . my soul is . . . tormented. I am . . . worn out with weeping. Each night I cry into my pillow. My . . . bed . . . is wet with tears."

Guillaume queried me on the correctness of Melisande's translation. I said: *She is a gifted young woman. Languages come easy to her. In the aptness of her poetics she is my teacher.*

Guillaume went to the window and looked into the storm. "We shall strike a fine bargain with her," he said.

He turned to go. The curtain flew back at the window and a spray of fine rain entered the room. Melisande closed the book and covered it with her apron. Guillaume paused at the door. He said: "Her talents will be appreciated in the effeminate courts of the north."

As Guillaume departed, Riculf came before his sister and pointed to the apron in her lap. Melisande was briefly perplexed, then uncovered the book and handed it to him. Riculf moved to the window. Rain flew into his face. He studied the book intently.

Melisande said, "Please, Riculf. The book will be wet."

Riculf closed the book and handed it to Melisande's maid, who held it close to her breast. Then he moved to his sister and, reaching out, touched her cheek with the knuckle of his hand. He looked only at Melisande, but he spoke to Guillaume's wife.

"Mechtild," he said. "Is she not beautiful?"

Mechtild did not respond, but gathered up her skirts and ran from the room.

Riculf laughed. "Pity me, O God, I have no strength," he said mockingly, mimicking Melisande's translation. Then he, too, departed.

He had not acknowledged my presence.

I sometimes accompanied Guillaume's steward into the forest for the purpose of cutting firewood and gathering moss. I took pleasure in this physical work, which came as a welcome break from the languorous mornings of study with Melisande. The wood of oak, maple, beech, and birch extended unbroken from river valley to river valley, and few persons of that region were brave enough to venture far into the dark interior. Only the verges of the forest were harvested—for wood, moss, bark for tanning, and charcoal for the smelter. Deer and boars were hunted for the table, and bears, aurochs, and wild goats. In the month of May, wolf cubs were exterminated with baited pits and poisons. Throughout all seasons, snares were set for wolves. On one of these excursions with the steward, we found a fat brown wolf in a snare, teeth bared, eyes gleaming like garnets.

The steward handed me the lance. "Kill her," he said.

I hesitated, balancing the spear upon my hand.

My guide was impatient: "She deserves no pity. She would rip your heart out if she could."

Gathering my courage, I thrust the lance into the wolf's throat, just where the wire constrained its neck. The beast's belly heaved and then was still. A pitch-black stream of blood flowed from the wolf's mouth and nostrils.

"She's a fine big bitch," said the steward. He took the lance from me and wiped the bloody point upon his sleeve.

⧗

A night of frightful dreams. I woke with a powerful sense of Melisande's presence beside me. I lay silently abed and listened. The wind from the mountain shook the leaves like castanets. Birds chirruped and sang from the forest's edge. And I heard from within my own flesh a cry, an awakening of physical longing, the carnal counterface of love. *O God, hold this one thing pure,* I prayed. I rose from my pallet and went into the forest, to a clearing at the base of a cliff where a spring of clear water emerged from the rock to form a broad pool. There I stripped off my tunic, broke a supple branch from a willow, and with it lashed my flesh. When at last I tossed the scourge into the crystalline spring, the overbrimming water trickled red.

As I quit the forest all of nature seemed to show the thin red stripes of repentance in harmony with my self-inflicted wounds, as the strings of a kesh vibrate in sympathetic resonance one with the other. The vineyards on the steep slopes across the valley were parapets of red in the slanting morning light, the river a crimson gash on the valley floor. I arrived early for our lessons. In the kitchen garden Mechtild, Guillaume's young spouse, was combing Melisande's hair. Melisande sat upon a stool, her eyes closed, her hands folded among fresh flowers in her lap, ribbons twined upon her fingers. She wore only her light undergarment of madder yellow. Her dark hair glistened. Unseen, I watched.

Mechtild drew the comb caressingly through Melisande's sun-brightened tresses, and with her hand she lifted each parted sheaf to her lips and bestowed upon it a kiss. I was distressed that I should be privy to an intimacy of which Melisande herself was unaware. Looking up, Mechtild saw me standing at the gate and her eyes turned cold and gray. She twisted the strands of Melisande's hair into her hand and closed her fist upon them.

At the height of summer we met in the herb garden for our lessons. In the first cool hours of the morning, Melisande's scales on the harp were like the music of a thrush, rising on scents of rosemary, thyme, and coriander. With my guidance, she had begun to set the verses of Solomon to music, and these she sang:

> *Who is this that comes out of the desert*
> *like a pillar of smoke,*
> *perfumed with myrrh and frankincense*
> *and every powder of the merchant?*
> *See, it is the bed of Solomon,*
> *borne by sixty valiant men,*
> *the bravest warriors of Israel,*
> *expert swordsmen all,*
> *and veterans of battle.*
> *Each man's sword is at his side*
> *against alarms by night.*

At *sixty valiant men*, her fingers marched like martinets on the strings, and I could see that she would soon surpass my own skill on the harp. In composition, too, she advanced rapidly, and effortlessly found turns of phrase—"the cicada's quickened call"—as fine as any that might have come from the mouth of Gerbert.

These sessions of Elysian happiness ended on the morning of Saint Swithun's, when Riculf rode into the garden mounted on a blue-roan mare. He carried a spear wet with blood, and behind him, flung across the mare's flanks, was the carcass of a deer. He wore green leggings and a ratskin vest; his wild hair and beard glistened with sweat. Melisande opened her mouth to speak but remained silent. Her eyes flamed with distrust and fear. I said nothing. Riculf reined his mount not six feet from us and, leaning down upon the mare's sweat-damp neck, surveyed us silently.

After some moments of this wordless inquisition, I rose and said, *Riculf, back away. There is no way we can study with you hanging there above us.*

A long silence ensued, and then he asked, "Why are you here?"

I answered, *I am here at your father's request, for the instruction of your sister.*

"The instruction of my sister." He repeated my words, lips curled in contempt. "To instruct her in what? In womanly things! How is it that you are so expert in womanly things?"

I did not reply to his question, but only said, *Riculf, back away. Your presence here serves no purpose.*

"Serves no purpose." Again he repeated my words. "How soft you are, monk, with your harp and your books."

He reached out with the bronze point of his spear and tipped open the book that lay at the edge of the bench. I picked up the book and passed it to Melisande.

"How soft you are," he repeated. And then: "How like a woman. I wonder if you have a prick."

With the tip of his spear he moved to lift the hem of my tunic. I reached for the spear and pulled it from his hand. My quick and unanticipated action nearly unseated him from his mount. I broke the shaft of the spear across my knee; the smooth ash snapped loud and clean. Riculf's eyes flared; his teeth were bared like a dog's. He threw his leg across his mount and leapt to the ground. With my hand I touched Melisande's arm, indicating that she should rise and move away (it was the first time I had touched her). Riculf came toward me. I lifted the two halves of the spear crosswise as a barrier to his approach. With a lightning-quick movement he lifted the wooden bench from its place by the path and brought it crashing toward my head. I veered sideward, and the bench struck my shoulder a crushing blow. There was a crack of bone as loud as that of the sundered spear. Riculf's mare bolted backward, trampling the garden herbs, churning the earth with plowing hooves. Melisande moved to restrain Riculf, who shoved her roughly aside. And now Melisande's maid, who had been sitting some distance away, ran forward to protect her mistress, but not before I had placed myself between the girl and her brother. I raised the two staves of broken spear, vertically, as a club. Riculf unsheathed a short steel sword, and with a powerful cast of his arm slashed cleanly through the two conjoined shafts of ash not an inch from my clenched hand. My shoulder was wrenched forward. Bolts of pain laced my body; I thought I saw the hand of No-Ear fly through the air, and I fell unconscious.

I do not know how Melisande quelled Riculf's fury or why my life was spared. I was carried by servants on a pallet to my hermitage, and doctored there by an old man of a nearby village, admired for his medical gifts. For three weeks I mended. Our lessons ended. Melisande was not allowed to visit me, though her maid came each day with some small gift—a fruit, a balm of herbs, and once, near the end of my stay at Argentat, a poem in Melisande's hand on a small panel of waxed wood, in which I could discern the transformed cadences of the Song of Songs:

> *I am a garden enclosed*
> *and a sealed fountain.*
> *He is the stream*
> *of milk and honey*
> *from the green mountain.*

103

I sleep, I sleep,
but my heart is awake.
He is the bed of spices,
the bed of green reeds.
My heart will break.

I opened to my love,
but he was sent away.
He is the orchard
of pomegranate trees.
My heart is in disarray.

There is no love so pure as love unexpressed. But Melisande's expression of love—for, yes, I took her verses as such—came to me as milk and honey. When I held her tablet in my hand I understood afresh everything I had heard or seen at Argentat. The tablet was the key to a grammar of love—a grammar I had been until now too unconfident to read. A hesitation upon a word of a song, a ribbon left untied, an herb lying on the page of an opened book, the words on the page: these things now became part of an unspoken vocabulary. Even what Melisande wore had been meant for me—as when she walked along the river in a scarf of vibrant yellow, that she might signal her presence to the person watching from the hill above. Her movements upon the riverbank were as carefully choreographed as a dance, and her mind was as attentively fixed upon her audience as mine was fixed upon the dancer. No physical touch, no coital act, could have been more intimate or full of intensity than that vocabulary of intangibles that separated myself and Melisande that summer at Argentat.

Skellig
May 1, 999
Aileran to Gerbert, bishop of Rome
From the door of my cell I observe two boats upon the sea. They are still far away, not yet as near as the Little Skellig, two black

dots moving in a halo of wheeling birds. This can mean but one thing: I am to be wrested from the island. I will be dragged off to Ardfert and interrogated concerning an absurd syllabus of "errors" by men who are themselves the credulous servants of superstition. It will be several hours before my adversaries arrive at the cove below. This letter, Gerbert, I shall seal and address to you, and if I am lucky they will accord it the privilege of confidentiality. You see, even here on this forsaken island, the power of Rome has useful currency.

These other scraps—these tattered recollections of a life so laboriously scribbled onto parchments, skins, and scraps of wood—I have wrapped in the hide of a goat (my faithful companion expired at last) and will bury with my chalice. When I can be sure of security I will tell you where they can be found.

Since last I wrote, I have passed through the valley of the shadow of death. I have looked into the abyss. I was not afraid. Death crept into my cell like a consoling cloud. I was not asked to give a yes or no. Death issued no threat or invitation. It simply enveloped me like a darkness, as the eclipse extinguishes the moon—and, like the moon, I have returned from adumbration. I was brought, Gerbert, to the very portal of eternity. I saw nothing.

And now I am faced with a decision: How shall I welcome those who are coming to take me away? Shall I resist? I have the strength to tip rocks down the face of the cliff. This place is well suited for defense; once, during the abbacy of Ciarán, six monks resisted the incursion of fourscore Vikings for three days. But I have no taste for violence. Then shall I go passively to Ardfert and submit to the indignities and insults of fools? Or worse, be carried off to Rome, that Whore of Babylon, leaving forever this God-struck island where I have vowed to spend my last days? Or should I simply step across the parapet and fall into oblivion? For this last I lack courage. So do I fear death after all? I have looked through the portal and I saw nothing. Yet might not God be the trickster who cloaks eternity in darkness? Perhaps death is the final trap, like a pit of stakes set for wolves and covered with twigs and leaves. One steps forward through the curtained portal, confident of safety, and then—the plunge into oblivion. Or perhaps my fear of the parapet is in fact a love for life. It is true, Gerbert, I feel that there is more to my story, another chapter yet to be told, which will bring together the separate strands of the tale and weave them into a cloth sufficiently strong to bear my life to eternity. An untold life is a tangle of fibers, like wool fresh-sheared from the sheep. A thousand short filaments twisted this way and that: The wool lies in a heap. The storyteller cards the wool, combs out the fibers into linear strands, then twists the strands into weft and warp and makes a cloth. I have not yet finished telling my story, nor—I think—is the story finished. I must therefore live some more, until the sheep is fully shorn and the cloth is made, and then—then, Gerbert, you may use the cloth as my winding sheet.

These two are the weft and warp of my life: Gerbert and Melisande. How accidental it seems that you, Gerbert, should have entered my life at all. Had I not been tending the vines, had you not slept, had your hair not shone like polished brass—subtract a single numeral from the sum and the life that I have lived would have added up to another. Had I not been sent to Argentat, had her eyes not been like doves, had her dress not been cinched at the waist with a sash of embroidered silk . . . A step, a spoken word, a word unspoken, the shrug of a shoulder, a glance to the right or to the left—of these trifles a life is made, like the straws of hay that are gathered into the cock. Does a life fall toward its conclusion like a feather in the wind, gusted this way and that, buffeted by chance, so that one destination is as likely as any other? Or does a life move as the leaf moves in a stream, turned and shaken by each gyre and ripple but drawn inexorably and inevitably toward a necessary end?

Gerbert, we approach the end of the journey. We look back along the path and try to put the best face on events. But the truth of the events slips away like water through a sieve. It resists summary. Every question has two answers. Did Aileran come to the Skellig for the love of God, or out of stubbornness and pride? Does he live in a stone cell on an ocean rock to honor the world, or to spite it? Does Gerbert occupy a Roman palace of cedar and marble that he might unify the world in Christ, or because he is seduced by ambition? Does he clothe himself in gold and silk because these are the necessary trappings of his office, or is the office an excuse for the gold and silk? And there is more. Did Aileran go to Verzenay to administer the sacraments to the house of Odo, or to consummate his love for Melisande? Did Gerbert intervene at Verzenay out of love for his friend, or because of guilt for the conclusion he had caused to happen? There is no end to the questions—as many questions as there are straws in the cock of hay. And the truth? Is it possible to know the truth? Does truth exist? Do we choose the trajectory of our lives, or do we simply fall toward death like the feather in the wind?

Perhaps when our stories are completed we will have answers to the questions. Perhaps when the stories have been told in full we will know the truth. If death is the empty door, then the truth of *this* life is all we have. You and I, Gerbert, must wrest the truth from our stories.

So I will not step across the parapet. Nor will I throw stones down upon the bailiffs of the bishop. I will go to Ardfert. I will place myself at the disposal of the bishop. The story will find its way to its just conclusion.

Aileran

❦

I remember Ovid's telling of the story of Pyramus and Thisbe:

> . . . *This chink, which no one had discovered*
> *Through the years (But what does love not see?)*

The lovers found, and made of it their voices'
Passageway, and through it safely whispered
Words of love . . .

From this place of my confinement—a small cell below the bishop's house at Ardfert—a single window looks out upon the light of day. No, hardly a window; a chink merely, a long narrowing embrasure, a hand's-width wide at my eye and no broader than a finger's breadth at the outside surface of the wall. Through this chink I court the world as Pyramus courted Thisbe. Through it I tell the passing of night and day; I hear the scream of gulls and the raucous chorus of the crows; I note the changing hues—blues, whites, and grays—of tumbling clouds; at night, I observe the stars, but cannot see enough of the sky at once to recognize their constellations. And through this embrasure for a few minutes each day streams enough of the sun's light to enable me to continue my memoir, so that this chink becomes, as in Ovid's story of the cloistered lovers, my "voice's passageway." To you, Gerbert, I whisper words of love, and to Melisande also. All night in total darkness, and through the Cimmerian shadows of the day, I whisper my story, over and over—this story of the two loves that have brought me at last to this place—over and over, until the words are committed to memory, as once I committed to memory the verses of Ovid's poem, until the hour of the day when the light, entering briefly as a single ray, permits me sufficient illumination to write the story down. For this, Gerbert, this latter use of my passageway of light, I am indebted to you. Your nuncio has recently arrived here and won for me the privilege of parchment and pen. More important, he has promised me the security of this memoir; to him I will consign the completed pages, and to him I will reveal the hiding place of my previous jottings. To you they will ultimately come.

There is an irony in the fact that my imprisonment at Ardfert represents an *improvement* upon my physical circumstances. My incarceration is no hardship. I have grown used to confinement. My room here in the bishop's palace is no less small than my Skellig cell. Darkness continues as my welcome companion. The silence of the dungeon sharpens my powers of recollection. The little bit of nature I am allowed to glimpse through my "window" is made more beautiful by its scarcity (*But what does love not see?*). And I am relieved from worry about what I shall eat and drink; once each day I am provided with a portion of food, tiny but sufficient, and indeed, by comparison with my diet on the island this past winter, my meals here at Ardfert are banquets. No hermit could have chosen a more desirable place of seclusion.

For an hour each evening I am interrogated by the bishop's seneschal, a young monk of stern simplicity and pious demeanor. He has but one objective: to root out from the garden of Christ every weed intruded there by Satan. This work he pursues with a keen self-righteousness. If there is an excess in his manner, then he is confident that it is justified by the urgency of his cause. The Millennium is near. The powers of darkness gather. The demons and fiends move among us, often in disguise. My young interrogator has studied Revelation and quotes it to me: *They will come swarming over the countryside and besiege the city of the saints . . . they will be made to drink the wine of God's wrath, which is undiluted in his cup of anger.*

Each evening I am asked to drink from my interrogator's cup of anger. "Is it true," he asks, "that you have made hosts from flour mixed with semen, and with this abominable bread celebrated a false Eucharist?"

No, I answer, *it is not.*

"Was it the procurement of semen that left your hands marked with the scales of Satan?"

My hands are scarred with burns.

"How burned? By hellfire?"

I would prefer not to answer.

"If you do not answer, it will be construed as an admission of guilt."

My hands were burned when those who would harm me placed hot coals into my palms.

"Who? Who would harm you?"

I prefer not to answer.

"Then you admit your guilt?"

I admit nothing.

"Is it true that while on Skellig rock you were visited at night by succubae, with whom you had unclean intercourse?"

I had no companion on the rock but a goat.

"Satan often presents himself to men in the aspect of a goat."

This goat gave milk and succor.

"And in your sleep?"

I had dreams.

"And those dreams: Were they unclean?"

Sometimes.

"And how do you know that they were dreams and not the visitations of succubae?"

They were dreams.

"Satan is clever; would it not be difficult to discern the visits of succubae from unclean dreams?"

They were dreams.

How did this come to pass? I spoke out against miracles, and now I have been made a thaumaturge. I questioned the power of Satan, and now I am the notorious instrument of Satan's power. Orthodoxy is like an arch of stones; remove one stone, and the arch falls down. There are no grays in the theology of my inquisitor; all is white or black. Once, embellishing my virtues, they thought I was a saint. Now, having fanned an ember of heterodoxy into a roaring fire, they proclaim me the follower of the Antichrist. I have not changed. I am the same Aileran they once admired. I love God, and I doubt. I see his face *as through a glass darkly.* I am a lover and a sinner, a believer and an apostate, a gray monk, damned by caution, uncertainty, and ambiguity. My interrogator knows the stakes; he quotes Father Augustine: *I classify the human race into two cities: the one consists of those who live by human standards, the other of those who live according to God's will. . . . By two cities I mean two societies of human beings, one of which is predestined to reign with God from all eternity, the other doomed to undergo eternal punishment with the devil.* This intense young monk, who once each day comes to my cell with his earnest questions and presumptions of guilt, is quite prepared to define "God's will" and prescribe for me eternal punishment.

At Saint Gerald's a part of the river Cére is channeled through the monastery to do God's work. The stream enters at the north wall, where it irrigates the garden. The monks of the brewery and the bakery draw off their shares. The stream is made to fill the kitchen cisterns. Then it passes into the monks' bath and the laundry. Finally, the waters pass under the latrine and flush the wastes of Saint Gerald's back into the Cére. Day and night, year by year, the water flows equably of its own nature, accomplishing its tasks. It does not reason, nor does it will; each part of the stream is like any other. Only when there is an obstruction, or the channel becomes clogged with weeds, does the stream draw attention to itself.

A well-ordered life is like the stream. For sixteen years following my return to Saint Gerald's from Argentat, my life flowed as equably as the channeled waters of the Cére. I did what I perceived to be God's will. With a single exception, I obeyed the Rule. I studied the Fathers of the Church. I prayed. Eventually I was asked to take Holy Orders and celebrate the Eucharist for my fellow monks. Within the monastery, ordination was considered a burden rather than an honor, dangerous to the humility and spiritual well-being of the person selected. On Sundays and the great feasts of the Church, the priest is lifted above his brothers, garbed in rich vestments, and allowed to take into his hands the Body of Christ. These distractions from the humility of cenobitic life I undertook because they seemed to answer God's call.

Abbot Colman was now old and feeble. Many of the tasks of administering Saint Gerald's fell to me, by his wish. It was widely assumed that upon Colman's death I would become abbot of our house. I found this prospect attractive, and at the same time frightening. What frightened was the attractiveness. Colman ruled Saint Gerald's wisely, efficiently, and with unaffected simplicity. He administered the monastery as another monk made butter, or swept the cloister, or carried dung from the cowsheds to the fields. This, I knew, I could never do. My will intruded itself into my every action. It clung to my spirit with the tenacity of a leech—a pestering worm of self that would not let go. If I was elevated to Colman's office, it would not be simply as abbot, but as Aileran, Abbot, and this exaggeration of self, I knew, was in violation of the Rule.

The Rule forbids that a monk should have any possession for himself: not book, tablet, or pen—nothing at all save by permission of the abbot. In violation of this rule I kept hidden a small tablet of wax on which had been written a poem, a poem I had carried from Argentat. *I am a garden enclosed and a sealed fountain. He is the stream of milk and honey from the green mountain.* The poem was a constant refrain in my life of prayer, an addendum to my every act of contrition. It was the talisman of my intruding will, a reservation on the love of God, the gift withheld. As long as the waxed tablet was hidden in my bed I knew I could not be abbot. It was a thorn embedded in my flesh . . . and a hedge on my ambition.

As I nursed my hesitant yearnings for greater authority, Gerbert's star continued to ascend toward the Roman zenith we had glimpsed that night on the strand at Narbonne. Astute politician, brilliant diplomat, flatterer, schemer: what was he? Even to our remote house at Aurillac the stories came: his contentions with the nobles at Bobbio concerning the possession of monastic lands; his desperate interventions on behalf of the Dowager Empress upon the death of Otto II, winning at last a secure throne for the heir, Otto III; his role as councillor and prop for Aldebero, archbishop of Rheims, and his bitter disappointment upon the election of Arnulf as successor to Aldebero. Intrigue, cunning, treason, rebellion: stories swirled about his name. Gerbert is here, Gerbert is there. Gerbert is the lover of the empress, or of the emperor. Gerbert has murdered Arnulf, or has been slain by him. Gerbert has been made pope, Gerbert has been excommunicated.

What was the truth? At last there came to Aurillac a messenger from Gerbert, now archbishop of Rheims, inviting me to come there as teacher-in-residence at the cathedral school. It is clear now, in recollection, that I had three motives for accepting Gerbert's invitation, although at the time I would have admitted only one. My first motive was to act in conformity with God's will, as perceived in Gerbert's request. Secondly, I was curious to discover the true Gerbert, by seeing him in person once again. And thirdly, at Rheims lived the author of a certain poem inscribed on a waxed tablet—as wife of the duke of Verzenay. With Colman's reluctant permission, I departed.

How shall I describe the Gerbert of Rheims? How was he different from the Gerbert I had known at Aurillac? His hair was still thick and blond (my own hair had thinned and grayed). He was somewhat heavier but carried the extra flesh well. Graceful, but now with a certain refined elegance in his motions, a patrician bearing, Italianate. Clean-shaven. Full, sensuous lips still tremulous with excitement. And the eyes! As luminous and unclouded as the waters of the sea at Narbonne. The debaucheries of Spain, and whatever vices and machinations had accompanied his ascendancy in the favor of the courts and the hierarchy of the Church, had left no residue in his eyes; his eyes proclaimed his innocence; they were the eyes of a child—darting, curious, credulous, chaste. He welcomed me generously. He flung his arms about me and kissed my cheeks. He took me with him, away from his courtiers and servants, into his private chambers, and queried me with honest interest concerning the events of the past two decades. Each and every episode of my clerical life was for him a matter of apparent importance—but we did not touch upon the interlude when I was tutor to Melisande at Argentat. For the space of the interview it was as if the intervening years had fallen away and we were again the Aileran and Gerbert who marched arm in arm on the roads of Languedoc. My love for him had not faded. I was immediately caught up again in the web of his affection, a web spun with guileless silver and flawless symmetry—irresistible, inescapable.

If Gerbert was the same, or nearly so, the circumstances of his life had altered drastically. His clothes were now of extravagant silk, acquired through Italian importers at Pavia or Venice. The outer garment, a splendid rose-colored dalmatic, was embroidered with a pattern of peacocks in gold and silver threads. His hands bore rings of semiprecious stones, and these he turned as we talked, first one, then another, round and round upon his fingers. The room was elegantly furnished, its chairs and benches decorated with a marquetry of rare woods or inlaid enamel. Tapestries hung on each of the four walls. One of these especially caught my eye; it depicted a young woman, bound to a bench, being mutilated by men with hammers and knives. ("The martyrdom of Saint Barbara," Gerbert informed me.) And against the wall, a chest I had seen before—on the front, three goddesses pose nude before Paris, and on the side, Venus throws a book into the fire.

"I have prepared two apartments for you," said Gerbert. "You may choose whichever one you wish."

The first was in the episcopal residence, adjacent to Gerbert's own chambers, and luxuriously furnished; the second, a small room in a tower of the church, containing only a cot, a table, and a bench. I chose the latter.

"The same Aileran." Gerbert smiled. "You see, I have anticipated your needs."

He threw a reassuring arm about my shoulder. From the window of my room he pointed out the various quarters of the town, and beyond the town walls, set in a parkland of birch and pine, the chateau of Odo, duke of Verzenay.

"I believe you are acquainted with the mistress of that house," he said. And added: "A ravishing woman, but unapproachable. God knows I've tried."

He laughed; it was unclear whether I was meant to take him seriously. I chose not to.

I asked, *Her husband?*

"A gross man, twice her age, interested only in the hunt, unless of course he can find an excuse to go to war. We do what we can to ensure that he has few opportunities for *that*."

And children?

"Three. A boy, two girls. And she has lost at least as many more. The old goat manages to keep her permanently with child."

Is she happy?

"Who can say? Is anyone happy? Am I happy? Are you happy? She seems happy enough. She enjoys her children. She is pious. She does good works about the town. The beggars all think her a saint."

And does she care for her husband? Odo? The duke?

"You *are* curious, aren't you. Are you certain that your interest is only that of a master for his pupil?"

I looked away. Perhaps I had revealed too much. Gerbert paid no mind. He repeated my question. "Does she care for her husband? I would say she probably despises the old rakehell.

115

Certainly everyone else does. But of course he owns everything hereabouts, so he has no dearth of feigned friends and sycophants."

Gerbert shook his head ironically. "One does not always have the opportunity of choosing one's friends. If I could choose my friends, Aileran, I would go off with you again on another adventure. God, what fun we had: sleeping in ditches, chasing *filles de joie,* debauching ourselves on Ovid and peaches. But I cannot. The irresponsibility of youth is a precious gift, given only once and not to be retained beyond maturity. There are more important things than youthful pleasures, more important even than friendship. We must keep the empire from crumbling further. We must assert and consolidate the power of the Church. The question is simply this: Is Europe to be united in the Body of Christ, or will it become a tatter of tiny princedoms, prey to the whims and fortunes of scoundrels like the husband of your pretty protégée? If cultivating the likes of Odo is what is required, then that is our duty. And so you see why it is that I wanted you here, dear Aileran. You are the only true friend I have. Everyone else is either scheming behind my back or waiting to lick my boots—or both. It will be good to have someone nearby who will take me as I am, who will love me for what I am and not for what I must sometimes pretend to be."

And I did love him, even as before. But in spite of his professed desire for my company, I saw little of Gerbert. He seemed always busy with letters, or negotiations, or travel, or entertainment. When we met, he engaged me with warmth and protestations of need. ("God, how I do enjoy you, Aileran. We really must spend more time together.") But quickly he would be called away, to the house of Odo, to the chapter house, to a meeting with his architects. ("We must knock down this old church and start afresh; build something new and immensely impressive, something that will give a visible expression to the optimism of the Church. If Odo and his fellow *primores* would be less stingy with their treasure, Rheims could have the finest cathedral in

Christendom.") And he was never alone. His house was crowded with retainers, favor-seekers, and petty officials—and guests, who seemed to come from nowhere and stay as long as they liked. Among the more or less permanent residents of the episcopal palace were the children of Borrell. ("Ah, Aileran, surely you remember John and Blanca? The son and daughter of our host in Barcelona. They are here for a taste of life in the cold north. Foolish, wouldn't you say, to have left sunny Catalan?") I would not have recognized them; they had lost all aspects of youth. But John wore on his wrist a familiar silver bracelet.

Among my students in the school at Rheims was Theodulf, the son of Odo and Melisande. A thin-limbed, gentle child, fourteen years of age: There was much to see in him of his mother, still vivid in my memory. (I had not yet encountered Melisande at Rheims, but I watched—in the streets of the town, in the cathedral precincts, in the almshouse and infirmary—for her familiar figure.) The boy had his mother's honey-lustered skin and dark hair. His mouth, like hers, was not quick to smile but soft, as if poised to whisper. His eyes, however, were black, not green, black like his father's, and fierce; there was in his eyes an anger, like scalding embers, and a Gaulish roughness that contrasted wildly with the measured temper of his disposition. I loved him; I loved him as I might have loved my own son, but of course it was Melisande that I loved, Melisande of Argentat.

Theodulf had inherited his mother's quick intelligence. He was a ready student. Our curriculum was set by Gerbert, who sought reforms not only in the school at Rheims but throughout the schools of Europe. Our subjects were the seven liberal arts—music, arithmetic, geometry, astronomy, grammar, logic, and rhetoric—but laced with elements of classical literature and learning, and, especially, in the case of arithmetic and astronomy, computational devices of Saracen invention. For arithmetic we were provided with the abacus, which Gerbert had brought from Spain, whose counters bore the nine Arabic numerals; with this instrument sums and differences could be performed with amazing speed. For astronomy we used fine brass astrolabes, contrived upon Saracen principles, and with them, at Gerbert's insistence, we made observations of the stars. For the study of music we had many excellent instruments, including the fine organ of the cathedral, and for the arts of language access to Gerbert's own remarkable library.

To each of my young scholars I assigned a part of Ovid's *Metamorphoses* as text for translation and analysis. To all of the boys save one I set such pieces as might give no offense to the most pious reader, but to Theodulf, perversely, I offered the story of Hermaphroditus and Salmacis. The boy responded at once to this tale of the son of Hermes and Aphrodite, who had a part of his features from each parent and his name from both, and who at the age of "thrice five years" traveled far to the lands of Lycia and Caria, where he encountered the nymph Salmacis. Theodulf began diligently to prepare a translation into the Frankish tongue, an awkward childish rendering that stumbled forward in the literal shoes of the Latin. I worked with him, as once I had instructed his mother, on meter, consonance, and rhythm. The next day he returned with this:

> He saw a pool, clear to the very bottom.
> No marshy reeds grew there, nor sedge,
> Nor spiky rush. The water was transparent
> But ringed about with springy turf
> And verdure ever green. A nymph
> Dwelt there. . .

Theodulf made no pretense that the work was his own: "My mother helped me," he confessed. No apology was necessary; I recognized at once the hand of Melisande. The piece was finely wrought. I showed the boy why the thing was fine, discussed the delicate internal rhymes and the music that took advantage of the rough, sedgy Frankish tongue while paying due homage to the crystalline clarity of Latin. Together we contrived a continuation:

> . . . *The boy, as if alone and unobserved,*
> *Walked to and fro upon the empty sward*
> *And dipped his toes into the lapping pool,*
> *Then his feet. And quickly tempted*
> *By cool waters, cast off the garments*
> *From his slender limbs. Then Salmacis,*
> *Gazing spellbound, burned with desire*
> *For his naked form . . .*

In this, "into the lapping pool" was the boy's own. His ear was quick to discern the nuances of sound, a gift that served him equally well when we turned to music. He objected to my "sward" and made a sour face; I stuck with the word and pointed out how well it worked with "unobserved." I set him more to do: "Can my mother help?" he asked. *Of course.* Of course. It was Melisande's translation I waited to receive:

> . . . *She scarce could bear to wait,*
> *Postpone her joy, so eager to embrace*
> *Him with her arms, so wild with love.*
> *He clapped his palms against his sides*
> *And dived into the pool . . .*

Each day scarcely passed quickly enough. I went through the motions of instructing my other students—but it was Theodulf's tablet I could not wait to see. How the boy felt about the subject of the poem I did not know; as he read the lines aloud, he did so without hesitation or embarrassment. "So wild with love" and "dived into the pool" he rendered in the same clear, well-modulated voice. He took pride in his own work but did not take his mother's credit. "That's hers," he said, indicating the first

lines; "the 'clapped' and 'dived' are mine." And looked to see if
I approved. I did; and I examined the boy as if he were the poem
itself, looking for fragments of the parent. Together we worked
on our next:

> . . . *flung off her clothes*
> *And plunged into the pool. She held him*
> *As he struggled, forced her kisses,*
> *Fondled him, and reaching down*
> *Caressed his breast against his will,*
> *On this side and on that. And finally,*
> *As he tried to break away, she wrapped*
> *Him round . . .*

I would gladly have forsaken my other duties to work with
Theodulf alone. (He left me earlier in the day than the other boys;
his father had no patience with the boy's schooling and insisted
that the afternoons be given to instruction in archery, swords-
manship, and riding.) My affection for Theodulf was real
enough, surely he sensed that; but did he know *why*? Did he
know that I was *in love* with him, or with that part of him that
confirmed my memory of his mother? I waited each day like a
patient suitor for this slim, black-eyed boy and his tablet:

> . . . *their bodies merged,*
> *One form and face, as when a gardener*
> *Sets a twig into a branch and sees*
> *Them both mature together. So when*
> *In firm embrace their limbs were knit,*
> *They were no longer two, but one—*
> *Not such as deemed a woman or a boy,*
> *Seemed neither and yet both.*

And what of Melisande? What was her stake in this shuttle-
borne translation of Ovid's verse? That it gave her opportunity

to exercise her considerable talent was clear enough. Her lines were fine, more graceful than my own; what I had achieved through study, she excelled by natural gift. And clear, too, that Theodulf was close to her heart and that in helping him with these poetic games she sought to ameliorate the harsh masculine influence of the father. But what more? With what emotions did she scan *my* lines? Did she copy out my translations (mine *and Theodulf's*) as diligently I did hers (hers *and Theodulf's*) before she smoothed away the words from the waxed tablet? Was my rekindled love returned? I searched the boy's face, sieved his words, and hoped to catch some hint of Melisande's heart, as if a part of her would cling to him as the tuft of thistle clings to a cat's fur. And sometimes the intensity of my scrutiny caused Theodulf to squirm uncomfortably, or become unruly, or simply refuse to work. One of the lines he had translated provided his own description: *The boy's cheeks blushed a rosy red; he knew not what love was.*

My love for Melisande was innocent enough—or so I believed. If God is love, then can it be wrong if part of Himself takes hold in our hearts? My love was physical; the love of God is spirit. But what is this spirit that is not flesh? Where can it be found? Upon what object can such a disembodied love be fixed? Did not Tertullian say: *Nihil est incorporale nisi quod non est,* "Nothing is incorporeal except what does not exist"; and again, *Quis negavit corpus Deum esse etsi Deus spiritus est,* "Who has denied that God has a body, even though God is spirit?" Then it must be true that God's body is the body of the world, for only the world is corporeal. And in loving Melisande, who is flesh and blood, I loved part of God's body. All love is carnal, I reasoned, and all love is divine, and only where there is an absence of love is God absent. The presence of God is more to be desired than propriety, law, and priestly vows. Is not a love that violates the laws of man a higher good than a law that violates love? Is not the fire that burns in the lover's heart the fire of divine life—even though it consumes what it inflames?

Gerbert showed me his clock.

He said, "You will notice how the force of the hanging weight makes the whole thing go."

Indeed, I marveled at the contrivance, which bore a resemblance to a device we had seen in Spain. The circles and catches were carved of fine-grained wood and turned upon brass pins.

"It is a small thing," he said. "I have made a larger one for the cathedral at Magdeburg, large enough to ring the hours."

The idea seemed preposterous. Even the object before me was implausible and seemed to move as if by magic.

It goes of itself, I said.

He corrected me: "When the weight is lifted by turning the cord upon the spindle, an impetus is stored in the machine, as heat is retained by iron when it is removed from the fire. This impetus is expended as the weight falls."

But it doesn't fall, I said; *the weight is motionless, and yet the circles turn.*

Gerbert laughed. "Oh, yes," he said. "It falls. Wait awhile, and you will see that the position of the weight has changed. The motion is imperceptible but inevitable, like the motions of the stars. Once set going, the hours and the minutes are unstoppable."

On Easter morning of the year 988, at the request of my lord bishop Gerbert, I celebrated the Eucharist in the private chapel of the duke of Verzenay. It was the hour before first light and the chapel was lit only by the flicking tongues of a dozen tapers. I was grateful for the darkness. My hands shook as I vested and performed the ablutions. As I entered the chapel and approached the altar I allowed myself only a brief glance at the congregation.

Odo and Melisande knelt at prie-dieux on either side of the altar, and behind them in the narrow room were their two older children and the members of their household. I spoke the prayers of introduction, and the *Gloria in excelsis*, and then turned to the assembly. I did not look at Melisande; instead I fixed my gaze beyond, on the figure of Theodulf (his eyes like small flames in the fuliginous light). *Dominus vobiscum.* I spoke the incantation, and heard in the answering murmur the voice I had not heard for more than thrice five years (*"Et cum spirito tuo"*), the voice I often imagined I heard at night whispering those other words—

> *I am a garden enclosed*
> *and a sealed fountain.*
> *He is the stream*
> *of milk and honey*
> *from the green mountain*

For the text of my sermon I took the question posed by the angel at the empty tomb: *Why look among the dead for one who is alive?* The incarnation, I preached, is the necessary condition for redemption. If Christ had not assumed a body of flesh, born of woman and susceptible to death, then there could be no resurrection. Against this great truth are arrayed the opinions of the heretics: Marcion, who disputed the reality of the incarnation; Apelles, who admitted that Christ had a body but denied that he was born of Mary; and the disciples of Valentinus, who taught that Christ's flesh was spiritual and illusory. These heretics denied that Christ's body could be formed of fleshly substance because they believed that all matter is intrinsically evil, the creation not of God but of the demiurge. But the Church affirms that the flesh of Christ is not merely accidentally but substantially part of the being that it clothed. Christ's fleshly resurrection redeemed all flesh, freed it from the sin of Adam and made it like unto his own. It was not matter that was destroyed in Christ, but sin; not substance, but guilt. In Christ's resurrection we celebrate the goodness of the material creation and the *rightness* of physical love.

Odo, a big man, full-bearded, feigned attention, alternately pitching forward to put his slablike hands on his knees, or collapsing back against the sooty wall with arms crossed heavily on his chest. His garb was entirely black and his skin dark; his body was like a shadow in the faint light. Melisande remained erect at her prie-dieu. Her features were less fragile than I remembered, her figure fuller, her hair cut shorter and caught up in a circlet braided with fresh flowers. She dressed simply; she wore no ring or brooch; her cloak was of green wool, gathered at the neck with a ribbon only. Her skin still glowed with a youthful radiance, flattered by the candlelight that danced upon her cheeks and brow. Her eyes did not meet mine—she looked into her folded hands—nor did I let my own eyes linger too long where they were inclined to stay. As I turned back to the altar for the *Credo* and Offertory, I could do no more than numbly recite the words of the prayers. What had I seen, if anything? Coolness. Not a hint of the passion that made my own hands shake as I lifted the cloth to uncover the chalice. She was not Salmacis, who *scarce could bear to wait, postpone her joy, so eager to embrace.* Was I alone, then? Were the verses of Ovid, so movingly rendered by Melisande, merely the transactions of a mother helping her son? And the poem—the poem from Argentat that had lain so long hidden in the folds of my bed—perhaps it, too, was a scholar's composition, a practiced mimicry of Solomon, a farewell gift of the student for her teacher. If I *was* alone, if my love for Melisande was unrequited, then my love was a sin, like the private fantasies that had tortured my days and nights during the time I frequented the brothel at Vich. Only Melisande had the power to transform my love; only she could lift it from the squalid shadows and let it burn with a Godly flame.

Consumed by uncertainty, I held aloft the bread and spoke the words of consecration: *Hoc est corpus meum.*

The congregation recited the prayer of the mystery: "We believe, O Lord, that in the breaking of thy body and in the pouring forth of thy blood we are redeemed."

The words of the *Dómine, non sum dignus*—Lord, I am not worthy—fell like lashes on my bare skin.

I turned from the altar to bring the communion to the master and mistress of the house. Whom should I approach first? Would Odo see and know? Would he rise up from his knees like the God of wrath and strike the chalice from my hands? I placed the host into his hands, into that dark basket of hairy, gnarled fingers. His eyes were black, emotionless, and unknowing. I turned to Melisande.

Corpus Christi, I whispered.

She lifted her head and I placed the wafer on her tongue. Her tongue furled back and carried the host into her mouth. She opened her eyes, and for a moment, perhaps only a second, I saw into her soul. I knew then that I was not alone, and that whatever followed was necessary and inevitable.

Quod ore súmpsimus, Dómine, pura mente capiámus, I murmured: What we have taken with our mouth, O Lord, may we receive with a pure heart.

Rome

Ardfert
June 21, 999
Oenu, bishop of Ardfert, in the province of Munster, Hibernia,
to Sylvester II, successor of Peter and bishop of Rome

My lord Father, first among bishops of Christ's Holy Church, I prostrate myself before you and beg your indulgence. These are troubled times. Some would say that we have seen in the heavens and the earth the signs spoken of by John that portend the coming of our Savior and the destruction of the world. Did not the Apostle say that Satan will be bound by the power of Christ for a thousand years, and that when a thousand years have passed he will be set loose out of his prison? Here and in other Christian lands there is considerable agitation, uncertainty, and fear. We are required to move carefully; we do not wish to fan the flames of anxiety, but at the same time we have the heavy responsibility of preparing souls for Christ. Many lands and possessions have fallen into our care as the faithful seek to prepare themselves for Christ's coming by affecting a Christ-like poverty. (The Apostle says, "Your riches will be destroyed within a single hour.") These new lands and possessions now in the care of the Church require inventory and administration, which places a heavy burden upon our offices. To this are added the dangerous pressures which are put upon the Church by Brian of Munster, who by consolidating temporal power into his own hands threatens the authority of Christ as exercised through his bishops. In the face of these heavy cares the case of Aileran of Skellig would seem to be trivial indeed. Certainly, the matter would have been dealt with judiciously and expeditiously by our episcopal authority had it not been for the intervention of your nuncio and the arrival of a letter from your own hand requesting that the monk Aileran be transferred to Rome. We can only guess at what *special relationship* exists between yourself and Aileran of Skellig that prompts this extraordinary and unfortunate abrogation of our authority. Nevertheless, in conformity with your will, we have dispatched the heretic Aileran into your care.

Let us remind you that the charges against him are serious:

—that he denies the power of God in nature;

—that he denies miracles;

—that he practices diabolic magic;

—that he blasphemes;

—that he has violated priestly vows.

These charges are fully documented in the dossier that is carried by my plenipotentiary. He also carries certain other materials which it may or may not be necessary to introduce into the trial, depending upon how vigorously you prosecute our intentions. These he will make known to you in full confidence. We trust, however, that your inquiry will uphold our writ of excommunication and that a stern and appropriate punishment will follow. The instructions of Our Lord Jesus Christ are unambiguous. Before the coming of a new heaven and a new earth, Satan, and those he has misled, must be cast into the lake of fire and sulfur. Only then will the earth be lit up in Christ's glory.

We are obedient to your will and trustful of your continued affection.

☧ *Oenu,* bishop

My memoir of Gerbert and Melisande has suffered a long and unwelcome interruption. My transportation from Ireland to Rome was made slow by my infirmity. Throughout most of the journey my hands were shackled, at the instruction of Bishop Oenu, so that in addition to the general weakness of my body my wrists were made sore and bloody by the pressure of the ropes. This new disability impedes my ability to write, but I confess that the pain inflicted by the bonds is scarcely felt. I have become, it seems, inured to physical discomfort. Indeed, discomfort has become an almost necessary condition for my body, so that here, in a cell at Castel Sant' Angelo, not far from the basilica of Saint Peter, I am made uncomfortable by the relative luxury of my circumstances. I have been treated by doctors, bathed, bled, fed absinthe for fever, aurone for weakness of limb, and fennel for constipation. All I lack is freedom, and *that* I forgo not by constraint of any lock and key (although lock and key are here) but by an act of the will. I have only one desire, and that is to complete this recollection, to recover the events of my life, and to discern, insofar as I can, the truth. No longer do I seek in these events the workings of a necessary fate, or an inevitable plan framed by God. Nor do I seek to justify myself by grand philosophical schemes. (I have abandoned the syllogism of youth: *God is love. Aileran loves. Therefore Aileran is God.*) Life is not logic. Life has no major premises and therefore no conclusions. Only minor premises—sex, love, fear, guilt. Now, at the end, I look only for truth. Not dogma, as defined by the officers of my tribunal, but the simple reality of the necessary, the substance of the present. Not God's plan but nature's. Not metaphysical treatises but scholia, marginalia, and glosses on the manuscript of life, inscribed in blood and tears. Saint Jerome said, "The work of the monk is to weep, not to teach." If God is here, in my blood and tears, then I have found Him. If He is not here, then He shall have to find me.

Gerbert has shown me no sign. I have been in his city for a dozen days and have had no communication from him. I am visited by theologians, who are presumably sent at *his* directive to interrogate me concerning the charges brought against me by Oenu. They have not mentioned their master, nor do they respond to my inquiries. These men are subtle; they are searching. They take my words and turn them on their heads. They squeeze my dispositions and protestations for drops of innocence or guilt. They have honey on their tongues and violence in their hearts. Are they my friends, sent by Gerbert to help me, or my enemies, who work in the cause of Oenu? I do not know. The investigation into the matter of my heresy proceeds apace. The inquest will begin shortly. Where is Gerbert?

Gerbert is everywhere. He runs through my narrative like an endless thread. Sometimes it seems as if Aileran was a poppet on Gerbert's hand. And Melisande: Was she another of Gerbert's poppets? Why did Gerbert invite me to Rheims, where Theodulf would be my student? Why did he send me to celebrate the Easter liturgy at the house of Odo and Melisande? And who was it that called me to that house again to minister the viaticum to Odo when he lay ill with fever? Was it Melisande? Or was it Gerbert? Yes. Gerbert! He knew. He orchestrated our love. He played his song upon the strings of our emotions—and we were his willing instruments.

Odo upon his bed . . . a mountain of gasping flesh. The eyes of Melisande's husband are wide and full of the fear of death. In the summer of 988 a fever ravaged Rheims. Rich and poor alike were stricken, the powerful and the weak, the licentious and the good. The sickness came like the effluvium of Avernus; like a malodorous breath it intruded the cracks of the houses, touched infants in their cradles, women at their milking, monks at prayer. Corpses lay stacked at the city gates like cordwood. Gerbert, who could have readily decamped to the safety of Pavia, stayed. He ordered works of sanitation. He made a part of his palace available as an infirmary for the scholars of Rheims. He provided from his own treasury for the purchase of food for those who could not farm. And for those who sought the consolation of the Church, he furnished relics. He caused the relics of Saint Barbara to be paraded through the streets. To Odo he dispatched a fragment of the True Cross, a sliver of wood from the tree of Christ encased in a vial of amber. This relic Odo clasped to his chest, the precious vial engulfed in his fetid fist. His black, fevered eyes searched mine for some thread of hope. I offered Odo the consecrated host and anointed his brow with chrism; the sacred oil sank into the furrows of the skin and ran down his cheeks like lava from Vesuvius. Odo's thick tongue convulsed against his lips, but he could not speak. Would he confess his sins? I spoke the words of absolution. The duke of Verzenay, brought low by an enemy he could not see, and now licked closely by the everlasting fires of hell, heard the absolving prayer as if it was a saving unction. But did I wish him saved? Did I pronounce the formula sincerely? Or did I falter in the absolution, withhold some gesture, and so wish him damned, this man who had bought himself a bride, possessed her as he might impale a stag upon a spear, and now, as he prepared to leave her, thought of nothing but saving his own rough skin? These thoughts were unworthy. I was a priest of Christ. I must not reserve Christ's saving grace. I repeated the words of the sacrament of the dying, and if those absolving syllables had the power to send this man into the arms of Christ, I was prepared to send him.

Melisande waited in the antechamber alone. Her eyes were wet with tears. I touched her hand.

Don't be sad, I said. *Perhaps he will live.*

She turned and moved away. Then she said, almost inaudibly, "I cry not because he is dying but because I wish him dead."

The words struck me like a ram. Wish him dead! Why? Why wish him dead?

Why?

She turned again to look at me. Her tears stood like drops of honey on her luminous cheeks. "Because . . ." But at that moment Theodulf entered from his father's bedchamber, red-faced and tearful. He stood gaping at his mother and then at me. He saw and knew, as surely as I, what it was she had begun to say.

With a candle I softened and smoothed the wax on the sandalwood tablet. I wrote:

> *Melisande,*
> *I have loved you since Argentat, and I know now that my love is returned. I am tormented by the thought of loss. Can God withhold such goodness? Can any earthly stricture be more forbidding than love's denial? Let us bring this one perfect thing to pass.*
>
> *Aileran*

This message I wrapped and sealed and sent to Melisande, with instructions that it be delivered to her alone. Hours and days passed without an answer. A hundred times I rehearsed in memory the words of the message. Had I offended? Had I presumed too much? Would it not have been more honest and manly to have approached her openly, faced Odo and demanded love's rights? What did I write? *Can God withhold such goodness?* What nonsense! What empty words! Of course God withholds goodness. The salmon is good, and the salmon is snared in the net; the vines are good, and the vines are seared by fire; the open graves of Rheims are full of the rotting corpses of innocent persons, unburied victims of the fever, good lives terminated in the midst of goodness. If God withholds the happiness of the innocent, why should he not also withhold the consummation of our guilty love? Odo, recovered from his illness, still possessed the rights of the marriage bed. It is *I* who should have withheld the message, shown restraint, thought of *her* happiness and not my own. She is the mother of three children, whom she loves; what could have possessed me to think that she would put my happiness—or her own—above that of her children? *One perfect thing!* No, not perfect, but tainted at the core. My obsession for Melisande was like a fever that would strike down the innocent and guilty alike. But still—drawing me toward hope—were the words smoothed deep into the wax of the sandalwood tablet, enfolded in softness like the secrets of a heart: *I sleep, I sleep, but my heart is awake.*

Early on the morning of the sixth day following the dispatch of my message, as I returned from morning prayer, I was approached in the dark aisle of the cathedral by a woman who introduced herself to me as Melisande's maid. She bade me follow. I went to Gerbert's stables and took my mount. We left the city by the east gate and moved along the river, on the lands of Odo's estates but in a direction that took us away from the chateau. The sun was masked by morning mist and the river wet with a nimbus of yellow light. From reeds at river's edge came a chorus of clicks, whistles, pules, pipings, and mewings. These sounds of nature were joined by the padded footfalls of my mount in dew-wet grass. The swish and jingle of caparison. Fragrances of water, soil, and willow. I experienced a fullness of the senses I had not felt since the hot summer days at Aurillac when I had helped Madalberta tend the vines. My flesh was like a pool with five flooding springs, filled to overflowing. We came at last to a cottage of timber and thatch. Melisande's maid retired. I dismounted and led my animal forward. Outside the cottage was tethered a roan mare, its mane braided in scented knots, its hide sleek with sweat.

Melisande.

She put her finger to my lips.

You are beautiful, I said.

She smiled; her eyes spoke consent. Then, more seriously: "Aileran, you must promise not to question what we do."

I nodded assent.

"When we are together," she said, "it must be as if our other lives do not exist."

That summer by the river at Verzenay we put our other selves away. We were not Melisande the wife of Odo, or Aileran, monk. Our cottage might as well have been in India, and our souls born again into other bodies. In our innocence and nakedness we lived life as it might have been lived before the Fall, before Adam's sin and Eve's folly. We worshiped the goddess Natura, in her own innocence and nakedness, as she existed before her corruption by philosophers, the goddess who unites in her own tempered disposition the two Venuses, *Venus legitima* and *Venus impudica,* who causes the heart and the flesh to come together into one harmonious *mundana musica.* We loved. We sat by the river and made music, I on the harp, she on the pipe. And we read, from a small book of beasts, which had been her gift from Gerbert, and improvised upon it.

"I am the bird Ercinee," said Melisande. "My skin shines so brightly with love's phosphorescence that I illuminate the overcast day. You shall find me by the telltale glow of my desire."

I am Hyrcus, I answered, *the He-Goat, burning for your sex. Adamant would melt in my hand.*

"I am Catus, who pursues the mouse. I catch it in my mouth."

I am Talpa, the blind mole, who burrows in the hollows of the earth. I nibble at the roots.

"I am Apis, who draws nectar from the flower. See the silver drop. I lay up honey in my comb. See how industrious I am, how agreeable."

I am Salamandra, who prevails against fire. I live in the heat

136

of the blaze without being burned. I extinguish the fire, yet I am not consumed.

"I am Turtur, the Turtledove. I love my first love only. I enfold him with my wings."

I am Grus, the Crane. I am never tired. I will watch you as you sleep.

We met at the seventh hour of the day. I try to recollect, here in the darkness of my cell in Rome, the reality of those sunlit mornings. The heat rising from the river. The warbling of the thrush in the river reeds. The scent from the fresh-mown hay that she had caused to fill our bed. The whiteness of the bedding. The touch of her skin. *Somnia, quae mentes ludunt volitantibus umbris:* Dreams, that mock us with their fleeting shadows. I see the bright colors of her garments in the grass by the river's edge. Her linen shift. The ribbons dispersed like poppies. I see her dark hair streaming on the water as she swims. I see her standing in the leafy pool, gathering her hair to the back of her neck with slim white hands, the water glistening on her breasts. *Mundana musica:* She made music of the elements. The earth was soft and warm against our backs. The water wet and cooled our kisses. The air quavered at her neck, in the hollow of her back, in her mouth. Her touch was fire.

On the days when we were not together she came into the town to nurse the sick in the infirmary established in the episcopal palace by Gerbert. The young scholars especially she minded, boys of Theodulf's age and younger, stricken with fever. Their bodies burned upon the cots; it was impossible to say which of them would live and which would die. She bathed them with cool water and offered words of encouragement. She had no patience for the bleedings of the physicians or the relics of the priests. She gave the boys simples made of herbs from her own gardens—

137

essences of wormwood, coriander, sage, and pepper. She seemed indifferent to the danger of contagion.

I was sometimes called to administer the viaticum to a dying youth, and on these occasions we met in a public place. No one who watched us at the bedside of a dying child could have guessed at the intimacy of our relationship. In this, as in all things, Melisande established the pattern of our intercourse. ("When we are together," she had said, "it must be as if our other lives do not exist.") As she moved among the cots, there was an otherness about her that I did not experience during our sojourns by the river. I wondered then about her other life, her life with Odo. I knew the many strictures that the Church places upon the exercise of the carnal act in marriage: Husband and wife must keep away from each other in the daylight hours and on the nights before Sundays and holy days; they are urged to forgo sex on the nights before Wednesdays and Fridays, by way of penance, and for the forty-day periods before Easter, Holy Cross Day, and Christmas; nor should a husband approach his wife during menstruation or the three months preceding and forty days following childbirth. These restrictions, I knew, Melisande would use to keep Odo away. I knew also that she had knowledge of herbal potions that might forestall Odo's ardor. But that the duke of Verzenay had carnal knowledge of his spouse was evidenced by her children, and the thought of him possessing her was more than I could bear, as I watched her move among the sick and dying. But there was a part of herself that was not Odo's, even when she was in his bed. Once she said to me, "I have given myself to no other man but to you, Aileran." Yet she was Odo's wife, and I did not forget the penalties prescribed by the Church for the sin of adultery.

You are beautiful, I said.

She wore a grass-green dress with flaxen sleeves, and her

unbound hair fell down across her breasts. I sat on the grass, she on the bench by the cottage door. She played the kesh.

I said: *At Argentat when we passed the wax tablet back and forth between us, our fingers almost met. Each time I strove to bring my hand a little closer to your own. Were you aware?*

"I was always aware of the nearness of our hands," she said, "but I thought it was my fingers that approached yours. I wondered if I risked too much, that you would think me forward, that you would see into my heart."

And what was in your heart?

"I loved you . . . so much, Aileran. I lay in bed at night and cried to think that you would go away. Since my mother died I had been alone. I was desperately alone."

Your father?

"My father was haughty and cruel. I believe that he loved me, but his temperament made it impossible for him to show his love. Riculf was dangerous. I lived warily. He often stood near to me—watching. I made certain never to be alone with him."

And Mechtild, your stepmother?

"She was kind to me, but she understood nothing. She was ignorant of my heart. Once she kissed me . . . on the mouth. I was startled and frightened. It was the only time I had been so kissed, and later, remembering, I wished it had been you."

And the poem . . . the poem that you sent me?

"Oh, Aileran, I was only a girl. You were older. You belonged to God. I did not have the courage . . . to tell you openly."

And now?

She laughed. "Now I have the courage to steal you from God."

In una flamma convertit tota natura: All of nature is changed in one great fire. Throughout the summer of our meetings at Verzenay, fever and conflagration ravaged Rheims. Hundreds died of a disease that found no remedy or cure. The cathedral begun by Ebbo in 816 and consecrated by Hincmar in 862 was destroyed by fire, and with it a hundred houses in the poorest quarter of the town. But for two of the inhabitants of Rheims, the transforming fire was desire. Three or four times each week we met at the cottage by the river; and when we were not together, Melisande's maid moved back and forth between us, bearing the well-traveled sandalwood tablet.

> At early dawn,
> Where Vesle's purling waters flow
> And summer gloves the hidden glade
> With cloth of green.
> The lamp of day begins to glow.
> I meet him in the greenwood shade
> At break of day.
>
> At early dawn,
> His kisses like the wakening dew.
> His touch dispels Aurora's rose
> Upon my cheek.
> The day (my happiness!) is new.
> My love, listen! The cock crows
> At break of day.

The garden was opened, the fountain unsealed. We slept together in the bed of reeds and spices. And never in all of that time did we allow ourselves to think of the consequences that might follow discovery. Love is blind. Blind and foolish. Discovery was inevitable. The fire burned too intensely. Its glow warmed everything around us. Even the sun (it seemed) flamed more fiercely. Poppies flushed crimson. The trout smoldered in the stream, their scales incandescent. Whatever we touched was ignited in our eyes. And anyone with eyes to see must have seen. And then, because they saw, the fire became real. The cottage exploded into flame. We awoke from the sleep of love in an inferno—a rushing, searing wind of fiery thatch. The bedclothes flew up in sparks about us, branding our naked flesh. *Melisande! Quickly!* The door—a blazing portal of escape. Blinding sunlight, stained red by fire. *Odo!* Mounted; his beard sucked wildly forward by the wind that gushed into the blazing cottage. Melisande's brother and son with weapons drawn, flames leaping from the polished blades. Riculf, the brother, straining with the fury of a mastiff chained, eager to complete the violence he had begun at Argentat long before; Theodulf, the son, frightened and guilty (our betrayer!), two boyish hands clamped whitely on the sword's silver hilt, the tip of the blade trembling. And six men-at-arms, awaiting Odo's orders. And now the answers to the questions asked by my interrogator at Ardfert become apparent, the true answers that I would not then yield my enemies. *Was it the procurement of semen that left your hands marked with the scales of Satan?* Burning embers were placed into my palms, my hands held outstretched. *Who? Who would harm you?* Odo, the husband of Melisande. Riculf, her brother. Theodulf, her son, my pupil. *And your genitals, how were they scarred?* Riculf took scalding ash onto the flat of his sword and tipped it into my groin. *Why did you not resist Satan's snares?* I did resist, with all my strength. I was held against the ground by Odo's men. Melisande, too, was held. Riculf pressed her naked body onto the earth and spat into her hair.

May God rejoice in his works, the earth trembles at his glance, his touch makes mountains smoke. Odo ordered his son: "Kill her. She is a whore. She is unworthy to be your mother."

The boy did not move.

"Kill the priest," said the father. "Cut off his cock."

Theodulf's hands shook on the sword.

Ecce deus noster: Behold our God! Gerbert, your game had gone dangerously astray. Your machinations—if so they were—had careened wildly out of control. Or did some greater deity control these events, plant our love, nurture it, let it come to fruition, and then take cruel pleasure in a carefully contrived dénouement of fire and blood? Was it the same God who with the

141

fingers of his hand orders the heavens, holds the stars in their courses, sends the watering rains, causes the fruit to ripen on the vine?

O Lord, God, how great you are! Clothed in majesty and glory, and robed in a mantle of light. And in his other hand, the sword; his eyes afire with lust; his tongue stained with blood. But wait! He teases us with fear. His nostrils have had their fill of the stench of burning flesh. He adds another turn to the plot. And you, Gerbert, will be his instrument. It is you whom God invokes to save the tormented lovers. You arrive desperate and alone on a lathered steed. *You knew.* How? Someone at the house of Odo had gone to warn you. Melisande's maid? Never mind; you knew, and you alone could save us. You possessed the one thing Odo valued more than vengeance. You had access to the ear of the emperor, and the emperor (as Odo knew) had plans to confiscate the duke of Verzenay's lands in Lorraine. And so you bartered Odo's land for our lives. What was the rate of exchange? How many acres of game-filled forest did you exchange for the foolish priest? How many villages and vineyards for the faithless wife? The bargain was struck. Aileran: mutilated, banished to Ireland. Melisande: hair shorn, body daubed with ashes, into the care of Gerbert, to be sent safely away. Theodulf's sword sheathed unblooded. Riculf's violence quenched. And in fulfillment of your part of the bargain, the land lust of the emperor Otto III, young protégé of the archbishop of Rheims, was distracted from Odo's estates in Lorraine.

❧

September 23, 999
the year of Our Lord
In the name of the Father, and of the Son, and of the Holy Ghost
Being a record of the interrogation of Aileran of Skellig, by the inquisitors of the Holy Office, at the instruction of Sylvester II, successor of Peter and bishop of Rome

—Aileran of Skellig, do you accept the authority of this Holy Office to inquire into the matter of your alleged offenses against the Keys of Peter and the laws of God vouchsafed to us by Christ?

—*I accept that the bishop of Rome has the power of life and death over my body. I accept the authority of Christ's church as it manifests itself in the hearts of men.*

—You have been accused of many serious offenses against the faith, offenses that carry the capital penalty. The most serious of these is the Pelagian heresy, well known to be endemic within the Celtic race. It is asserted: that you deny that man requires redemption from his sins; that you hold Our Lord Jesus Christ came only to *inspire* men to goodness, not to save them; that you deny original sin; that you teach that physical death is a part of nature, present in creation since the beginning of time, and not the penalty of Adam's sin; that spiritual death is not the consequence of Adam's sin but comes to each individual through the power of free choice; that by the existence of free will alone, and without the intervention of divine grace, men can avoid evil and do good. Do you deny that you have taught and affirmed these pernicious doctrines?

—*I do not deny that man can sin, and sin repeatedly. Sin is committed by the free choice of any man. Every human being is responsible for his own sins. I have sinned. Adam sinned. Insofar as Christ was a man, it is not inconceivable that Christ sinned.*

—Beware of blasphemy, Aileran. Your soul is in danger of hellfire. Did mankind fall with Adam?

—*Like all men, I have within myself the power to commit sin or avoid sin. And I believe that in spite of Adam's sin, human nature remained intact, just as it came from the Creator's hand. Nature is basically good, and we are part of nature. I cannot believe that a good God would punish all men for the sin of one man.*

—You have asserted that Christ is capable of sin.

—*Christ is our model for goodness. His life stands as a shining example for all men. In our imitation of Christ we become initiated into the goodness of the creation.*

—Do you deny that Christ is the Son of God and fully coequal with the Father? Do we not live in eternal life by his resurrection?

—*You try to put words in my mouth. I have never preached that Christ is not the Son of God. Nor have I ever publicly asserted that Christ is not divine.*

—Heresy is not only a matter of public teaching. We are here to ascertain what is your private conviction. God sees into the human heart.

—*Do you pretend to be God, that you would pry into my heart? I am unqualified to possess an opinion on these weighty matters. I am a simple priest, not a theologian. I will say only this: I am aware of my capacity for sin, but I will not excuse my sin by invoking the sin of Adam. Adam sinned. Aileran sinned. Both Adam and Aileran are damned or saved by God's justice and mercy. Conversely, when I seek the good, I seek what is manifest in nature: order, beauty, love. In seeking what is good in nature, I seek God. I desire only to become one with Him.*

—You are aware that these opinions have been condemned as heretical by the councils of the Church?

—*As you say: God sees into the human heart.*

—Be aware, Aileran, that we know certain things concerning your life at Vich and at Rheims, things you might think are hidden. It is said: *Fornax horum est ignis concupiscentia, quia causa omnia heresis est vel luxuria, vel cupiditas, vel superbia*— Their furnace is the fire of concupiscence, for the cause of all heresy is either lechery, cupidity, or pride. Can it be, Aileran of Skellig, that Satan has possessed your reason through concupiscence and lechery? When your body was examined by the bailiffs of this Holy Office, your genitals were found to be marked with scales of horn. Your genitals have the appearance of the organs of the Fiend himself.

—*My genitals were scarred by fire.*

—The fire of concupiscence? The furnace of lechery?

—*The fire of violence.*

—Is it true that you have made a pact with Satan, and that to curry his favor you have renounced Christ and trampled the holy cross? Is it true that you worship Satan, that you have done him homage on bended knee, that you have offered him the obscene kiss, and that you have had unnatural sexual intercourse with him? Is it not also true that your genitals were in fact corrupted in the caldron of foul lechery, in the service of the Prince of Darkness?

—*I have never encountered the Prince of Darkness, unless he sometimes assumes the figure of a man. My genitals were scarred by one who was manifestly evil, but it was not Satan.*

Day by day my interrogation continues. Why doesn't Gerbert intervene? Why did he have me brought to Rome if only to abandon me? And what do my interrogators know of my life at Vich and Rheims? Only Gerbert has knowledge of the events that transpired in Vich. Has Gerbert placed this information into their hands? The outcome of these interrogations is inevitable. My inquisitors have assured me that I shall be found guilty of heresy and handed over to the secular authorities for execution. They seek only to affirm from my own mouth what they already know. What little time I have left I must use to complete this memoir. The security of this document, at least, has so far been respected by my jailers.

The bargain struck by Gerbert with Odo specified that I should leave Gaul and forgo forever the company of Melisande. So in the early winter of 988 I returned to Reask, or rather to the site of that former settlement. Thirty years had passed since a savage raid that had turned the Eden of my youth into a charnel house.

Time had softened the wretched place of memory. The stench and smoke were gone, and gone, too, the churned-up earth of blood, mud, and dung. The walls of the rath and the stones of the clochans were tumbled and in disarray. The wooden buildings and thatch roofs of the clochans, burned in the raid, had vanished into the earth, together with the blood and bones of my fellows. Bramble covered all. Rabbits burrowed into tangled banks.

The day of my return to Reask was soft and still. A gray quiescence infiltrated stone and vegetation, wet and palpable; dewdrops glistened on bramble thorns. I stood for a moment at the kiln where No-Ear dried the malt—its corbeled dome collapsed, its fire-baked belly open to the sky—and called up from the darkling bog of memory the image of Maire: Maire of the white skin, the curve of her breast bared from her shift, her mouth open in a scream I cannot hear, her eyes agape with terror as her body is torn asunder. And then, inevitably, the image of Maire became Melisande, driven from the blazing cottage, her face pushed into seared earth, her skin glowing with the heat of the inferno. I had helped her from the cottage. Firebrands fell upon our naked skin as we stumbled toward the door. Behind us, the bed ignited—sheet, straw, a globe of flame. The blinding sunlight, shimmering, crimson. Brutal hands tore us from one another, forced us onto the ground. The futile struggle. The flash of swords. Across an unbridgeable gulf of pain I see her eyes made blind with fear, her face, breasts, and belly black with ash, her shorn hair on the scorched earth at her bare feet.

Who is this monstrous magician, this Janus-faced conjurer who devises dreams of the utmost sweetness and then with a snap of his fingers turns them into nightmares? The followers of Mani teach that whatever is carnal is evil, the creation of a Prince of Darkness who is coeternal with the Divine Messenger of Light. The flesh is malefic, say the Manichees, and irredeemable, and since flesh is sinful, God and flesh are never one. Can the Manichees be right? Was it he, then—this Prince of Darkness—

who split Maire's body with his ghastly phallus, who spat into Melisande's hair and touched her naked flesh with the point of his sword? Was it the Prince of Darkness who worked his depraved sorcery through my own genitals in Vich, violating the innocent flesh of the child Joveta in imitation of Gerbert? And was it he who lay with Melisande in the cottage by the river, who touched her gently in quavering summer light, who whispered the praises of Solomon's Bridegroom into her ear, who swore fidelity, and then—turning his cruel mask to reveal his precedent purpose and awful intent—unleashed treachery, violence, and betrayal, and having finished his deceit, left the willing instrument of his malfeasance hideously scarred and forever unworthy of the Bride?

No. The Manichee dichotomy is too simple. It is not possible to say: *This is love, this is lust; this is the longing of the soul, this the prompting of the flesh.* Even our love for God is tainted with lust. The voluptuary is sometimes moved by beauty, the rapist by pity. Good and evil are so inextricably entangled in the fabric of the world that it is impossible to isolate the one from the other. Matter is manifestly beautiful, and the spirit demonstrably capable of evil. The Messenger of Light and the Prince of Darkness are one, a single divine being coterminous with creation, who rages against himself.

As I stood near the bramble-bound kiln at Reask, surrounded by the beauty of nature but stifled by the atmosphere of sin, I remembered a night on the hill when Brother No-Ear told me the story of Dinah: *Dinah was the daughter of Jacob. She crossed the river from the camp of her father and entered the town of the Hivites. She went to visit the women of the town, but soon her beauty attracted Shechem, the son of Hamor, who was ruler of that region. Shechem carried Dinah to his house and raped her, and so dishonored her. But his love for the young girl was such that he comforted her. Shechem said to his father: "Get me this girl; I wish to marry her." So Hamor went to the camp of Jacob*

147

and asked for Dinah. He proposed an alliance between the two tribes, to be sealed by the interchange of marriageable daughters and by a large bridal price to be paid by Shechem for Dinah. Meanwhile, Simeon and Levi, the brothers of Dinah, who had been away in the countryside with their cattle, returned. The brothers were outraged that their sister had been dishonored. They said to Hamor: "You have given our sister to an uncircumcised man. You have disgraced us." And to Shechem they said: "We can only agree to the marriage on one condition: that your people be made like ours by the circumcision of all your males. Then we will give you our daughters, taking yours for ourselves, and we will stay with you to make one nation." Shechem did not hesitate, for he loved Dinah deeply. With his father he talked the men of the town into letting themselves be circumcised. Then, on the third day, when the men of the Hivite tribe were tormented by pain, Simeon and Levi, the brothers of Dinah, took their swords and went into the town and killed all the males. They slew Hamor and Shechem, took Dinah, and came away. And they took with them the women and the children, the animals, and all the riches of the town. Jacob was unhappy, for he knew that by this treachery he had placed his people at risk with all other inhabitants of that region. But the brothers, Simeon and Levi, retorted, "Is our sister to be treated like a whore?"

In the mouth of No-Ear the story of Dinah was a tale of violation and just revenge. But is it so simple? *Where* in the story of Dinah does good lie? Where evil? Might not a scribe of the Hivites have recorded a different version of the story than the author of Genesis? *Dinah crosses the river into the town, alone and without permission, ostensibly to visit the women but in reality to satisfy her curiosity and to show off her beauty before the men. She laughs, she teases. Soon she is noticed by the son of Hamor, and to him she gives special attention. Smitten by her youthful beauty, Shechem invites Dinah into his house. She goes, half willing to be seduced, but she is surprised by the vigor and force of Shechem's pursuit. She yields. But now she is fearful of the response of her father and brothers. Shechem is intoxicated by Dinah's innocence and sensuality. He cannot now live without her. She gives him to understand that her willing favors will be his only in marriage. And so the son of Hamor acts honorably; he offers an alliance with the family of Jacob and a generous settlement for Dinah. But Simeon and Levi see the opportunity for something better, something violent and treacherous.*

Now, as I stood near the kiln at Reask, as evocative of memories as once it had been redolent with the odors of malt, it became clear to me that the story of Dinah had two poles: the attempt of the fathers, Hamor and Jacob, to find a just resolution, and the slaughter of the mutilated men by Simeon and Levi. Between these two extremes of good and evil the affair of Dinah and Shechem was played out. The threads of their love were like the strings of a cat's cradle that bind together the two hands of God—good and evil, light and darkness, beauty and violence.

If every human act has the capacity for both good and evil, then to live rightly one must struggle in every action with weighing and measuring, with searching and circumscribing, and without knowing with certainty if one's actions ultimately add to the total measure of good or of evil in the world. Was my inability to emerge from the kiln to help Maire an act of cowardice or an act of prudence? Was No-Ear's confrontation with the soldier foolish or brave? Did Melisande, trapped in a hateful marriage that was not of her own making, have the right to pursue love at any price, or was the price too high? Did Aileran selflessly love Melisande, or did Aileran selfishly expose her to evil? Even now, as I write this narrative, I cannot say that I know the answers to these questions. A person acts, and the moral consequences of the action ripple outward like a wave on a pond. Every good action has a potential for evil, and the bravest and most passionate actions have the potential for the greatest harm. But there is another way: One can withdraw from the world, and so limit the perimeter of one's contact with others that any action soon dissipates its moral effect. If to be good means to do no wrong to others, then the most certain way to goodness is to be alone. Or so it seemed to me then as I turned my back to the bramble-choked ruin of Reask and climbed the ridge between the hill of Croaghmarhin and Brendan's mountain. And there I saw a pyramid of black rock standing afar off in the western sea.

My passage to the Skellig was by wicker boat—a frame of willow, bound together with leather thongs, covered with cowhide, and sealed with the grease of goats—oared by monks of Ballinskelligs. To be in that craft upon a sea turned suddenly rough was to be in the belly of a beast. The day had been fine as we set out from Darrery, but as we progressed across the ten miles of open water that separate the island from the mainland the wind turned westerly and freshened. By the time we approached the island the sea was running high, and waves smashed against the black rocks of the landing place like the flats of Viking swords. The island was more daunting than I had imagined. It rose from the sea like a pillar, like a smooth spike driven into the floor of the ocean, a violent afterthought of creation. Our craft brought provisions for the seven monks who lived in the huts above, but there was no way in this rough sea of bringing the goods ashore. I slung the sack containing my few personal possessions about my neck and leapt onto a wave-swept rock. The boat backed off and I was alone.

The way up to the monastery was by hand- and footholds cut into the sheer cliff. As I climbed I vowed that having ascended these steps I would not come down. The way to heaven, I was convinced, was through the needle's eye. The narrower the eye of the needle, the more likely that I would find God on the other side. Above, on the Skellig, I would find what was needed for life:

150

shelter, a modicum of food, a woolen garment. What more? In my bag I carried a copy of Ovid's *Metamorphoses* and my small harp. As I climbed I began to feel their burden, weighing me down, drawing me back to Rheims, to Aurillac, and to Vich. When I had gained the security of a ledge and the free use of my hands, I removed the bag from my shoulder and flung it into the sea.

My brothers on the Skellig had been hoping for butter, cheese, and milled grain. What they got instead was another member for a community whose resources were already sorely pressed. Nevertheless, they welcomed me warmly; indeed, this sudden turn in their fortunes, like every other "misfortune" that afflicted them, was embraced as a further God-sent test of the sincerity of their faith. What little food the island provided was willingly shared. Each brother offered straw from his pallet to make up my own. Pallets were moved closer together to allow room for one more monk in the tiny dormitory huts.

These men—my brothers—lived together with a marked lack of strife, and this equanimity flowed from the abbot, Ciarán. At forty-seven, I was the oldest of the brothers, except for Ciarán, who surpassed my age by twice a dozen years. I was accorded no precedence because of my years; indeed, I was considered to be a novice anchorite and treated with something akin to benign condescension. In one way, however, I was different from all of my brothers, including Ciarán: I had taken orders. It was for this, my capacity to perform priestly duties, that I had won permission from the ecclesiastical authorities at Ardfert to transport myself to the island. (Those authorities did not, of course, know of my transgressions at Rheims or of my removal from the Rule of Saint Gerald's. The regularization of my return to Ireland had been attended to with care by Gerbert. The appropriate documents had been forwarded. The scars on my hands excited great curiosity, but these I explained with an appropriate pre-varication. The scars on my genitals were known to no one but myself.) No priest had lived on the Skellig for a generation, and no Eucharist had been consecrated there for as many years. Monks of the island did occasionally go to the mainland at Easter for the purpose of attending Mass, but to leave the Skellig in the season of Christmastide was generally impossible. My arrival meant that Christmas, Easter, and other important feasts of the Church would be marked by Mass celebrated in our little chapel, my own scruples notwithstanding.

My scruples I kept to myself. If the violation of my vows and my own apostasy (now in full bloom) had abrogated my right to consecrate the Eucharist, and if therefore the "miracle" of transubstantiation was rendered ineffective, then my brothers were no worse off than before, and indeed consoled by the illusion that the Body and Blood of Christ were present among them. On the other hand, if my priestly powers had not decayed along with the fervor of my faith, then the miracle of transubstantiation occurred for my brothers in spite of my private failings and, indeed, with sublime indifference to my own transgressions and doubts.

On the Skellig my doubts found a perfect venue for disguise. Ciarán did not allow theological or philosophical discussion to trouble his monks. Such debates (he believed) incur a risk of agitation that is not compatible with "contemplative repose." They distract the spirit from the undivided search for God. In our abbot's view, questions, objections, and argumentations rapidly lead into an inextricable forest of disputation, a *nemus aristotelicum*. In place of these intellectual quibblings a single quest must be substituted: to seek God, and not to discuss Him. Ciarán defined holy simplicity as an unchanging will in pursuit of a changeless good. He quoted the Psalmist: "My heart has no lofty ambitions, my eyes do not look too high. I am not concerned with great affairs or marvels beyond my scope. Enough for me to keep my soul tranquil and quiet like a child in its mother's arms." Love itself is knowledge, said Ciarán; the more one loves, the more one knows.

Nor did Ciarán pry into my past affairs, nor would he let the younger brothers ask questions concerning the places I had been or seen. Our world—our entire cosmos—was this ledge of rock that could be crossed with a dozen strides. The four rivers of Paradise in the east and the Isles of the Blessed in the west were beyond our ken; we were surrounded by a desert of sea, and our eyes were necessarily directed upward to heaven. And so it was that I had found a refuge in which to hide my soul and chasten it. In place of the verses of Ovid (which I had cast into the sea) I took as my text the island itself; in place of my harp, the songs of the wind and the birds. And what at first seemed to be a place of forbidding austerity I soon came to know as rich with a wild and delicate beauty. Whenever my duties of work and prayer allowed time for study, I watched and listened. I entered, insofar as I was able, into the lives of the birds that nested in astonishing numbers upon the island. I noticed, for example, a most peculiar correspondence between the plants and birds of the island: sea spurry near the burrows of the puffins, mayweed and sorrel with the nests of gulls, orache and scurvy grass with fulmars. I took note of the prevailing winds and changes in the weather. I studied the weeds that grew upon the rocks, and the fishes that swam in the sea. There seemed enough of nature's fullness attendant upon our tiny island to reward the examination for a lifetime. For the rest, I gave myself to silence, obedience, and prayer. Each of the brothers had particular responsibilities—gathering the eggs of birds, building up the terraces with seaweed and soil, tending the garden, milking the goats, cutting steps into the cliffs, shoring up the terraces with stone—and these Ciarán wisely exchanged among us. Our community possessed the few books necessary for the execution of the Holy Office, but unlike our brothers at Innisfallen or Ardfert, we compiled no manuscripts and illuminated no texts; the damp climate of our little island did not allow for proper work with inks and vellums. But this, too, suited Ciarán's plan; in his view, books distracted the mind from its proper object, which could more readily be found within the human heart than on the written page.

As I look back upon my early years on the Skellig, what seems to me most worthy of note was the way in which eight men (seven upon the death of Brother Ultán) lived together in such close proximity with so little discord or contention. This I must now insist was due to the moderating influence of our abbot. The method by which Ciarán pacified our brotherhood was not by forbidding strife but by discouraging familiarity. For himself, he showed no excessive affection or favoritism for any member of our community. When he saw the spark of closeness or friendship flicker between any two of us, he acted quickly to extinguish it. For such a course of action to be successful (and not provoke bitterness), it was necessary that Ciarán recognize the beginnings of love even before we (who would have been love's victims) were aware of it ourselves. Where none had love, none wanted it; where none had love, there was no jealousy. What brotherly love there was between us (for it is impossible that love not exist) Ciarán strove to ensure flowed equably among all, as water rises to the same level in connected vessels of different capacities or shapes. If one of us began to shine in the esteem of the others, Ciarán acted to soften the offending luster; if one of us began to darken, he added gloss. And so he kept our spirits polished as uniformly bright as holy vessels, which indeed we were—practical but not ostentatious, worthy of receiving the Body and Blood of Christ but not so gaudy as to attract attention to ourselves.

If I had learned earlier the lesson of Ciarán's success, things might have gone better when later on I became personally responsible for the well-being of the Skellig community. As it was, my abbacy would be marked by discord from the beginning—jealousy, selfishness, laxity, dishonesty, scandal—ending in full-scale rebellion and the unhappy sequence of events that would bring me at last to a prison cell in Rome. Only once in Ciarán's time did the concord of our community falter, and the cause of that episode was inevitably love, and regrettably involved myself in a most unworthy way.

Between the youngest of our brothers, Ultán, and myself there began to grow a kindly affection. For my part, I felt a fatherly solicitude for a gentle young man (he was no more than twenty) who had perhaps embraced a more demanding discipline than his age and disposition allowed. My attentions took the form of occasional encouragement, or the sharing of certain of my enthusiasms—birds, plants, stars and constellations. I did not notice—or chose not to notice—that Ultán's affection for me had begun to stir in a deeper, more physical way. I recognize in retrospect the culminating moment of the unintended seduction: I had taken Ultán's hand in my own to demonstrate the sign of the cross in the way of Aurillac. *In nomine Patris,* I said, and with the tips of his fingers I made a tiny cross on his forehead . . . *et Filii,* to his lips . . . *et Spiritu Sancti,* to his breast. I had forgotten the desideratum of touch, how cruel and perfect a proffered touch can be in a place where touch is forbidden. Ultán was affected. Within his heart began a struggle that eventually led him to confess to Ciarán.

The young monk's penance was severe; he was sent down along the cliffs near the southern landing to cut into the living rock a stairway that led from nowhere to nowhere, fourteen steps with no obvious point of departure and no destination. Upon this task Ultán worked for many weeks, isolated from the community, until the unhappy day when he somehow slipped from his perch and fell into the sea. His death was a severe test of the bonds that held our little group together. All of the brothers felt remorse. They blamed Ciarán for the severity of the penance. I was blamed, and certainly none could have been more responsible than I, who had acted, or so it seemed, entirely out of charity and love. But now in my own mind doubts began to grow. Was my affection for my companion pure, or was it tinged with carnality? Did it unconsciously invite a sensual return? Did my solicitude for Ultán hide itself from Ciarán, so that the response

155

evoked in the heart of the young monk went unnoticed and uncorrected? With the affair of Ultán I began to be uncertain of my capacity to love innocently even within the confines of a narrowly constricted society. Whether my lapse was a failing of love itself, or of my own heart, I did not know. All I knew—then as forcibly as now—is that love and hurt are inextricably bound up together. If love is the salmon that glides through the silvery pool, love is also the spike and the net. If love is the sparrow on the wing, love is also the falcon that brings it down. Ovid, I remembered, had written a book on the remedies for love, and that book had been used by Gerbert at Vich and Ripoll to inflame the passions of his hesitant companion. Love has no remedy. The only *remedia amoris,* I concluded, was to isolate myself in such a way that the sole object upon which love might fix itself was God as manifest in his untrammeled creation.

To this end I sought from Ciarán permission to build myself a hermitage apart, as penance for my part in Ultán's tragedy and for the practice of a harsher eremetical discipline. And so it was that I created for myself a tiny cell on the bleak and shrill north face of the Skellig rock, three hundred feet above the pounding sea, in a place impossible to obtain without considerable danger. Above this cell I constructed a catchment basin for water. My food was dropped to me from above at appropriate intervals by my brethren, no more than was necessary for the sustenance of life. In that forbidding place I lived for three years, out of sight and sound of any human companion.

What transpires in the midst of such complete solitude? How does one still the interior voice? The answer, Gerbert, is that one does not. The voice speaks continuously, an unceasing mono-logue that snips at the roots of madness, prunes back the branches, and stunts the dark demonic flower. The voice strives for clarity. It was mostly to you, Gerbert, that I spoke. It was to you that I sought to explain myself by describing the world. *There: a pool of water no larger than a hand, held in a triangular chink of rock. The water is clear. In the water floats a single leaf of sea thrift, slender and green.* It was as if I wished for you to see the world through my eyes. *A single storm petrel tests the evening air. It slips across the swell with no more substance than a passing thought. Then another. And another. Now the sea scuds with birds. They scull the billows with their tiny feet.* It was as if I saw in these things the face of God and wished to teach you to see what I saw.

I did not know it then, but even as my silent voice was engaged in this enraptured monologue, you were being drawn inexorably toward Rome. First, to the archbishopric of Ravenna, the second most important ecclesiastical office in Italy. Then, as the charmed protégé of the emperor, to Rome. And what was it that passed through *your* mind as they consecrated you the successor of Peter and crowned you with the triple tiara? Did you think of Aileran? Did *your* interior voice describe for *my* benefit the pomp and grandeur of the occasion? For my benefit did it speak the name of each notable who knelt to kiss your ring? And if it was not to me that you directed your silent conversation, then to whom?

To you, Gerbert, I felt then (as now) a necessity to justify myself. It was only against the antithesis of *your* life that my own life had meaning. As Gerbert rose, Aileran fell. Which of us moved toward God? Was God in the basilica of Saint Peter, or in the blade of sea thrift that rests in the triangular pool? Was God garbed in the vestments of cardinals, or in the feathers of the petrel? *Look, there: far away on the western horizon, the sun in its setting has turned for an instant green, coloring the sea topaz and emerald. The cormorant turns its head this way and that—its jeweled eye burns, as a girl turns her ringed hand and lets a fiery garnet shine.* I spoke, Gerbert, unceasingly to you.

And Melisande. Where was she? It was not to her that I spoke, although she was never far from my consciousness. My awareness of Melisande was like the root of the Skellig—solid, dark, and hidden in the flesh of the sea, unmoved by wind or wave, enduring, unreachable. My love for her was intact. To her I had nothing to explain. I imagined her voice, gentle, intelligent, and wise. I heard her songs, the songs she sang by the river at Verzenay to my accompaniment on the kesh. I heard her whisper the vocabulary of endearment in the silence of sexual love. During the time we were together, Melisande tolerated no inquiry, no recriminations, no dialogue of conscience. If I opened my mouth to speak, her finger stopped my lips. The inner voice was stilled. She instructed me in a grammar of eyes, lips, and hands—a grammar of declaration and repose. It was a grammar I could not retain in my self-imposed isolation on the Skellig.

September 29, 999
the year of Our Lord.
In the name of the Father, and of the Son, and of the Holy Ghost
Being a record of the interrogation of Aileran of Skellig, by the inquisitors of the Holy Office, at the instruction of Sylvester II, successor of Peter and bishop of Rome

 —Aileran of Skellig, do you accept the authority of this Holy Office to inquire into the matter of your alleged offenses against the Keys of Peter and the laws of God vouchsafed to us by Christ?

 —*Get on with it.*

 —Your parents. Who were your parents?

 —*My father was a sailor from Spain who was cast ashore on the coast of Ireland. My mother was the child of an Irish lord.*

 —Were they bound by the sacrament of holy matrimony at the time of your conception?

 —*They were not married.*

 —Then you are illegitimate?

 —*My parents were not married.*

 —Are you aware that it is forbidden by church law that the

offspring of an illegitimate union should be allowed Holy Orders?

—*I am. But I was not aware of such a prohibition at the time of my ordination.*

—You were not questioned on this matter by your superior?

—*The matter never came up. I was asked to take orders by my abbot, Colman of Saint Gerald's. I have sought faithfully to perform my responsibilities as a priest.*

—Was Colman aware of your illegitimacy at the time of your ordination?

—*He did not ask. Nor do I think that it occurred to him to ask. Colman was a man who lived according to the spirit of Christ's law, not the letter. My abbot was more expressly concerned with the goodness in a man's heart than with the circumstances of his birth.*

—Apparently, then, your ordained service to the Church began with a breech of God's law. Did you subsequently break any other laws regarding your priestly vows?

—*I sought to live faithfully as a priest.*

—And what of the time when you were appointed to the school of Rheims?

—*I taught to the best of my ability.*

—And your relationship with Melisande, the wife of Odo? You should be aware that things will go better for you if you volunteer the circumstances of your transgressions.

—*I knew Melisande. I was once her tutor at Argentat.*

—And were you her paramour at Rheims, at a time when you were bound by the vow of chastity? Were you apprehended *in flagrante delicto* by Odo?

—*How do you know these things?*

—It is not your place to ask questions, but to answer them.

—*Did Gerbert tell you this? Where is Gerbert?*

—The Holy Father does not hold conversation with heretics.

—*Why does he place into your hands the information which*

you require to torment me? I had thought he was my friend and benefactor.

—We remind you again that it is not your place to ask questions. Did you have carnal knowledge of Melisande, wife of Odo?

—I loved Melisande.

—Did you have carnal intercourse? We are well aware of your lascivious proclivities, even from the time when you were resident at Santa Maria de Ripoll and consorted there with whores.

—So! Gerbert is your informant. Why does he turn against me?

—We ask once more. Did you have carnal knowledge of a married woman, in violation of your priestly vow and God's commandment?

—What occurred between myself and Melisande were acts of love.

—Does not the law passed to Moses on Mount Sinai forbid adultery?

—Jesus Christ forgave the woman found in adultery.

—Do you put human love above the law of God?

—I do not claim to know what God desires.

—Do you believe in God, the Father almighty, creator of heaven and earth?

—I believe that God is beyond the grasp of human reason.

—Do you deny that God exists?

—Whether God exists or not depends upon what you mean by existence. If this stool on which I sit exists, then God does not. If, on the other hand, you wish me to say that God exists, then I must conclude that the stool does not exist. Surely God and the stool partake of different kinds of being.

—We are not here to play with words. And might I remind you that you are ill trained as a theologian. A simple answer will suffice. Do you believe that God exists?

—I believe that nature exists, for nature is keenly present to my

160

senses. If nature exists, then God does not. And yet I would not therefore wish to deny God. God is Himself unknowable and only makes Himself known insofar as He reveals Himself in nature. God is created in every creature. How this happens I do not know. God is unreachable, and yet He offers Himself to us. He is unseeable, but shows Himself. Unthinkable, He enters our minds. Hidden, He reveals Himself. He is nature and above nature. He is no thing who becomes things. He is love, and we know Him only when we know love.

—What you say of God—that He is nature, that He can be identified with human love—are heretical opinions vigorously condemned by the Church. To affirm such views puts your life and the salvation of your soul in jeopardy. You would be wise to recant these opinions.

—*I cannot recant what I do not know. And what I know, I cannot recant. I do not know God, so I cannot deny Him. What I do know, I cannot say is not God.* Omnis creatura simul eterna et facta est—*He is the maker of all and is made in all. By requiring a confession of faith, you ask me to limit what cannot be limited. You ask me to make simple what is complex and to make complex what is simple. I can only say this: There have been certain moments in my life when I felt the presence of God intensely, and at those very same moments I have also felt the precariousness of my faith. At other times, when I have felt abandoned by God, I have felt most deeply the need to affirm Him. It is as if God makes His presence most keenly felt through His absence. I am aware of the paradoxical nature of these statements. As you say, I am not trained as a theologian. Nor am I prepared to debate the definition of God with such eminences as yourselves. I am willing to place my fate in the hands of Gerbert. Inform him of my wish. He knows me as well as I am known by any man. He will confirm the orthodoxy of my faith. He will confirm the absurdity of the charges against me.*

Only Gerbert has knowledge of the events that occurred at Vich. Only Gerbert could have exposed my relationship with Melisande. Why has he betrayed me? Why did he effect my escape from Bishop Oenu, only to place me in the hands of the more highly practiced inquisitors of Rome? Unless I perjure myself, I will be condemned as a heretic, and the ultimate penalty will be exacted. Do I fear death? I have slept in the arms of my own mortality. I am not afraid of death, but I am not yet ready to die. The story is not over, the story of Aileran, Gerbert, and Melisande. Only when I have understood all that has gone before, only when the tangled threads of the narrative have been unraveled one from the other, will I willingly let go of life.

The conditions of my confinement slowly deteriorate. Twice each day I am given bread and cheese. The bread is maggoty and the cheese rancid. Patiently I pick the worms from the bread and drop them onto the floor of my room. Soon this place will swarm with the disposed residents of my food. My interrogator took note of this and said, "You will have worms enough in Hades; they will feed upon your flesh." Twice each day I am interrogated. My Roman examiners are less earnest than the young man who questioned me for Oenu, more practiced, and motivated not so much by the desire to save my soul as by the requirement to take my life in conformity with the strictures of the law. They seek not truth but guilt.

I must now tell how it was that Aileran became the "Saint of Skellig" and then, in the eyes of his enemies, the agent of the Prince of Darkness. It seems there was a necessity to all that happened, an ordained conclusion to the story that human will could have done nothing to forestall. But I know the appearance of necessity is only an illusion, a failure of the imagination to understand the plenitude of possibility that exists in nature. At every instant a life turns upon the nexus of chance. If Theodulf had not seen into his mother's eyes at the time of Odo's sickness, my affair with Melisande might not have been betrayed. If Ultán had not fallen into the sea, I would not have given three years of my life to seclusion and solitude. And if on the day of the Viking intrusion—which I now recount—the wind had been from the north rather than the south, or if the wind had been foul rather than fair, then I might still be clinging to that ledge of rock on the bare north face of the Skellig.

Three years! Three years alone in a hermit's cell. Three years that even now seem to have passed as an uninterrupted interval of innocence. Some might have thought so spare an existence to be the foreshadowing of hell. Once, when I was a child, Brother No-Ear told me how, after sailing upon the Western Ocean for seven days and seven nights, Saint Brendan and his companions saw a man sitting upon a rock in the sea, with a veil like a sack hanging from two iron forks, so that one might have thought that what they saw was a ship. Brendan commanded the monks to steer toward the strange apparition, and they found a misshapen, unshorn man, clinging to a rock, buffeted by waves, and lashed by the wind-whipped cloth. The man's flesh hung from his body in scorched tatters. It was Judas, the betrayer of Christ, and his present condition (he informed Brendan) must not be counted as torment, for the day was Sunday, and on Sunday he is allowed respite from his tortures. At other times he burns like molten lead in an iron pot, in the midst of the rock itself, his flesh gnawed by toads, salamanders, and serpents, and of food or drink there is none. For three years, like Judas, I was alone upon a rock in the sea; for three years I was lashed by wind and rain; for three years I had only such food and drink as was necessary to sustain life. Rainwater was my wine. The minuscule flesh of a whelk was my feast. If Brendan's company had found me, they might have thought me, like Judas, afflicted by the torments of hell. But they would have been wrong. I was neither happy nor unhappy in my self-imposed exile; neither exuberant nor depressed. I found instead a certain equanimity of spirit, a suspension of bodily needs. I spoke unceasingly, in a silent voice—description, petition, I knew not what it was. The hours, days, and months flowed by, sleeping and waking were all the same, bright days and storm were indifferently accepted. More than all else I felt release, from the responsibility of conscience and the terrible paradox of love.

Unknown to me, the legend of the "Saint of Skellig" had begun to take hold in the regions round about. The circumstances of my isolation on the island were a source of wonder to all who heard. It was said that my exile was an expression of exceptional holiness, but this was not true. There was no courage in my exile; rather what I sought was an existence where courage was not required. In my solitude I addressed no words to God; my silent conversation was only with Gerbert. But the illusion of my sanctity acquired a life of its own, and indeed was carefully nurtured by the ecclesiastical authorities at Ballinskelligs on the mainland shore, for it enhanced the stature of their community. And the myth was dangerously enlarged by the episode of the Viking raid and the baptism of Olaf Trygvvesön.

The Vikings came in two ships from the south, and so their approach was unobserved by me from my hermitage on the island's north face. For three days Ciarán and his five companions resisted the incursion by throwing down stones onto the heads of the invaders. A dozen Northmen were knocked from the face of the cliff as they sought to gain access to the monastic terraces. But their losses only made their determination more fierce. On the fourth day, as the defenders slept exhausted, the Northmen gained the terraces and the butchery began. One by one the brothers were taken and tortured in grotesque ways, that they might reveal the hiding place of the "monastic treasures"— our pitifully poor collection of waterlogged books and holy vessels. Brother Rolle was blinded with a dagger and thrown from the cliff. Brother Scoithín had each of the digits cut from his hands, one by one, until with the single remaining finger of his left hand he was asked to point out the hiding place of the "treasure"; he refused and was slain. Brother Felix was castrated, before he, too, was tossed into the sea. All of this transpired without my knowledge, out of my sight and hearing. Not until Brother Richard somehow managed to slip away from his captors and come to my cell was I made aware of the tragedy that had embraced our settlement.

It was in the sixth hour of the day. I lay prostrate upon the narrow porch of my tiny cell, reciting from memory the seventy-first psalm—*In you, Lord, I take shelter; you are my rock and my fortress*—when from within my aloneness I became aware of a human presence. I opened my eyes and saw the stump of a handless arm, and for a moment considered that I had dreamed of No-Ear, for often I had seen this same vision in troubled sleep. But this was no dream. It was Richard, the youngest of the monks of our little community, and his was the first human face I had seen for three years. Ghastly face! His eyes were pools of fear, his lips obscenely swollen, and he wore a tonsure of blood. And the arm! The bone gaped from the putrid wound like a stake from which the vine of flesh had been cruelly torn. I begged his mercy and forgiveness for an atrocity whose source and dimensions I could only dimly guess.

No speech passed Richard's lips, nor could words have formed upon his ravaged tongue. His eyes alone told the story of his affliction. I bathed those frightened eyes with the cloth of my sleeve, taking water from cold pools of rain. He died in my arms. Gently I composed his body, drawing shut the lids of his eyes and covering his wound with his garment. Then I climbed the narrow crevasse that led to the shoulder of the island above and to the monastic terraces. The muscles of my arms and legs, made feeble by long disuse, gave me scant purchase on the rain-wet rock, and often I thought that I must fall into the sea. When at last I had gained the height that separates the north and south faces of the island, a most horrible scene was revealed below. Two longboats stood moored at the southern landing, sails furled upon the masts. The eyes of fierce dragons, carved onto the prows of the vessels, gazed upward, to the monastery. And there, on the terraces, I saw the glitter of bronze and steel in the arms and ornaments of the invaders. Lashed with ropes to two stone crosses—those meticulously carved crosses, the pride of our foundation—were Ciarán, abbot of Skellig, and Brother Lawrence, the sole surviving members of our community.

Wail, you shepherds, and cover yourselves in ashes, for the day of your slaughter and dispersion is come, you shall fall like fattened rams. Gerbert, as I think upon the events of that day and consider the harsh inhumanity of man against man (as if we were not all of the same race of Adam, as if in our breasts there did not beat the same hearts of flesh and blood), I cannot help but feel that your dream of uniting the nations of the earth into the one Body of Christ is a foolish fantasy. Like wolves out of the north they came ravaging. The steel of their swords was like an icy wind. They cut us down like wheat, they slaughtered us like lambs. No! Even heathens must show to the slaughtered lamb more compassion than the Northmen gave to the monks of Skellig. For Lawrence they had prepared the torment of his namesake, a priest of the early Church who was roasted upon a gridiron by an emperor of Rome; as I arrived on the monastic terraces, ashes still smoldered under the bare soles of his feet where a fire had recently raged; his skin was scorched black and his screams were like the shrieks of gulls. Ciarán's body was yet unmarked by steel or flame, but he was bound to the stone cross in the posture of Christ and stripped naked. The body of the old man was pale and translucent, like a carving of ivory, and the ribs of his chest stood out like the strings of a kesh.

I pretend no bravery. I am not a courageous man. I walked among the Vikings in a kind of sleep, the sleep of the solitary hermit from which I had not yet fully woken. I walked among the Vikings on the monastic terraces, fourscore warriors armed with broadswords and axes, and they sat or stood stock-still and stared, as if I were an apparition. I walked to Ciarán, lashed upon the cross of stone, and begged his forgiveness. *Father, I was not here. Selfishly I secluded myself.* His eyes brimmed with tears. With serenity and sadness he spoke my name.

The threads of history must be knotted in the selvages or the fabric falls apart. My life was spared that day by a knot of which I had no knowledge, a knot that bound together threads that reached back in time to my infancy and across the space of the sea to faraway lands. I turned away from Ciarán, who was, in any case, not long for this world. I raised my hand to bless the heathens; it was a reflexive gesture; I do not know why I did it. A Viking raider—the spell broken—lifted his blade to strike me down. Death seemed inevitable, expected, even desired; I turned my head to accept the blow upon my neck. But the blow never fell. The blade was blocked by the raised ax of Olaf Trygvvesön, leader of the Vikings.

He said, in the language of the Celts: "The old priest spoke your name—'Aileran.'"

Olaf's face was fierce and clean-shaven; his black eyes glowed with the coruscating light of the aurora; a torc of gold constrained the blue sinews of his neck.

"Tell me," he asked, "who is your mother?"

There was no need to answer; I knew at once the meaning of the question, and he of the unspoken reply. Olaf Trygvvesön swept his helmet from his head, a helmet of glistening iron and gold.

He said: "She was my father's concubine . . . and my nurse; she was to me as a mother."

Was the appearance of the man who was my mother's nursling an intervention by the Divine Author of the book of life? Or merely coincidence? Perhaps neither. Vikings from the same ports of Norway had swept our coast for generations, sons following the stories of their fathers in search of treasure. Many Irish women were carried to pagan lands, and many bastards were begotten on our shores, so that soon the blood and history of our races were hopelessly mingled. Olaf Trygvvesön followed the wake of his father's atrocities; in his veins flowed the blood of the man who destroyed Reask in the time of Fergus Mor and who abducted for his pleasure the most desirable human spoil of that unfortunate community. Olaf Trygvvesön's father was a chieftain of his people; the son would rise higher still.

Gerbert, can you know that the present Christian king of Norway, with whom you are engaged in delicate negotiations regarding the consolidation of Christendom and the adoption of the Latin script, was six years ago the godless butcher of the Skellig? No, not godless; for he and his retinue worshiped a grim plethora of gods—gods of iron and stone, wind and sea, dragon gods, gods with insatiable appetites for blood, gods appeased by the ravishment of beauty, a pantheon of lust and shame presided over by Wodan, the bringer of death and battle, whom each man served and sought to satisfy by filling the chalice of his wrath to overflowing with the entrails of his enemies. In the days and weeks that followed the savage murder of my brothers, while the Vikings were still resident on our island, I had ample opportunity to witness the excesses of their pagan faith. One man showed me a leather pouch that he carried against his chest, containing more than fourscore rings of bronze and gold that he had taken from the hands of women he had violated and slain; these he intended to carry back to his homeland as an offering for the god of a well or spring. Another man had threaded the testicles of his male victims onto a kind of belt. Others painted their bodies with the blood of the vanquished; not even Father Ciarán, that most innocent of men, was spared this indignity, for upon his death he was taken down from the cross and disemboweled, his blood being collected in a bronze bowl for that obscene decorative purpose. Lawrence, my brother in Christ, was allowed to live, but only upon the intercession of Olaf, and only after that worthy monk had suffered terrible wounds.

Olaf Trygvvesön told me of my mother, of whom I have no memory. He told me of her beauty and spirit, and how upon being returned from Ireland to the coast of Norway she became his nurse and surrogate mother; during his youth, he said, they were inseparable. She told him of Ireland, and of Reask, and of how she had given birth there to a dark-skinned son named Aileran, a few years older than himself. Of all the people in her new community only Olaf knew her secret—that she retained her Christian faith while pretending to adopt the religion of the north. She still lived, said Olaf Trygvvesön. My mother was nearly seventy years of age and blind. Except for her prayers, she had forgotten the Irish tongue.

Olaf accepted me as a brother. He was impressed by the rigor of my solitude and the courage of the Skellig monks in facing the Vikings unafraid, and asked to hear more of our faith. He was an intelligent man, with an acuity of mind that seemed strangely inconsistent with the barbarism of his actions. His own companions he treated with cruelty and contempt; with them his language was fierce and strange, but with me he was gentle and quick to understand the subtleties of theological debate. For twenty days he remained upon the island, while his men grew restless and spiteful. For twenty days I shared with him my knowledge of the greater affairs of Europe and of the history and practices of the Christian faith.

Before embracing the Christian faith, Olaf Trygvvesön required a sign. What he did next I begged him not to do, and offered myself in the place of Lawrence. I quoted the words of Christ on the Mount: *Blessed are the merciful. Blessed are the gentle.* Olaf showed that he had learned his lessons well. "Blessed are they who are persecuted in the cause of right," he cynically said. "If your friend dies, he shall inherit the kingdom of Heaven." He ordered that Lawrence and one of the Viking warriors be lowered by ropes to the base of the cliffs at low tide.

They would be left to hang until one or the other cursed his god—Christ or Wodan. Olaf's men were not pleased that a comrade should be subjected to this trial, but Olaf bullied and threatened and chose for the experiment the man who protested loudest. We watched from the parapet above as the waters rose. The waves impelled the two men repeatedly against the cliff, at last breaking over their heads. When the curse was heard, it was in the Viking tongue. Olaf took his ax and slashed one of the two ropes where it crossed the parapet. It was not Lawrence who fell into the sea and drowned.

Upon the Feast of Pentecost in the year 994, Olaf Trygvvesön was baptized a child of God by my own hand on the island of Skellig. Then, the weather turning inclement, Olaf and his entourage boarded their ships and sailed away. The remainder of his story, Gerbert, you know better than I, for the Viking's faith held fast, and on his ascent to the kingship of Norway he entered upon the affairs of the great world and brought his people with him into the fold of Christ. And surely, Gerbert, the irony of these events is not lost upon a person of your wit: The blood-drenched heathen became the much-solicited Christian king, courted by popes, and the man who poured the waters of baptism upon the Viking's savage brow has been dragged low into the dungeons of Rome.

But all of that came much later. The baptism of Olaf Trygvvesön brought a respite to the pillage of the Irish coast. And for this "miracle" of the baptism I was given the credit, indeed the adulation, of all Christians of those parts. I was lifted by the See of Ardfert to the abbacy of a restored foundation on Skellig, and to our island came a dozen monks, drawn by the saintly reputation of the abbot, so inadvertently acquired. It was an honor and a responsibility I had not sought. The "Saint of Skellig" existed only in the minds of those who invented him, but to that idol I sacrificed my humility and my pride as readily as the godless Viking threw into a sacred pool the rings and ornaments of innocence.

Rome
Easter Day, 996
Melisande to Aileran, abbot of Skellig

Reverend Father. Today, at our noon meal, the Reader presented for our edification the story of Aileran of Skellig—of the holiness of his life, his chastisements of his flesh, his long solitude, his conversion of the heathen king, his devoted abbacy. And so, dear friend, the particulars of your life have become common knowledge throughout the Christian world and have been embroidered into tales that serve the moral instruction of holy women.

As the words fell upon my ears—and I realized who it was of whom the Reader spoke—I found myself weeping. This was the first I had heard of you since our unfortunate parting! It was as if Aileran, like the Easter Christ, had risen from the dead. I asked myself what was the cause of my tears. Was it my love for you—the knife that still twists in my heart? Was it pride in your accomplishments? Or was it something else: a feeling of betrayal, of abandonment, a resentment that out of the fire of our love you have snatched an eternal reward, leaving me with ashes?

Or was it guilt, that terrible guilt that for so long has sapped my spirit, guilt for the desecration of your body, for the terrible wounds you suffered on my behalf, for the spark and for the tinder that gave rise to the conflagration of love's destruction. Eros is Janus-faced; his names are love and hate. The dark side of the love I felt for you is self-hate, a self-hate that overspills into a bitterness that negates all love, including, dear Aileran, so often, my love for you.

Could any love have been strong enough to survive the circumstances of our separation—the nakedness, the shame, the wretched negotiations, the callous mercy? Was any love ever dragged so low, crushed so unhesitantly into filth and dust? Where does love reside, that it is so easily susceptible to change?

In the head? In the heart? Is it like the lead in the crucible of the necromancer that is suddenly transformed into gold and then back again to lead, a metal both noble and base—see, now it glistens like the sun, now it is cold and gray.

When I was removed from the house of Odo, I was sent by Gerbert to the convent of Saint Anne in Rome. Here I have lived with the nuns for seven years, sharing their meals and their prayers. I could not begin to tell you of the loneliness I have suffered. Most desperately I miss my children—Melissa, Lucia, and Theodulf—especially Theodulf, with whom I was so close during those last days at Rheims and through whom we communicated the messages of love. I need only close my eyes, or touch metal, to see him with the fire-rimmed sword quavering in his two white hands. You can't imagine the humiliation, to be cast naked before him; nothing, not the presence of Odo, or Riculf, or Odo's men, could have exposed my heart to half such grief as seeing myself in the eyes of that gentle boy, now commanded by the premature requirements of his manhood to do violence against his mother. Was it worth it? To have known love, to have tasted the sweetest wine, to have been intoxicated by the fullness of the senses, and for this to have paid so terrible a price, to have had my children taken from me, to have seen only hatred in the eyes of my son, to be locked up in a grim world of prayer and silence with no paramour but God?

It is true, Aileran, I despise God. Nightly, I curse Him. How perverse is His creation! How heartless His denial of our happiness. Not even Odo, in his most despicable self-centeredness, approached the arrogance of God. So miserable have I been in my loneliness—in this bed unwarmed by God's least grace—that I have sometimes longed for Odo—yes, Odo!—for the rough security of his body, for the touch of his clumsy hands. Even to have endured the brutish thrusts of his sex was not without reward—the full womb, the child at breast, a son's kiss. From God I have received nothing but pain. His embrace shrivels the womb, dries the milk in the pap. The only happiness I have known in His company I have wrested for myself.

How would you comfort me if you were here? The Saint of Skellig! God's favored child! "And so God filled Aileran's heart with courage and the love of Christ, so that the Viking king was smitten with the force of grace and surrendered his soul to God's unbounded mercy." Yes, those were the words that I heard in refectory. *God filled Aileran's heart.* And my own heart, Aileran, who will fill it? It is like an empty vessel. I search it for love of you, for the gentleness of your touch, for the way you listened to my words, for the self you made me feel. In a world of men you made me feel most fully woman, and for that I gave you all that I had to give—my heart, my body—and at last surrendered for the love of you even the fruits of my womb.

I want to love you. I want our love to survive as the one relic of our happiness. But it is hard, so hard not to let the bitterness of abandonment overwhelm the tenderness I once felt. I know that you are not to blame for my present exile—the first step toward intimacy was mine. And yet it is you that I blame. Who else? Not Odo, who had no choice but vengeance; his honor among men demanded it; both sacred and secular law sanction the aggrieved husband's violence against a faithless wife. Nor Gerbert, who as bishop of Rheims had every obligation to condemn adultery; his intervention on our behalf was taken at risk to his own advancement. Instead my fate was in your hands—those same hands that touched my flesh with such tenderness, that taught me to play songs of exquisite sweetness upon the harp, that in sympathy with mine moved the stylus upon the wax tablet—those same hands were powerless to protect me against Odo, against Riculf, against God.

But I am not writing this letter to accuse, nor to reprimand, nor to hate; but as a necessary step to purge the rancor from my heart. Perhaps then I can understand the inevitability of my present aloneness, and find again the capacity to love.

Melisande

The letter is destroyed. But memorized, so that even now I can reproduce in this memoir every syllable. How the letter came to me I do not know, save that the last step of the journey was in the hands of a priest who had friends in Rome. Melisande! Even the script upon the parchment evoked her physical presence—the curl of her fingers about the pen, the motion of her wrist, the studious intensity of her eyes. I read her words again and again; they were like a bitter wine I could not swallow or live without. And, of course, what she said is true: I was a coward. When bold choices might have been made, I did not make them. When love demanded action, I equivocated. I wanted everything: God's favor, obedience to vows, the respect of superiors—*and* the consummation of love. I try to remember what was in my mind as I lay on the ground outside the burning cottage at Verzenay, a boot on each wrist, the point of a sword at my throat, the blazing embers tipped into my groin. Of whom did I think: Of Melisande? Of myself? And why, when Gerbert had won my freedom, and she was sent to Rome, did I hurry at once to Ireland—no, beyond Ireland, to the Skellig rock, to the outermost compass of creation, a recreant's flight, a fugitive from love, from responsibility, from self?

God filled Aileran's heart with courage and the love of Christ. The epitome of fraud! The life I lived then on the Skellig as abbot of that little establishment was a lie. Even as my reputation for holiness and wisdom grew, I had begun my separation from God. As I reveled in the exaggeration of self, I became more completely alone than I had ever been, more alone even than when I had lived for three years in solitary isolation. No wonder, then, that I destroyed her letter, tore it into a hundred pieces and scattered it to the wind; it stood as a rebuke, a patent reminder of the enormity of the lie.

As abbot of Skellig I set my monks Herculean exercises of mortification, and nothing of Ciarán's common sense tempered my expectations. The hours of sleep I reduced to three, broken by night prayers into two segments. Our diet was hard. For physical work, I set the brothers upon the construction of a path of penance to the highestmost western peak of the island, a stairway to Heaven cut into solid rock, from Christ's Saddle to the precipitous pinnacle six hundred feet above the sea where I caused to be set up a stone cross at the end of a narrow ledge. Our days were filled with an unending regimen of work and prayer, a regimen that attracted to the island the bravest and most devout monks of the region. But it was *my* sins that the labors of the monks were set to expiate. In the commission of these fraudulent demands my reputation grew, and I sank deeper into the slough of pride.

❧

Public virtue and private vice: By a paradox of causality these two opposites feed upon each other. With ostensible virtue come pride and power, the motive and the instrument for sin. And the guilt that invariably accompanies sin is exonerated (in the mind of the sinner) by public respect. Between these two reacting poles I lived a lie. Carefully I cultivated the myth of sanctity, drawing upon my failing stores of integrity as the spider spins a web of his own substance. Inwardly my heart turned cold and false. The sin that corrupted was *amour propre or féin-grá,* self-love—the love that once was fixed upon another now found no object but self. Only twice in my life had I experienced the assuredness that the outward and inward selves were the same—with Gerbert on the road to Spain and with Melisande in the cottage at Verzenay. Only those two knew Aileran whole, without posture. Love was the liberating force that lifted the self out of self and made it whole in the eyes of another. And now—without Gerbert, without Melisande, without any loved other—the worm of self-love grew fat on the substance of self and like a growing viper sloughed off skins of virtue.

"In my bed at night I sought him who my soul loves." I hear still those words of Solomon's Song in the mouth of Gerbert. At night, in the darkness of my Skellig cell, I sought myself, by rehearsing in my mind the events of my life. I remembered the whisper of Melisande, as we lay together at Verzenay: "I want to intrude myself into your very soul, I want to know the secrets of your heart." I had answered: *My heart is an open book.* In other cells on the monastic terrace the brothers slept, exhausted from the rigors of their labors and their prayers. They spent themselves upon a divine love that admits no questions. Their hearts were open to the object of their love, and if God was mindful of our small island in the midst of the great sea, then their hearts were His to read. But the heart of the abbot of Skellig was sealed, undisclosed even to himself: In my bed at night I sought him whom my soul loves. I sought but did not find him.

The culminating crisis of my abbacy was attained in the matter of Brother Alcuin, a young illuminator who came to us from Britain. He had resided first at Innisfallen, where he produced some of the most beautifully ornamented manuscripts in that house's illustrious history. No other artist then working in Ireland could create such compelling designs, at once intricate and simple, incorporating wondrous elements from the world of nature—hares, birds, stags, hounds—each serving a didactic purpose for the greater glory of God. Alcuin came to us on the island that he might create within his own life the simplicity and grandeur that characterized his art. He enthusiastically embraced the rule of our foundation, but at the request of the abbot of Innisfallen returned there in the summer months of each year to continue his artistic endeavors.

In the late summer of Alcuin's second year, rumor came to the island that the young monk's travels to and from Innisfallen were interrupted by sojourns in the mountains near Ballinskelligs.

Therefore, at the time of Alcuin's scheduled return to the island, I sent two monks to seek him out. Together with the bailiff of the bishop, they apprehended him at a hut in the hills, in the bed of a shepherdess. The assignation had been arranged and presided over by the girl's brother. Also confiscated were erotic drawings in Alcuin's hand, on parchments and vellums taken without authorization from the scriptorium at Innisfallen. The girl was handed over to the abbot of Ballinskelligs, who caused her body to be branded. The brother was tried by secular law and garroted. Alcuin was remanded to my authority, with the expectation that a suitably harsh penalty would be exacted.

The errant monk was brought to the island, together with the incriminating drawings. And now began the inevitable decay of my authority. The monks of the Skellig, jealous of Alcuin, waited for the penalty to be imposed, for it was assumed that a minimum of fifty lashes were required to expiate so severe a transgression. I delayed . . . one day . . . two . . . a week. At last, at the prodding of the bishop's bailiff, I had Alcuin stripped and bound to the outer wall of the monastic compound in anticipation of the lash. Twice the lash fell, cutting deep into Alcuin's flesh. And then, remembering Joveta, I recognized the enormity of the lie. I ordered the punishment stopped. Losing patience, the bishop's bailiff insisted that Alcuin be returned to the mainland and to the jurisdiction of the abbot of Ballinskelligs. I consented. As the boat that carried the prisoner entered Ballinskelligs Bay, the young monk leapt into the water and attempted to swim ashore. A week later his body was cast by the sea upon the strand at Hog's Head, his feet still bound by thongs. I was doubly blamed—for irresolution in the matter of the punishment and for Alcuin's death. As a consequence of the affair, I was lessened in the eyes of my brethren and in the confidence of my bishop.

Alcuin's drawings I destroyed, but not before I studied them carefully; indeed, I kept them long after they should have been committed to the fire. Some were sketches of the nude girl; others portrayed acts of forbidden human conduct. The drawings were remarkable, indeed revelatory. Their content was provocative, all the more so in that the style was very different from that employed by Alcuin in the illumination of manuscripts. Here were many of the same elements used in the ecclesiastical decorations—scrolls and mazes, animals and plants—but now woven with a surprising delicacy into scenes of such fidelity to nature and fineness of line that they caused me to see the world in a new way. It had not occurred to me before that the human body—or the human genitalia—could be expressed graphically in such a way that the beauty of the image derived entirely from the thing itself, served no didactic purpose, required no textual complement. I saw at once the profound significance of Alcuin's work, beyond and in spite of its venereal purpose. I had seen sculptured art of such surpassing realism before, in the south of France and Spain, art of a Greek or Roman origin, but had not realized how fully alien it was to the Christian concept of creation as expressed by Tertullian and the Fathers. The subjects of Alcuin's art might have been rendered in Eden, uncorrupted by Adam's sin, without need of Christ's redeeming grace. Here, in these forbidden drawings, was the visual correlate of the works of Ovid that I had studied in Spain, and an echo of something I had learned long before at Reask, from a gentle one-eared man, who was unlearned in philosophy and theology but a skillful interpreter of nature.

October 2, 999
the year of Our Lord
In the name of the Father, and of the Son, and of the Holy Ghost
Being a record of the interrogation of Aileran of Skellig, by the inquisitors of the Holy Office, at the instruction of Sylvester II, successor of Peter and bishop of Rome

—Aileran of Skellig, by the authority of the Holy Office we

inquire into the matter of your alleged offenses. Have you anything to say before the interrogation begins?

—*Might I have a bit of food? For three days I have had nothing but water.*

—If you wish food, you would do well to cooperate fully with those who have charge of the salvation of your soul. By denying Christ, you have forfeited your own body.

—*I do not deny Christ.*

—Do you deny that Christ's physical flesh and blood are fully present in the Eucharist?

—*We have gone through all of this before.*

—Answer.

—*I believe that the spirit of Christ is present in the Eucharist, as his spirit is sacramentally present in the waters of Baptism, the chrism of Confirmation, or the oil of the Anointing of the Dying. I have not seen Christ's physical flesh in the Eucharist, nor have I tasted his flesh, nor have I smelled his flesh. I have seen enough of flesh and blood in my lifetime to know it when I see it.*

—Careful, Aileran. The Church does not say that the accidents of Christ's Body are present in the Eucharist, but only the substance. The bread and wine become fully and substantially the Body and Blood of Christ, while retaining the appearances of the natural species.

—*Such things surpass my understanding. I have not studied the philosophers. I know nothing of substances and accidents. In my own experience bread and wine and water and oil are only that—bread and wine and water and oil. If they are sacred, it is because all of nature is sacred. If they contain the spirit of Christ, it is because Christ is present in all of nature. Which is not to say that these things cannot take upon themselves a special significance in the sacramental practices of the Church, wherein their goodness and perfection are exploited for our moral edification. But . . .*

—You condemn yourself, Aileran. The words you speak are

manifestly heretical. So blatant is your apostasy that it would seem that Satan himself speaks through your mouth.

—*So it was said on the Skellig: that I consorted with Satan, that his words were on my tongue, his appetites in my belly, his concupiscence in the organs of my sex.*

—Why?

—*Why not? A belief grew up in those parts that the year 1000 would be the time of Christ's coming. People began to embrace the most extreme mortifications of the body. Others abandoned their worldly goods or consigned their properties to the Church. Certain people, including my lord bishop, Oenu of Ardfert, encouraged these fanatical practices and grew rich. I preached against these excesses, even as I held the monks of the Skellig to a severe discipline. I demonstrated that the so-called signs—comets, storms, diseases—were natural, that they signified nothing. An ancient tradition in those parts held that no rainbow would appear in the sky for forty years before the end of the world, and so people began to say there had been no rainbow since the year 960. This was patently and obviously false; rainbows were then no less common than at any other time, and I said so. But people heard only what they wanted to hear, saw only what they wanted to see, believed only what they wanted to believe. To discredit me, rumors were spread concerning my allegiance to Satan. It was said that Satan spoke through me, so that souls would not be prepared for the coming of Christ. And if a rainbow appeared, it was said to be a false bow, artificially contrived by me through Satan's power.*

—The Scripture says: "I shall set my bow in the clouds and it shall be a sign of the Covenant between me and the earth." A bow is set by God as a sign and withheld as a sign. If God chooses to withhold the bow, then surely that is within his power. To deny this is to deny Scripture.

—*I say only this: When a bow appears in the sky it is always in the same posture with respect to the sun, always when the sun is low, and always when there is water in the part of the sky opposite to the sun. Whenever these conditions concur, there is a bow. Often I have successfully predicted when a bow would appear. This was taken as a sign of my ability to conjure the bow. But I did nothing of the kind; I only recognized the conditions in the sky that are concomitant with bows. These conditions occur inevitably in the natural course of events.*

—Do you deny God's ability to act within nature, or to suspend the ordinary workings of nature's laws?

—*In a perfectly contrived creation, there is no need for the intervention of the Creator. Natural events have natural causes. And it is precisely that—the power to discover the natural causes of things—that makes us men, different from the beasts and created in the image of God.*

—Excessive curiosity is an invitation to heresy. After Christ we have no need to be curious. The Church satisfies our intellectual needs, by interpreting for us the word of Christ as revealed in Scripture and Tradition.

—*You are captured by the pretensions of authority; you are led as by a bridle. Brute animals are led by a bridle, not knowing where or why they are taken, and plodding along behind the rope that binds them. To be bridled by authority is to be constrained like a beast. Surely, God did not endow us with the ability to reason and to know, and intend that we should be led in blinders, brute and dumb.*

—Do not impiously think, Aileran of Skellig, as do the heretics, that things contrary to the accustomed course of nature cannot occur, from certain mysterious causes that are hidden from men by God. Many such things happen to show men God's grace. Our Holy Father has himself expressed the opinion that the recent marvelous signs in the earth and sky are God-given, not to prefigure the end of the world but to herald the coming of a new millennium of peace and justice, the beginning of which we may assume to have coincided with the enthronement side by side of a new pope and a new emperor, Sylvester and Otto, who shall resuscitate the Christian empire and bring together the two halves of God's dominion, spiritual and temporal. Such a spectacle has not been witnessed since the departure of Constantine for Byzantium.

—Gerbert knows better than anyone that the so-called signs are in no way exceptional. Gerbert knows better than anyone else their natural causes. If a new era of peace and justice is to begin, then I welcome it. But I doubt that peace and justice will ever reign as long as men pretend to interpret the mind of the Creator. There is in nature a wonderful harmony. The supreme artisan created the world like a great harp upon which he placed the strings to yield a variety of sounds, all in perfect consonance one with the other. All parts of nature blend harmoniously as they observe with due measure the laws implanted within them, and so, as it were, emit their natural sound. A harmonious chord is sounded by matter and spirit, fire and water, earth and air, sweet and bitter, hard and soft, as each acts according to its nature. Only man, it seems, has the ability to strike the discordant note, to untune the strings, by ignoring nature's fit measure. If God's plan for the world is to be known at all, it will be discovered within the fabric of nature, which is and endures as a perfect thing. If Gerbert, or Otto, or any other man, pretends to know God's plan, and at the same time denies nature, then he is a fool. Such men, no matter how well intentioned, cause mischief.

Days have passed since my last interrogation. I have been moved from the basement of the Castel Sant' Angelo to an upper floor. My new quarters are not without amenities: There is a bed, and a table on which to write; I am again provided with ink and parchment. A small window, uncurtained, looks out upon the Tiber and Rome, and from this window, for the first time since I was brought into the city, I have viewed the great metropolis that Otto and Gerbert intend to make again the center of the world. More than once I have heard the shouts in the streets—*Gaude, Papa! Gaude, Caesar! Gaudeat, Ecclesia! Gaudeat, Roma!* Crowds swell. There is agitation. The bridge across the Tiber is guarded by a regiment of men; their halberds glisten like diamonds in the sun. At night, on the hills in the southern and eastern precincts of the city, fires burn.

The stench that rises to my nostrils is unlike any I have known. I search my memory to identify its elements, and nothing comes so close to what I now experience as an almost forgotten fusion of fermented grain, smoke-baked kiln, vomit, blood, and excrement. It is, I know, the smell of *urbs Roma,* the stinking cesspool of creation, to which all power comes. The river below my window carries the excreta of ten thousand people; it is a brown serpent that slithers from the plains to the sea on a belly of offal. *Alas! alas! thou great city, thou mighty city!* And one of the seven angels of Revelation said: "Come, I will show you the judgment of the great harlot who is seated upon many waters, with whom the kings of the earth have committed fornication, and with the wine of whose fornication the dwellers of the earth have become drunk." Seven great anthills, built upon a ruin of marble, a new Jerusalem rising from the putrid flesh of Imperial Rome, whose inevitable destiny Gerbert dared to dream those many years ago on the strand at Narbonne.

And Melisande? Is she still here, in this city? Is she still alive? Perhaps from this window I can see the Convent of Saint Anne. Perhaps if I shouted she might hear my voice, unrecognizable among the din and babel. And now I will confess a most terrible thing: I have forgotten what she looks like. I command my memory: The elements are there—the color of the hair, the texture of the skin, the eyes, the lips—but the composite, the person who was Melisande, I can no longer conjure. I close my eyes, and I see her; but no, it is not her. I can recollect no fixed image, no *Melisande* that is not an artifact of my own invention, a collage of fragments assembled from the detritus of time. And for this she paid the price of exile in the belly of the lion.

And now Rome and the Leonine City are Gerbert's. He has

taken them with Otto, a boy of twenty, the child of a Greek mother and a German father, who learned his Latin at Gerbert's knee. My Roman interrogators inform me that when Otto captured Rome, the leaders of the city, Crescentius and twelve other nobles, were beheaded and hanged by their feet on a hill near the city wall. The eyes of Crescentius were plucked from his head and his bones broken. These facts were recounted with considerable pride, as confirmation of God's approbation for the German enterprise. Is this cesspool of violence, then, the City of God? Is Gerbert's thousand-year reign of peace and justice ushered in by the hew of steel against flesh, by the release of a Tiber of blood? Do Christians execute Christians where pagans once exacted the blood of martyrs? The city burns. Soldiers patrol the streets. Corpses rot on the gibbets. *The woman was arrayed in purple and scarlet, and bedecked with gold and jewels and pearls, holding in her hand a golden cup full of abominations, and on her forehead was written a name: Babylon.*

From my jailer I have learned certain details of Gerbert's life. He is both loved and hated by the people of Rome—loved for his office (*Gaude, Papa!*), hated as a foreigner. He has struggled with great energy to reform the city, to establish hospitals, schools, convents, markets, works of sanitation. He has ordered the restoration of baths and aqueducts. He has gathered to the Vatican artisans and craftsmen for the purpose of embellishing the basilica of Saint Peter. For these corporeal works he is admired, but the endemic violence of the city and the teeming thousands of the poor threaten to overwhelm his efforts. Rumors circulate: He has established Frenchmen and Germans in every office of the Vatican and Lateran; he has ordered the massacre of the Roman nobility; he has looted the churches of the city to enrich his private treasury; he has filled the papal apartments with pederasts and whores.

Have you seen him? I asked my jailer.

"Few have seen him," he replied. "It is said by some that he is grossly fat, by others that he is as thin as a reed from the Tiber marshes. Some say he decorates himself with precious stones plucked from the necks of the dowager countesses of the Aventine, as sometimes he plucks the treasure from between their legs; others say that he wears an unadorned shirt of raw wool. I have heard that he is confined to his bed by the pox, an affliction he has supposedly shared with his German princeling."

This information—or misinformation—supplied by my jailer makes me all the more desirous to meet Gerbert, to see for myself what he has become, and to discover why he has betrayed me.

⚇

Rome
October 31, 999. All-Soul's Day
Johann, secretary of the Holy Office, to Oenu, bishop of Ardfert, in the province of Munster, Hibernia

My lord bishop, greetings. The secretariat of this most Holy Office, acting on behalf of Our Most Holy Father, Sylvester II, supreme and universal pope and vicar of Saint Peter, after extensive interrogations and deliberations, have now decided in the matter of Aileran, abbot of the monastery of Skellig Michael.

With respect to specific charges brought against Aileran by yourself, we have made the following dispositions:

—that Aileran of Skellig denies the power of God in nature we find in the affirmative, and condemn him for heretical perversions of the truth contrary to Scriptures and the teachings of the Church.

—that he denies miracles: guilty, of a most blasphemous heresy, contrary to reason and revelation.

—that he practices diabolic magic: not guilty, and we caution those who have the care of souls against ascribing to Satan's influence what might more properly be attributed to human arrogance and perversity.

—that he blasphemes: guilty.

—that he has violated priestly vows: guilty.

185

Many of the opinions of Aileran, said abbot of Skellig, documented in the course of these deliberations and in supplementary materials submitted to this Holy Office by yourself, have been found expressly to contradict truths of revelation. That these opinions have been condemned by councils of the Church and by the Fathers cannot be doubted. Further, the heretic Aileran has shown no sign of reform or remorse but stands steadfast in the affirmation of said contrary opinions, and having been offered every opportunity to recant his heresies, he has refused to do so. Accordingly, we consider his life forfeit and have condemned him to death by hanging upon the Monte Malo.

In the course of these deliberations it has become apparent that certain excesses have been encouraged by the ecclesiastical authorities of the province of Munster, Hibernia, regarding the supposed coming of Christ and the end of the world in the year 1000. Our Holy Father, Sylvester II, has expressly asserted that there is no foundation in Scripture or in reason to assume that the millennial events foretold by the Apostle are imminent. Rather there is every expectation that Christian nations will enter upon a time of unparalleled peace and prosperity, the establishment of a City of God on earth. We therefore encourage you, as our brother in Christ, to use your apostolic influence, which derives from the See of Peter, to bring the souls of your diocese into conformity with Roman law and Roman wisdom.

Obediently in Christ, *Johann,* secretary of the Holy Office

Aurillac

Aurillac
July 1000

The wheel of fortune has turned full circle. In the vineyards of Aurillac the grapes grow fat as plums. The smoky haze of summer is made sweet by the fragrances of orchards and meadows. In the kitchen the cook's baskets brim with figs, quinces, apples, and pears. Cakes made heavy by walnuts and almonds are spread upon the table. In the heat of midday the chant of the monks rises from the valley like a cooling wind: *For God alone my soul waits in silence, from Him comes my salvation.*

On the bench beneath the fig tree in the cloister, Brother Madalberta shucks peas into his lap. He is old, his sight and his memory are failing; he did not recognize me upon my return. I took his hands and held them in my own; his fingers were as brittle as winter vines, the palms like ancient parchment. Few monks from the time of Colman's abbacy remain at the monastery of Saint Gerald's. I returned unheralded, and none of the present brethren know of my condemnation in Rome or of my escape from the gallows. Few things have changed since last

I was here, twelve years ago. The stones of the cloister paths, polished by the strop of time, cool the feet. The fig tree spreads its shade. The voice of the bell consoles. The Psalms, chanted in new voices, fill the valley with a familiar sweetness. In the library I examine, one by one, the books that once I read with such passionate intensity. They have, in my hands, a palpable nobility, a *largeness* that cannot be found in any other thing fashioned by human artifice—but their contents no longer interest me. Here among the others is *De fabrica mundi* by Victorinus of Pettau. It is the book that nearly cost Gerbert his life as a result of his dispute with Paulinus over the accuracy of a translation. *"Dóim ifreann,"* Gerbert had whispered as he lay consumed with fever; "I'll burn in hell." *God forgives,* I had said, to console him. "If He does," Gerbert responded, "He is a fool."

As a doe longs for running streams, so my soul longs for you, my God. Oh, yes. Now more than ever my soul longs for God. But not for forgiveness. Nor even for recognition. Only for peace, a stillness of heart, the forgiveness of friends. Gerbert is dead. Otto is dead. The Holy Roman Empire that would have lasted for a thousand years has crumbled into its fractious parts. The heirs of Crescentius and the counts of Tusculum have divided Rome between them, like jackals dismembering the body of a stag. The empire is in disarray. East is set against west, north against south. The Gauls are set against Germans, the Germans against Slavs, the Romans against all. The millennial *Urbs Dei* is a shattered dream—but the world endures. The stars keep their courses and the moon its phases. The sun climbs again toward its place of solstitial rest. And here, in the valleys of the Cére and Dordogne, there is a summer peace.

Peace, Gerbert—now you have it. In the palace of the popes I watched you die. The bedclothes were of Damascus silk and Saxon linen, your nightgown was embroidered with Egyptian gold. And under the gown there were leeches, Roman leeches from the Tiber marshes, applied by the doctors to rid your blood of the poison that made you shake upon the bed. This time you did not fear hell, nor fret for God's forgiveness. You wanted only life. "All the waters of the earth are one," you had said one night long ago on the strand at Narbonne. I watched you then, loving you. Water droplets glistened on your skin. The blue cloak, white shirt, and saffron leggings lay on the sand. "This is what it means to live," you said, and ran plashing back into the sea.

Now my friend has the peace of the grave, and still I address this memoir to him. All of the pieces of the story are assembled—the fragments of parchment I had buried on the Skellig, the recollections I maintained in the dungeons of Castel Sant' Angelo, the letters to Gerbert—all restored to me by Gerbert upon his deathbed. And, yes, the documents from the Skellig are included. These were discovered by the agents of Oenu, after my letters to Gerbert had been intercepted and read. So it was not Gerbert who provided my inquisitors with the information about events at Vich and Rheims. Those parts of the story, recorded in my own hand in this memoir, were supplied by Oenu to the Holy Office to ensure my condemnation—and, since Gerbert himself was implicated, to make certain that papal power did not intrude upon the course of "justice."

"It was essential that Oenu be placated," said Gerbert, when later we were joined in the papal quarters at the Lateran Palace. "The political position of Ireland and the Celtic church is precarious enough without alienating the authorities of that region. Roman power is not sufficiently secure at that great distance to bring Oenu into line. If there had been any appearance of intervention on my part in your interrogation and trial, it would have exacerbated an already dangerous independence on the part of the Irish church. And Oenu would have used what he knew of my own past to undermine my authority here. Surely you must know how delicate is my position in Rome, surrounded as I am by enemies on every side, and particularly by the Crescentian faction, who have never forgiven the part I played in the execution of their leader; they would make effective use of any shred of gossip that might damage my reputation."

I said: *The comets, the earthquakes, and eruptions of fire, the so-called signs—you of all people knew that these things are not exceptional, and yet you urged them upon me as "miracles." You fed the fires of superstition that threatened to consume me.*

Gerbert responded: "Aileran, you will understand my position here. In politics one must be ready to use any stratagem to ensure success. If people are superstitious, then one must play to superstition. Do not forget that we worked for a higher good, the establishment of Christ's reign on earth."

And why, if you intended all along to save me, did you allow me to believe as I was taken from the Castel Sant' Angelo that my destination was a gibbet on the Monte Malo?

"A necessary precaution, my friend. Our lives matter little in relation to the course of history. Make no mistake: I would have let you die if it would have served the unity of Christendom."

Oh, yes, on the day arranged for my execution a body was hung up on that gibbet beside the wall of Rome, a body that wore my tunic. From my hiding place in a cart belonging to the Holy Office I saw the rope yank taut, I watched my surrogate's limbs thrash. I smelled the stench of rotting flesh on the nearby gallows and of the heads impaled on pikes. Carrion crows strutted on the bare earth of the hill, perched on the severed heads of the enemies of Rome, and flapped up into the leafless trees with bits of flesh in their beaks. It is said that at night wolves come to the Monte Malo from the forested hills to feed upon the criminal refuse of Rome.

On the morning appointed for my execution I was awakened at dawn by warders, two men I had not seen before during my confinement. They were, I now know, agents of Gerbert, but of this they gave no sign. They had come, they said, at the instructions of the Holy Office to remove me to the Monte Malo, where a gibbet was prepared, and only then did I learn of the finality of my sentence. I cannot remember if I was afraid. I was reconciled to my fate; death had been my long companion. My request for pen and paper was refused; I had thought to write a last message to Gerbert, forgiving him the crime he was about to commit. The warders stripped my tunic from me, bound my hands and feet, and dragged me to the cart that waited at the gate of the Castel Sant' Angelo.

I do not know who it was that died in my place, in my tunic: a common criminal perhaps, or another "heretic," one who was not so fortunate as to have a pope as his protector. That wretched soul did not cry out as his feet were kicked from the plank, for a clod of soft earth had been stuffed into his mouth. As the rope crushed the sinews of his neck there were no earthquakes or drumrolls of thunder. There was only a great and terrible silence under blue Roman skies. Far off to the west the morning sunlight shone on the purple Tyrrhenian Sea, whose waters flow to and from that greater, blacker ocean that encloses the world.

⚭

"Melisande is at Argentat," said Gerbert.

We were dining in the papal apartments. With us was John of Barcelona, now a cardinal. I would not have recognized the son of Borrell had Gerbert not introduced him by name and parentage.

Your father? Your sister? I asked.

"With God," said John. His face was old and wizened, and the pouting lips now curled sourly into a gray beard. A glass goblet shook in his hand. "With God," he said again, distractedly.

Gerbert's silver bracelet was still on John's wrist, and with it many bangles; rings bound his fingers. The old man seemed helplessly encumbered by the volume of his garments, layer upon layer of fine fabrics, the outermost trimmed in ermine. Gerbert, by contrast, though heavier than I remembered him, retained

193

something of his youthful character. He wore no jewelry other than the papal ring. His habit was rich but simply styled, and rested comfortably upon his body. He was a man at ease with his authority. I loved him still; the lapse of years stood as no impediment to the affection of our youth.

I had a letter from her, I said. *She was in Rome.*

"Yes, she was here," replied Gerbert. "And then her son, Theodulf, came to fetch her. Her father, you see, had died. Riculf, the brother, had slain the emperor's cousin in a fit of temper and was executed by law. Melisande inherited the estates on the Dordogne."

And Odo?

"Long dead. All of his lands are Theodulf's now. Melisande is safe enough. She is protected by her son, who has powerful allies. There was no need for her to stay in Rome."

Such a surfeit of death! It was as if a great wind had passed through a forest, felling all but a few trees. Which trees survived? The strongest? Those supple enough to bend with the gale? Those that were sheltered by others?

"She is still a handsome woman," said Gerbert; his finger traced circles on the rim of his goblet.

I said nothing, but searched my memory for her image.

He continued: "When I came to Rome I invited her to live *here*—in the Lateran, or in my apartments on the Caelian, or at my estates in Etruria. She could have had anything she wanted. Instead she chose to stay with the nuns, in that hopeless hovel of a convent at the foot of the Aventine hill—all of the sewers of the poorest district run down about that place."

Gerbert searched my eyes for a moment. Then, in his own eyes and at the corners of his mouth, I caught a glimpse of the Gerbert of Aurillac who would tousle the hair of the younger novices and throw his arm exuberantly across my shoulders.

Your guile was like honey, I whispered, remembering. I was grateful that Melisande had removed herself from him and that

194

she was now far away, and I knew that I must go to her if only to prove my loyalty.

Why did you save me? I asked Gerbert. *Why did you intervene in my execution when you knew there was risk to yourself?*

He smiled. "Need you ask? You were—and are—Aileran, the only one who ever loved me . . . for myself alone." Gerbert glanced at John, who was preoccupied with stilling a tic in his hand.

I should thank you, I said.

He laughed broadly. "Not too generously, I hope, for if I say that I saved you for love, it is a lie. I had much to gain by keeping that rope from your neck."

How?

"In the matter of Olaf Trygvvesön. For a long time I had heard stories of your triumph with the Viking, of the so-called miraculous conversion of the heathen king, but never took them seriously. You know how these stories grow up around supposed saints."

He paused; recollection of the past lighted his eyes.

"Do you remember the story of Gerald, our founder, and the peasant girl—how God made her ugly so as to save his virtue?"

I acknowledged the memory.

Gerbert laughed. "I always wondered why God did not make *Gerald* ugly; it was, after all, *his* virtue that needed saving."

Then he continued: "I did not realize until I read your memoir that the barbarian Viking of the Skellig was one and the same person as the present Christian king of Norway, and that he considers himself a kind of half-brother to you. So I will use you, Aileran, in my negotiations with Olaf. Perhaps I will send you there as my emissary—a plenipotentiary of the pope. Would you like that? We'll dress you up like John there, in scarlet . . . like a whore of Rome . . . and send you off to impress those savages in the north. They are spiritual troglodytes who have need for a little of the sophistication of the empire."

I answered simply: *If I am free to leave Rome, I will go to Aurillac.*

Gerbert had been drinking for some time. Now he became serious and melancholy.

"You know, Aileran," he said, "the trouble with power is that with enough of it you can have anything you want. And I wanted everything. Honesty. Integrity of spirit. Good works. And, yes, comfort too. The pleasures of the flesh. If you are powerful you can have them all—but not necessarily at the same time. There is an old hermit, Nilus, who lives in a hut near the Esquiline Gate. He is ninety-six years old and noted for his holiness. The emperor Otto went to him once and begged for his prayers. Nilus said, I ask of you only one thing, to think of the salvation of your soul. At that, Otto began weeping and placed his crown into the hands of the old man. All Rome heard the story and briefly considered Otto a saint. And then—guess what? When Otto returned to his palace on the Aventine, he had another crown fashioned, more richly encrusted than the last one. And so it has been with me, Aileran. I have never been able to make a choice. I love God, but I also love myself. I have used whatever power has been given me to advance the work of God's kingdom. I have won more souls to Christ than any pope since Gregory. I have brought the secular power of empire into alliance with the Church. I have made the clergy answerable to moral law. I have established peace where before there was wickedness and war. And at the same time I have cultivated vices that are secret to everyone but God. And to you, Aileran. You know who I am."

There were tears in Gerbert's eyes. I sought to console him.

Do not think, I said, *that any one of us is without a secret sin.*

He responded: "And how will God weigh our sins, Aileran? God is omnipotent. If He is all-powerful, then He is familiar with the gratification of weakness. Artists show Christ Triumphant in garments grander than those of any pope. The robes of the saints have threads of silver. It is said that the streets of heaven are paved with gold. So God does not eschew luxury. Or beauty. He will see that I have done more good than evil. He will welcome me to Paradise."

I was Gerbert's guest in the Lateran Palace for three months. I had ample opportunities to observe his activities as pontiff, including his successful efforts to direct the young emperor.

"Otto is not Charlemagne," said Gerbert. "My task is to give the emperor direction and purpose. He is young and foolish. Where he sees a problem he can think of nothing to do but to throw an army at it. If he is allowed to blunder about on his own, he will destroy the unity we have striven to achieve."

A dozen secretaries were required to handle the huge correspondence that Gerbert poured across Europe (I had myself been the recipient of several of those letters). He used letters the way generals used armies.

"Throughout the empire scales are delicately balanced," said Gerbert, "abbot with bishop, abbess with patron, bishop with prince, prince with prince, yes, even emperor with pope. The City of God requires that the scales tremble in equilibrium. If one scale of a balance becomes heavier, it is necessary for me to throw a letter into the opposite pan, restoring poise. One man's ego must be inflated, another's pricked. One man's power must be augmented, another's diminished. Balance. The scales must tremble. Then Europe will have peace."

Emissaries and ambassadors filled the papal antechambers. Clerks and auxiliaries moved among them, hearing petitions, accommodating differences, examining credentials.

"The art of diplomacy is timing," said Gerbert. "It is best to make them wait . . . to make them deal with underlings. It takes the edge off their confidence. But if we make them wait too long they become resentful and recalcitrant. For every envoy there is a precise moment when our advantage is at a maximum. To know when that moment is, is everything."

Most astonishing of all was the deftness with which Gerbert bent the emperor to his purpose.

"Otto must not be allowed to rule," he said; "Otto must only think he rules. As long as the emperor is surrounded with the trappings of power he will be happy. His palace must be bigger, his retinue longer. As for the actual government . . . the Church has the instrument of literacy. Education is in our hands and we must use it to our advantage. The more efficient numerals of the Saracens must replace the Roman. Mechanical principles—the abacus, the clock—must be given to the abbots and bishops. Latin must be universal among clerics, while the secular authorities are made impotent by a babel of tongues. Most important, we must exploit the Keys of Peter, the divine mandate that invigorates our efforts. What we seek to create is not the dominion of Caesar but the Body of Christ."

On the last day of the nine hundred ninety-ninth year since the birth of Christ, on the eve of the millennial year, Gerbert took me to a high window of his palace on the Caelian. Gray clouds steeped with silver heaped the horizon; the river was refulgent in moonlight, its turbid burden masked. Rome lay before us. Pagan Rome, Christian Rome. The Rome of Romulus, the Rome of Peter. We saw the imposing mass of the Colosseum, the triumphal arches of the Caesars, the monastically crowned hills, the dome of the Pantheon, the Campus Martius, the walls of Aurelian and Leo.

"She is beautiful," said Gerbert.

I acquiesced halfheartedly, aware of the ruin, putridity, and violence that festered unseen.

Then he said: "Since I came to Rome I cannot sleep."

And I remembered his sleepless nights at Vich; in the mornings he had shown no sign of weariness.

"All men fear the night," said Gerbert. "They live for the cock's crow. But I abhor the coming of the day. Night is my disguise."

And the morrow? I asked. *The new millennium? Out there, in the city, the churches are full, the air is thick with incense and prayers; the people are fearful and uncertain. Will tomorrow dawn with fire and glory? Will the graves open and the dead wake? Or will there be more morrows?*

That night, I woke in darkness. Someone was moving within my bedchamber in the papal palace, a sensed presence. Half awake, I searched the shadows until a hand pulled back the drape at the window and a waning moon illuminated the room. The tenebrous presence moved near to my bed. A dream? Was I awake? A young man stood silhouetted against the window. He was naked—his features as delicate as a girl's, his body lithe and thin, his skin like Frankish silver.

"He asks you to come," the young man said.

Was I addressed by the angel of death, come to fetch me? With a struggle I shook off sleep and endeavored to come fully awake, to return from the porch of death into the light of reason. My visitor did indeed appear angelic, but he was real enough. His body was familiar . . . like a statue . . . Antinoüs.

Who asks me to come?

"Gerbert," he said. "It is Gerbert. Please come."

I was led by my otherworldly guide to the bedroom of Gerbert. My friend was propped against pillows wet with sweat. His hands shook on his chest.

"I've been poisoned," he whispered. "They have sent for the doctors."

With a nod of his head he indicated the boy, my angel of death, now curled up in a chair at the foot of the papal bed, intently watching. "Tell him to go—and to put on clothes."

I waved the boy from the room.

Who did it? I asked. *The boy?*

Words formed hesitantly on Gerbert's lips, with a froth of involuntary spittle: "Nct him; he is too simple, though God knows he may have been their agent."

Then who?

"The cardinals of the Crescentian faction. The Tusculan princes. Who knows? I have enemies in every quarter of Rome."

What can I do? How can I help you?

"Absolve me," answered Gerbert. "You know my sins. Absolve them."

With the edge of the coverlet I wiped the foam from his mouth. *It is not for me to forgive you,* I said. *God forgives you.*

One by one the doctors lifted thumb-thick leeches from a bronze casket and placed them on Gerbert's chest, that they might draw the poison from the blood, but it seemed to me that the beasts must draw the lifeblood itself.

"For all I know, these men . . . are in league with the murderers," Gerbert stammered in the dialect of Aurillac, which only I would understand. And then, drawing upon his waning resources of strength, he said: "What happens to us after death? Aileran, you . . . you have studied the philosophers; was Pythagoras right when he said that at death our souls take up residence in new bodies, passing . . . from beast to man . . . and back again . . . from man to beast? All in flux, nothing dies; earth is reduced . . . to water, thinned again, becomes air . . . at last . . . empyrean fire, and fire congealed and thickened becomes earth; souls migrate too; the carcass of a . . . bull, slain for sacrifice, gives rise to bees from its flesh . . . the corpse of a stallion produces hornets; bury a crab in the sand and it becomes a scorpion; a grub . . . emerges from its shroud as . . . a butterfly . . . or moth; mud contains seeds from which frogs are born. . . . And so a spirit moves . . . from place to place, now a pope, now a slave, or a bull, or . . . a moth. Nothing constant. Nothing dies. And what . . . what do Christians have in place of this? A universe fixed from the first moment of creation; souls that have no existence except their own, that are . . . created out of nothing and fly . . . upon death . . . beyond nature, to heaven or hell, to reside eternally, immutable . . . cold as the planetary spheres. It is a frightful world we Christians have inherited . . . as brittle as glass. We carry our souls like glass vessels in our hands . . . and if we drop them . . . they are shattered forever. Only God in His mercy can restore a soul to its pristine form."

This long, halting discourse cost Gerbert considerable pain and expended his last frail stores of energy. It was characteristic of the man that at the moment of his death he reverted to philosophy. There was no talk now of politics. He lapsed into a long silence, and then he said, "I will not ask you to follow me, Aileran . . . for I do not know where I'm going . . . but if we meet there . . . we shall be friends."

At dawn he died. The sunrise came like a curtain of pure yellow silk that moved across the city from east to west, entering at the Tiburtina Gate and filling at last the chambers of the Vatican with a cold midwinter light. A seaward wind carried the wakening scents of the city to our nostrils: odors of rotting fruit and composting debris from the empty markets, the fetid marsh, the sweat of sleep. The doctors composed him, carefully removing the leeches from his chest. John of Barcelona returned the silver bracelet to Gerbert's wrist and wept copious tears.

Nature abhors a vacuum. Beyond Gerbert's chambers news of his death kindled action. Fear of Armageddon gave way to ambition and greed. There was a stirring in the courtyards, a slow assembly of arms, a congealment of purpose; power moved toward the papal precincts from across the city, flowing like an estuarine tide toward the gates of the Lateran. I knew I had little time to make good my escape. I slipped from the palace and made my way across the waking city to the Porta Flaminian. I waited there until the gate opened to admit early tradesmen bearing produce for market, and put Rome at my back. The long road stretched northward, toward Melisande and Gaul.

Argentat
Midsummer's Day, 1001
Melisande to Aileran of Saint Gerald's

Word has reached us of your return to Aurillac. For a long time I did not know if you were dead or alive. You have been described to me by one who recently visited Saint Gerald's, and I try to match the fragments of that description with the Aileran of memory. Have you changed? So many years! So much to remember.

I live in my father's house with my daughter Anne. We are watched over by Theodulf, who has been everything to me a loving son can be. My father and brother are dead. And Odo too. Most grievously, I have lost my daughters Melissa and Lucia, who were stricken by pestilence while I was in Rome. And now, at the rear of this procession of death, comes one who lives.

Will you visit us?

Melisande

From Saint Gerald's I made my way to Argentat. So eager was I to see her that I left the river road and took the steep mountain path between the valleys of the Cére and the Dordogne. I entered the forest at daybreak and arrived in the hills above Argentat at midafternoon. The path was perilous. I met no one until, near the end of my journey, I came to the forest spring where once before—nearly thirty years!—I had gone to discipline my flesh. On the grass near the pool's edge a girl sat reading. Behind her a dappled pony grazed upon sedges.

I knew at once that the girl was the daughter of Melisande. She resembled her mother in face and form, though darker-skinned. She wore the light garment of madder yellow that once had been her mother's, and her hair was bound at her neck with ribbons in her mother's fashion. I entered the clearing, taking care not to startle her. When she saw me she stood, cautiously, and retreated to her pony; she slipped the book into the pocket of her shift.

I said: *I have known only one other woman who can read.*

She did not speak.

I believe that woman is your mother. Are you the daughter of Melisande?

"I am the daughter of Odo and Melisande," she answered.

She slipped her arm under the pony's neck; the animal nuzzled against her side. And then she added: "How is it that you know who I am?"

I am Aileran, I replied, *and I was once your mother's tutor.*

The girl became less wary. "A hedge of trees surrounds my hermitage . . . ," she began.

It was a poem I had written long ago. I continued the verse: *A blackbird sings.*

We laughed.

"My mother has told me of you," she said. "You were her teacher here at Argentat, when she was my age. You taught her Latin, and music, and poetics."

She was an apt pupil, I said. *And she was beautiful, as you are beautiful.*

The girl smiled faintly. What more did she know of my relationship with her mother?

Yes, she was about your age, I said, remembering. Then: *What are you reading?*

She took the book from her pocket and held it to her breast. "Virgil," she answered.

I knew of the Roman poet but had not read him.

She said: "I have it from my mother. She is using it to teach me Latin. It was a gift to her, from the pope."

Can you take me to your mother? I asked.

The girl did not answer. She put the book into her pocket and led the pony forward. Her movements, her gestures, were familiar—it was Melisande risen phoenix-like from the cold ashes of memory. We walked together to the verge of the forest and then down through fields of yellow flax to the castle. The girl tethered her pony at the gate in the kitchen wall and beckoned me toward the orchard. The trees were burdened with fruit—apples, quinces, and pears. There were odors of sweetness and must.

⬥

The verses that follow are my gift from Melisande, presented upon the occasion of my return to Argentat. They are a part of her translation of Virgil's Latin epic into the Frankish tongue. The original, bound in African leather, she had received from Gerbert upon her departure from Rome. Now, at Argentat, she turns the cadenced lines of the Roman poet into Gaulish song. In this task she is assisted by her daughter Anne—dark-skinned Anne, born in Rome, carried there Camilla-like in her mother's womb.

The tale of Camilla, retold from the Aeneid of Virgil by Melisande of Argentat. The year of Our Lord 1000.

> *In the first rank of the Latin armies came*
> *The warrior-girl Camilla, of whose fame*
> *The gods have spoken, leading soldiers clad*
> *In sun-bright bronze. Her thin white hands had*
> *No experience of spindle or teaseled wool,*
> *Minervian skills; instead, armed with a quiver full*
> *Of arrows and a myrtle-shafted spear, she ran*
> *Into the fray more gallantly than any man.*
> *Her hair was bound with golden clasp, her tabard*

Royal silk. She fought with one breast bared
That she might wield her weapons unimpeded.

This fair-haired, fleet-footed girl who heeded
Not the demarcations of her sex was child
Of Metabus, despised tyrant of Privernum. Exiled
From his city, the Volscian despot fled
With infant girl upon his breast. He led
His enemies a swift, unequal chase until he came
To Amasenus stream in flood. The game
Was up, his passage blocked, he could not swim
Lest he put the child at risk. He tore a limb
From a stout oak and fashioned a kind of spear,
To which he lashed the infant. "Diana, hear
My prayer," he said, "I swear my child shall be
Thy servant if my throw succeeds." With cork-tree
bark he wrapped Camilla, then he hurled
The spear and babe across.

                        In wooded world
The father raised the child, and when she made
Her first small steps he armed her with a blade,
A javelin, arrows and a bow, and tutored her
In skills of war. No dainty garments did she wear,
But skins; her hair fell free and loose, her feet
Touched the earth unshod. No swan or egret
Winged above that she'd not fell it with her dart,
No forest beast escaped her spear. Her heart
Had place for naught but hunt and arms. At last
The child became a maid. Whoever Camilla passed
Was stricken by her beauty. Young men vied
To possess her. The mothers of Tuscany cried
In vain that she might be their daughter.

                                           Then
The Trojan armies came, and with their Tuscan
Allies laid siege to Latin towns. Battle pitched
Ensued, a clash of arms, the line was breached,
Then mended, bright steel met flesh and dark blood
Drenched the wretched ground. Into this dread
Carnage rode Camilla, quiver at her back, a two-
Edged ax and javelins in her hands. With hue
And cry she led her chosen comrades—Larina,
Tulla, Tarpeia—virgins all, the cohort of Diana,
Women soldiers into battle. Savage girl:
Whom first did your hard-thrown spear impale?
How many men partitioned by your ax? Euneus
Faces her; she hacks him down. Brave Pegasus
Lifts his lance; her arrows fly. Each javelin cast
Finds its mark. A troop of Trojan warriors massed
Before her—swept away! Ornytus turns to flee;
She wheels her mount, a flash of steel, and see
The splash of blood.

                          One Arruns, marked by fate,
Begins to stalk Camilla, waits for her mistake.
She spurs her steed; he gallops too. She tarries;
He holds back. He follows like her shadow, wary,
Cautious, seeks his chance. Camilla spies Chloreus,
Phrygian knight, in splendid gear—his harness
Linked with bronze, his armor gold, the bow
At his shoulder of silver-encrusted ash. She knows
This finery will be hers. Headlong she charges,
Reckless, gives no heed to the man who forges
Her undoing. Now the javelin flung from Arruns' hand
Strikes true; the point, as if by a god's command,
Pierces beneath her naked breast. Camilla tries
To pull the barbed dart from her flesh. Her eyes

Close; cold death embraces her, the rosy glow
Of youth drains from her cheeks.

Diana's bow
Answers Arruns' shaft. The goddess will not let
Her favored daughter fall without revenge. She sets
An arrow, lets it fly; across a high celestial arc
It soars and strikes deep in the girl-slayer's heart.

"Look," said Melisande. "Here is Gerbert's presentation verse."
On the title page of Virgil's epic Gerbert had copied this phrase:
Tum, si quid non aequo foedere amantis curae numen habet iustumque memorque, precatur—Then she prays to whatever god in justice cares for the grief of lovers unequally bound by love. Melisande was not ignorant of Gerbert's meaning.

I had found her in the orchard, gathering pears into her apron. These, upon seeing me, she spilled upon the ground. There was no salutation, no embrace. My knowledge of her instantly returned—the features, expressions, and gestures that had once been the very substance of my consciousness. Yet she was different. The girl of Argentat was gone (re-created, as I had seen, in the face and form of her daughter Anne); gone, too, was the impetuous and passionate young woman of Rheims. The woman I found in the orchard was possessed of a certain . . . tempering, a pride of bearing, like a willow that has withstood the stream in flood.

She smiled. "So, Aileran, it is you."

You are beautiful, I said.

"Yes," she laughed. "We are all older."

A thousand years have passed since Virgil wrote his poem, a thousand years since Christ was taken down from the tree of the cross. And the world endures. Trees in the orchard at Argentat that were placed in the ground when I lived in the hut near the forest now bear fruit. The pears lie plump and round in the grass; they are the color of Melisande's shoes. Below, beyond the water meadow, the river flows in gray-green eddies through marsh grass and willow roots. The otter glides through darkling pools. Nothing remains the same; everything lasts. I have seen a place where the ocean has been turned to dry land, and another place where dry earth has been engulfed by sea. Seashells are sometimes found far from shore; Ovid tells of an anchor centuries old found on a mountaintop in Spain. The hills are cut down by streams; a marsh is drowned by windblown sand. A thousand years pass, and the world is arranged and rearranged and rearranged again. Gerbert's millennial City of God is stillborn; Otto's universal empire is but a shadow of Charlemagne's. And still the world endures. No trumpet sounds to announce a new Paradise, the clouds of heaven do not roll back to reveal a kingdom paved in gold. The year 1000 has arrived and the world is whole. The Four Horsemen of Revelation that were to bring war, famine, plague, and predation have been here all along.

Was it wrong of me to come? I asked.

She answered: "It was wrong of you to leave—then, in the aftermath of the fire."

I had no choice.

"You could have followed me to Rome."

I felt . . . I was honor bound to Gerbert.

"Honor? What honor was there then? Odo's honor? You and I might have died to hold Odo's honor intact. Gerbert's? His purpose was power, not honor. Our own honor we had compromised by our liaison. What honor was there then that might have kept us apart?"

I do not believe that Gerbert acted dishonorably.

She shrugged. "Honor is a man's concept. I do not understand it. It seems to me that honor is a man's way of esteeming himself in the eyes of other men. But what of self-esteem? How did Aileran judge himself in his own eyes?"

I could not answer.

She continued: "Let me tell you about Rome. How I was put in with the nuns of Saint Anne's and forced to participate in their silence and prayers. The silence was unbearable. The prayers were like profanities on my lips. And all the while I grew fat with child in the eyes of their disapprobation. When at last my time came I was forced to give birth in a squalid cell, hidden from the nuns, without midwife or friend . . . only an old woman, a servant, to lift the baby from my womb . . . the afterbirth left to lie between my legs. Never have I been so alone. I swore then never to love any person, nor God."

She paused. There was no bitterness in her voice, only sorrow.

"The child was baptized Anne, for the patron of the convent. I was not even allowed to choose her name."

I stepped toward her: *Melisande, I am sorry. I . . .*

She reached out her hand and stopped my words with her fingertip. That touch, that gentle momentary pressure of her finger against my lips, unleashed the memories that had been so long unremembered, and like a spring unstoppered they gushed forward: *I place the host upon her tongue, the current of desire that flows through Christ's flesh from her body to mine in the candlelit chapel, her husband lapsed in shadows. . . . Her hands undoing the laces of her gown, letting the cloth fall from her shoulders; offering herself, she says, "I have given myself to no other man." . . . The smell of her hair as she steps from the river, her hand moving the wet tresses from her eyes, the ribbons dangling unloosed between her breasts.* A flood of sensation, not desire but knowledge, the phrasings of memory, a person restored. *Sunlight streaming through the window, a hush of breeze and purling water, Melisande on the bed, her skin like honeysilk; she moves her hand to her sex and with the moistened fingertip touches my lips.*

A spring unstoppered. I turned from her and wept.

I stayed with Melisande and Anne at Argentat for three days. It was a busy, productive household, much softened since the time of her father, Guillaume. The gardens and orchards flourished. A fish weir had been established in the river, and a race and mill for grinding corn—the first water-driven mill I had seen in all of Gaul. Melisande's pride was her herb garden, the very garden where on summer days long ago we made together songs and verse. In memory I saw her thin fingers marching on the strings like Nubian soldiers and heard her child's voice singing,

> *See, it is the bed of Solomon,*
> *borne by sixty valiant men . . .*

In the garden she had planted a remarkable variety of herbs, not only those, such as anise and fennel, that might be found in the kitchen garden of any manor house, but others she had brought from field and forest or purchased from afar. Here were lupine, coriander, nettles, rosemary, iris, borage, onion, hyssop, rue, chives, celandine, and many more. With these she practiced the arts of healing. "The friend of the physician and the praise of cooks," said Melisande of her herbs. Of marigold she made a healing salve, of angelica a tonic against pestilence, of mentha a cure for disorders of the stomach, of oxlip a refreshing drink. When I cut my foot on a stone, she stopped the blood with a balm of herb Robert. "God makes the grass for the cattle and the green herbs for men," she said, and packed me a small wooden casket of the dried leaves and roots of assorted plants.

On the bench by the mint pool, where once we sat at lessons, she instructed Anne—in music, Latin, and poetics.

"Anne is my treasure," said Melisande. "I have lost two of my children without ever knowing them, and without being able to comfort or heal. Theodulf is far away, maintaining the properties of his father. Anne is all I have. Once she was taken from me in Rome . . . from my breast—she was only an infant—and brought here to Argentat to live with her grandfather. If she were taken from me again I would die."

She will marry, I said. *She has all of her mother's beauty.*

Melisande was silent. Then she said as if to herself: "*. . . quae nunc dubiis committitur auris . . .*"

The line, I supposed, was from Virgil, and might be translated: "whom I now commit to an uncertain wind." It was a great pleasure to sit near the wall of the garden and watch Melisande and Anne as they worked at their lessons or gathered herbs. Once, in the cottage at Verzenay, she had said to me: "You spend all of your time searching for meaning, considering, analyzing, God-chasing, and what you are looking for may be right in front of you"—and reaching out she had touched my bare breast. Now, at fifty-seven years of age, in the company of these two women, I saw what I had looked for all my life, and knew was not mine.

That night, as we sat at evening meal, I said to Melisande: *Once I left you when I should not have gone. Now, if you want me, I will stay.*

She answered: "No. . . . I have suffered too much to obtain my freedom to give it up now. We will be friends, Aileran. And except for Anne, you are my dearest friend. I will visit you, and you me. I will want to share with you my translation of Virgil. But we cannot be together. All of that is past."

And Anne . . . , I began hesitantly.

"Anne is my treasure," she said.

It was not as a husband or a lover that I wished to stay with Melisande. Sexual desire is now no more than a memory, like the glow of an aurora faintly perceived on a distant horizon. Perhaps it was to experience what she gave to Anne that I wished to stay—to shelter in her quiescence, to come at last to rest. (At Verzenay she had said, "You must promise not to question what we do.") But of course she is right. My presence at Argentat would infect the very thing I wished to share. Within my heart I

211

bear the ineradicable worm of doubt, the nattering consciousness of guilt. Death was attendant at my birth and left its barbed dart affixed in my flesh. Of my affliction she is properly wary.

From my pocket I took a slip of parchment on which I had copied from memory the poem I had received upon my previous departure from Argentat (*I am a garden enclosed and a sealed fountain* . . .). I passed it to her across the table. She read the verses and folded the parchment carefully, tucking it beneath her girdle. As I departed for Aurillac she embraced me and said: "Aileran, I have not forgotten."

I have been made welcome at Saint Gerald's. Upon my arrival the place was without a priest; the abbot, a German, allows me a hermitage on the hill above the monastery in return for the performance of the sacraments as required by the members of the house and the celebration of the Eucharist on feast days. I give my days to the tilling of a small garden and to meditation. Melisande sends plants, which I place among my own, and herbal balms and elixirs. I gather wood from the forest for my fire. Occasionally I tutor a young monk who comes up from Saint Gerald's. At night I consider the stars. I watch them move in their crystalline courses, as they have moved for a thousand years—as they will move for a thousand years more. I trace the familiar constellations that I learned at No-Ear's knee half a hundred years ago. The Milky Way arches like a silver bridge from earth to heaven . . . the Eagle beats toward the zenith . . . the Swan dives on extended wings to tropic rest.

> *O King of Stars! Eternal king,*
> *These are the gifts that summer brings.*

There is but one miracle, my gentle instructor had said, and that one miracle is the Creation.

This memoir I now bring to a close, and the whole—a tattered packet of scraps and pages, some already decayed with age—I will wrap and send to Melisande.

Argentat

Argentat
September, 1003
In the hand of Melisande

Aileran came back to me on the woodsman's cart, his body mauled by wolves. He lived for but a few moments in my presence; his eyes moved in a pathetic searching way, his lips trembled, and there was stillness. He died unshriven.

He lay throughout the night in the herb garden. In the morning I dressed his body, cleaning the wounds and applying sachets of aromatic herbs, and wrapped him in a cerecloth of silk. I wept to see the terrible scars inflicted by Odo. I wept to see the ravages of age. With the assistance of Theodulf I buried him near the edge of the forest, at the place where once his hermitage stood, at the place were he wrote:

> *A blackbird sings*
> *(An announcement I shall not hide);*
> *Above my lined book,*
> *The trill of chorusing birds.*

It was important to Aileran that his story have a conclusion. So I will add this final chapter and tell how it was that he died. Then I will recopy the entire story, on vellum, and have it bound. It will be his testament and his legacy.

What I write now must necessarily be partly conjecture, but I have ascertained what facts I could from the monks of Saint Gerald's. Aileran's final tragedy began on the night before Anne's wedding feast. Yes, Anne has wedded, even as Aileran assumed she might. Her husband is a fine young man, Robert of Laon, a friend of Theodulf's, a knight of refinement and courteous demeanor. So I have not lost her after all; as their wedding gift I gave them the house and lands at Argentat; here they will live, and here, too, they have welcomed me to stay.

On the evening before the wedding feast, Aileran was wakened from an uncertain sleep by a coruscant light in the night sky. At first he took it to be the aurora, and immediately went out to study the shimmering lights. What lit the sky was Saint Gerald's in flames. The entire monastery was ablaze: the church, refectory, dormitories, infirmary, even the famed library. Not waiting to don his sandals, Aileran hurried down the hill. The fire had been ignited by brigands from Languedoc who were raiding along the valley of the Cére. Their attack was swift. They killed the abbot and stripped the sacristy of the holy vessels. The monks they secured in outbuildings and put the torch to the cloister. It was a windy night and the flames spread quickly along the roof of the cloister until the fire took hold in all of the connecting buildings. By the time Aileran arrived the villagers had freed the monks and together with them were endeavoring to extinguish the flames. The criminals responsible for this sacrilege had moved on down the valley toward the junction of the Cére and the Dordogne.

Now Aileran began to fear for my safety, and for the safety of

Anne. Foolishly he set out to warn me of the danger, not by following the path of the brigands down the valley of the Cére and then up the Dordogne, but through the forested hills that separate the valleys of the two rivers. In this way he thought to arrive at Argentat before the raiders. He did not count on the darkness of the night or his own infirmity. He lost the path. The forest canopy was too dense for him to use the stars as guides, and the undergrowth impeded his progress. Before dawn he had fallen exhausted and unconscious, still within the forest but not far from Argentat. It was then that he became the prey of wolves.

He was found by my woodlands steward and carried to the house at the end of a day of merriment. Darkness had fallen, and the wedding guests were reveling and well drunk, when a maidservant came to whisper the news. I slipped from the banqueting hall to the kitchen yard where the woodsman waited with his melancholy load. The juxtaposition of my sadness for Aileran with my joy for Anne was almost more than my heart could bear. Poor Aileran. His fire-rimmed eyes searched me out. They swam as if his soul sought an anchor that would hold him to this life. Perhaps he tried to speak. I sent for the bishop of Rheims, who was among the wedding guests, but before he came Aileran died.

"Who is this man?" asked Erchambald, the bishop, a big man, wise but haughty, an ally of Theodulf.

I begged him to confer upon Aileran the sacrament of the dying.

"Aileran of Skellig? The heretic?" whispered Erchambald, and I could see that he was searching his mind for fragments of the story. "I have heard that he was executed in Rome."

I answered: "He is a friend of Gerbert's . . . and of mine. I beg you to shrive him."

The bishop cupped his chin in his great palm and considered my request. He said: "My daughter, my heart goes out to you, and I am distressed to offend against your hospitality, but I cannot anoint this man. He has been condemned as a heretic. To shrive him would offend against my responsibility as a bishop of Christ's church."

I reminded him: "He is Gerbert's friend. Gerbert was your predecessor as bishop of Rheims. Gerbert's patronage helped achieve your appointment as bishop."

He responded: "My dear Melisande, Gerbert is dead. There are others in authority now in Rome who are not sympathetic to Gerbert's memory . . . or to his alliance with German power. You must know that my position in this matter is precarious. My allegiance is necessarily divided between Rome and the emperor. Gerbert forged a unity between those interests, but that unity has been severed."

With the tip of his heavy finger, encumbered with the episcopal ring, Erchambald closed Aileran's eyes, then rubbed his fingertip against his thumb as if to wipe away the odor of heresy. He said: "Because of my friendship with your family, I will keep secret the fact that this is the man who is presumed to be buried in the heretic's grave in Rome. But I will not shrive him."

Then Erchambald returned to the guests. From the open windows of the house came sounds of music and laughter. And I prayed for Aileran in the words of the Song of Solomon that we had shared so long before:

> *Awake, north wind,*
> *come, south wind!*
> *Blow upon my garden,*
> *to spread its perfumes round.*
> *Let my Beloved come into his garden,*
> *and taste its pleasant fruits.*

This same Erchambald, who refused to Aileran the last anointing of the Church, had preached at the wedding of Robert and Anne.

He quoted Saint Jerome to the effect that Adam and Eve had remained chaste in Paradise. Not until after the Fall were their bodies united. The sexual act is accursed, said the bishop, even in marriage. The only justification for sexual love between men and women is procreation. The bishop exhorted the young couple to continence. He urged an *honesta copulatio, amicitia,* friendship, and fidelity.

As the bishop spoke, the children knelt before him, their gaiety undiminished. I was saddened for my daughter and prayed that she might find with Robert what I had found with Aileran, however briefly, outside the bonds of matrimony. But Erchambald was not finished; now he drew inspiration from Augustine and Ambrose. Adam represents the spiritual side of the human condition, he said, and Eve the sensual side. Satan triumphed in Eden by winning over the spirit through a weakening of the flesh. Evil comes from the body, and therefore from woman, who is inferior and carnal. Between husband and wife must be established an affective relationship—*delectio*—which is primordial and excellent, except that in the conjunction of the sexes the direction—*praelatio*—belongs to the man, and the submission—*subjectio*—to the woman. In a harmonious marriage the cunning of the female and the roughness of the male are mitigated by the *commixtio sexuum,* or fusion of the sexes. But in all these things, in the interest of the higher life, it is the man—Erchambald insisted—who is prelate.

Anne's faced beamed with love. She was radiant in a dress of yellow silk. Fresh flowers crowned her hair. She knew nothing yet of *praelatio* and *subjectio.* Nor did she yet know that she was other than the child of Odo. The terrible events that occurred at Rheims long ago had been carefully reconstructed by Theodulf, who now, by way of repentance for his betrayal, sought only my comfort and peace. The conflict of loyalty between father and mother that once had violently divided his spirit was resolved upon Odo's death. Into Theodulf's hands and judgment I now place my trust.

But not my freedom. With Aileran I tasted the *delectio* of freedom—if only briefly—and I will not now surrender my new-found liberty to Theodulf, or even to Aileran or Anne. In the three days that Aileran stayed with us at Argentat before returning to Aurillac, he often observed Anne, searched her features. His eyes betrayed his love; his heart overbrimmed. But he could not bring himself to speak of her parentage, nor did I allow him release from that final act of cowardice. I love Aileran, and I pity him. Even at Verzenay, in the fullness of our freedom, he was not free. God held his soul at ransom, God selfishly possessed him, the same God here preached by Erchambald, the God of Augustine, Ambrose, and Jerome, whom I despise and curse. If I rot for eternity in hell I will not acknowledge Aileran's God as prelate of my soul.

As Anne and Robert were accompanied to the bedchamber by reveling guests, Aileran came home to me—in a woodsman's cart. I was grieved by the anguish in his eyes, the confusion and the guilt.

"He spoke your name," said the woodsman.

I touched Aileran's hand, and what was left of his fragile spirit departed. The body in the cart was like a heap of broken twigs, streaked with blood. "I am Grus, the Crane," I whispered to him. "I will watch you as you sleep."

In the morning, I cleansed him. I anointed his body with vervain, the herb of grace, and with endive. Of endive it is said that the herb will break all bonds with the earth and render its wearer invisible. I sent him invisible into eternity.

AUTHOR'S NOTE

The characters in this story are fictional, although Gerbert and several minor characters are based on historical persons. There is some historical basis to believe that Olaf Trygvvesön, the first Christian king of Norway, was baptized by a Skellig monk. The medieval foundation on Skellig Michael remains today, remarkably intact. The ruins of the medieval settlement at Reask, on the Dingle Peninsula, have been excavated and are open to the public.

The verses of No-Ear and Donatus, the blessing of Fergus Beg, and Aileran's "blackbird" poem draw their inspiration from early Irish verses compiled in *1000 Years of Irish Poetry,* edited by Kathleen Hoagland (Old Greenwich, Conn.: Devin-Adair, 1975). My renderings from Ovid were guided by several existing translations, including A. D. Melville's *Metamorphoses* (Oxford) and Peter Green's *The Erotic Poems* (Penguin). Melisande's tale of Camilla is rather more a paraphrase of Virgil than a direct translation.